"Few know what they have been producing. They see great quantities of material going in and they see nothing coming out of these plants, for the physical size of the explosive charge is exceedingly small. We have spent two billion dollars on the greatest scientific gamble in history—and won."

—President Harry S Truman, August 1945

Praise for Atomic Express

Mark Zimmerman's historical fiction brings to life the most unusual transportation of Uranium 235 from Oak Ridge, Tennessee, to Los Alamos, New Mexico, for use in the world's first atomic bomb ever used in warfare, Little Boy. His effective approach to storytelling, because of his lengthy career in journalism and based on his extensive experience doing research, enables him to show the intricate details of such a unique transportation method. He blends in characters (historical and fictional) that both interest the reader and add authenticity to the story.

The Oak Ridge history story, within which the *Atomic Express* fictional story occurs, is one of our nation's most renowned. Zimmerman is true to the history as he was a reporter for *The Oak Ridger* newspaper early in his journalism career and thus understands the history of the East Tennessee area. He also realizes the need to retain accuracy even while creating fiction within the parameters of that history.

Being a historian, I enjoyed reading *Atomic Express* and found the history to be accurate. Basing his story on what was itself a most unusual transportation method considering the enormous value of the highly enriched uranium, Zimmerman has created details that make the important mission more readily understandable. I found *Atomic Express* to be a welcome addition to the Oak Ridge story and the Manhattan Project mystique.

Ray Smith
Oak Ridge City Historian
Tennessee Historical Commission Commissioner

Mark Zimmerman spent his career as a journalist. He has the eye of a historian and the ear of a great storyteller. While most of us are familiar with the newsworthy events surrounding the development of the first atomic weapons, Zimmerman creates a compelling and authentic novel that explores the what-ifs and maybes of the transport of uranium between Oak Ridge, Tennessee, and Los Alamos, New Mexico. From the opening pages of *Atomic Express,* you know that this story will take you on a fascinating tale of history and imagination.

Dr. Jay Thomas
Professor of Educational Psychology
Aurora University

**Non-Fiction by Mark Zimmerman
available from Zimco Publications LLC**

*Fortress Nashville:
Pioneers, Engineers, Mechanics,
Contrabands & US Colored Troops*

*Mud, Blood & Cold Steel:
The Retreat From Nashville, December 1864*

*Iron Maidens and the Devil's Daughters:
U.S. Navy Gunboats versus Confederate Gunners
and Cavalry on the Tennessee
and Cumberland Rivers, 1861-65*

Guide to Civil War Nashville, 2nd Edition

*God, Guns, Guitars & Whiskey:
An Illustrated Guide to Historic Nashville,
Tennessee, 2nd Edition*

*Gone Under:
Historic Cemeteries and Burial Grounds
of Nashville, Tennessee, 2nd Edition*

Land of the Free, Home of the Brave

*The Zone:
True Tales from the Heartland*

Atomic Express: The 1945 Plot To Destroy Amerika
Copyright © 2025 Mark Zimmerman
Zimco Publications LLC
Website: zimcopubs.com
Email: info @ zimcopubs.com

ISBN Paperback   979-8-9988292-0-8
ISBN eBook   979-8-9988292-1-5

Printed in the United States of America.

This book is a work of fiction. Even though it is set during a certain time in history, it is a story from the imagination of the author, and any comparison to the actual events, persons, places or actions is completely unintentional and coincidental.

Content related to this publication can be found on the publisher's website at: zimcopubs.com

ATOMIC EXPRESS

THE 1945 PLOT TO DESTROY AMERIKA

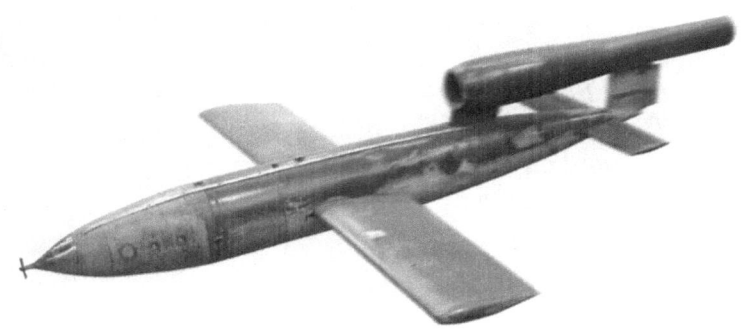

A Novel

Mark Zimmerman

Author of Mud, Blood & Cold Steel

ZIMCO Publications LLC

AUTHOR'S NOTE and DEDICATION

This book is a work of fiction. Even though it is set during a certain time in history, it is a story from the imagination of the author, and any comparison to the actual events, persons, places or actions is completely unintentional and coincidental. The characters in this book are fictional and do not represent real people; they are the product of the author's imagination. Some wording reflects attitudes of that time period, which may not be appropriate today. One of the guidelines in writing this book was that it be fun. Hopefully, it's as much fun to read as it was to write. This work is dedicated to all the men and women who fought in World War Two, especially those making the supreme sacrifice. Any and all errors are those of the author's.
Glory be to God.

THE RENDEZVOUS

The two of them had planned and rehearsed many months for this moment but separately. Now they have to come together. One is a deep National Socialist plant in the US; the other a superbly trained Nazi infiltrator.

Timing is everything. The pilot is directing the small airplane in a north by northwest direction from Tennessee into Kentucky airspace, droning along slightly higher than the pine treetops. He knows the terrain well, having practiced several times, at the exact same location, for this moment. About two miles south of the Grand Gulf Trestle over Laurel Hill Lake he catches up with the northbound train, descending and trying to match the train's speed exactly. Then he sees the man climbing on top of the baggage car near the end of the train. The tracks curve through the woods and the steep limestone cuts. There is really only one place along the route that the rendezvous can be made and that is on top of the tall railroad trestle. The top of the spindly trestle consists only of track and bed, with no superstructure overhead. But only for 1,125 feet, about the length of four football fields. The exposed man is securely braced by the inertial force of the train, facing toward the back of the train. He wears a backpack, goggles, a package strapped to his chest, and holds a rigid loop. All the time the train keeps up its diesel-propelled pace. The pilot closes in on the train, aiming for the crew car just in front of the baggage car, trying not to overcompensate with the controls. The train is now approaching the trestle.

The train wobbles slightly on the track, exuding a rhythmic metallic beat. The wind presses against all moving parts. The aircraft engine whines and the propeller whirls. Flocks of birds zigzag in murmurations caused by the variations of frequency in these unnatural waves of noise.

Coming closer now, the aircraft hovers over the baggage car, matching the speed of the train. The pilot employs full flaps to slow the plane without stalling.

The acrobat now holds the loop upright to try to catch the hook hanging below the aircraft. He pushes the loop forward with the wind but just misses contact. It takes all of his strength to turn the loop upright again. The plane bobs slightly from an updraft but settles down for another harried attempt. The opposite bank with its gauntlet of tall pine trees is rapidly, relentlessly approaching. The side window pushed open, the pilot yells wildly at the man on top of the train, caught up in the excitement of the moment.

Atop the train, the man lunges forward again with the loop and misses the hook. He cannot see the end of the trestle; he's facing toward the back of the train, watching time disappear. In a split-second of disappointment he realizes there is no time left for another try, or is there? He has to make the hard decision fast...

PROLOGUE

The Appalachian mountains in Tennessee are at least 240 million years old, and natives have hunted in the dense primeval forests for 14,000 years. Much closer to modern times, around 1900, eccentric farmer John Hendrix, after spending 40 days and nights alone in the foggy foothills of the Smoky Mountains, emerged at the Black Oak Ridge crossroads and proclaimed:

"In the woods, as I lay on the ground and looked up into the sky, there came to me a voice as loud and as sharp as thunder. The voice told me to sleep with my head on the ground for 40 nights and I would be shown visions of what the future holds for this land.... And I tell you, Bear Creek Valley someday will be filled with great buildings and factories, and they will help toward winning the greatest war that ever will be. And there will be a city on Black Oak Ridge and the center of authority will be on a spot middle-way between Sevier Tadlock's farm and Joe Pyatt's Place. A railroad spur will branch off the main L&N line, run down toward Robertsville and then branch off and turn toward Scarborough. Big engines will dig big ditches, and thousands of people will be running to and fro. They will be building things, and there will be great noise and confusion and the earth will shake. I've seen it. It's coming."

And so, did it all begin with a fevered dream...?

THE INTERVIEW
Tues., Feb. 4, 2020, 9:45 am Eastern Standard Time

The rain was freezing on the ground the morning I got the phone call. It was Gruenwald, an old acquaintance from college days. I hadn't heard from him in years. He sounded impatient, even concerned. He wanted me to interview an old man whose last days were numbered. He had an astounding story to tell, my friend claimed. I was warm and snug at home in Knoxville enjoying my morning coffee and a chocolate doughnut. My wife was just dragging herself out of bed, making all kinds of weird noises, as she always does when awakening. The dog wanted outside for the usual reasons.

"What's this all about?" I asked.

"This guy I know has a story about World War Two that needs to be told. And if you don't interview him and get his story it will be lost to the ages."

I was interested but dubious. If nothing else, I am inherently curious. That's a good trait for a journalist.

"He can't leave home. He's in pretty bad shape but still sharp. He's also kept notes. He said he hasn't talked to anyone about this. All the others involved are gone."

"What's your connection?" I inquired.

"His wife knows my wife. But she's recently deceased—his wife. It's a long story and doesn't matter."

"Where does he live?" I asked, glancing out the window at the nasty weather.

"He lives up in Norris, that tiny town near the dam. He worked at Oak Ridge during the war and after."

"You're talking about the Manhattan Project?"

"Yeah. It wasn't called Oak Ridge back then, of course. It was the Clinton Engineer Works or CEW for short."

"This have something to do with the bomb?"

"I believe so."

"National security?"

"What he has to say doesn't necessarily involve current national security, no."

"When's a good time?"

"He said he can talk today. He has a live-in nurse, by the way."

He gave me the address and the old man's name. He said he'd call and let the nurse know I was coming. "Bring him a bottle of whiskey. He'd like that. Some good stuff."

"Alright, I can do that. I'll go see what he has to say."

We pledged to get together soon and I hung up the phone, an old-fashioned land-line. To write, I use an IBM Selectric typewriter. I'm old school. I told my wife what was going on. She didn't ask too many questions; she knows better. We've got an all-wheel-drive husky vehicle so I wasn't too worried about the roads. It wasn't cold enough for the pavements to freeze over. Cloudy, overcast day nonetheless. I let the dog out and urged him to do his duty quickly. He didn't listen to me. Fifteen minutes later, back inside, I got properly dressed, poured some coffee into a travel mug, and made sure I had some cigarettes, a notebook, and a small digital recording device. I added some fresh batteries. I kissed my wife on the cheek and headed out the door. She told me to be careful. The dog looked anxiously at me but remained in his warm bed.

The windshield was covered with sleet, light enough that I could use the wiper to clear the glass. I made sure to switch on my heated seat. Just outside my Old City neighborhood, I bought a 375ml bottle of Evan Williams at Ralph's Liquors and pointed my Jeep northward on I-75. Took me half-an-hour to get there, turning left past the living-history Museum of Appalachia. Norris was a small town built the same time as the TVA dam, back in the 1930s, and touted as an "ideal town of the future." Most of the one-level homes had a yard and were powered totally by electricity. The picturesque town had lots of common green spaces and traffic round-abouts. I noticed that there were no utility poles; the cables and lines were all underground. I found the old-timer's house at the top of a hill. It was a neat brick cottage covered with ivy with one huge pine tree in the front yard. A dog across the street announced my arrival. At the door I was greeted by the black female nurse. She was in her forties probably. Polite and straight-forward. The house was quite warm. I kept the whiskey bottle in my coat pocket.

The sitting room was warm and stuffy and smelled of must and overly sweet medication.

"What he's got is not contagious," she explained.

The old man was submerged in a overstuffed recliner with a comforter over him. He wore a plastic breathing tube connected to a small oxygen bottle. He showed no intention of rising to meet me. He shook my hand rather limply. Hardy in his own day perhaps, but now he was close to skeletal, his face a mask of jagged angles and wrinkles. One eyelid drooped. Wispy white hair billowed around his scalp. You get to a certain age you don't bother keeping up appearances.

The nurse introduced me. He eyed me wearily with an obvious mistrust of strangers. Years of cigarette smoking and drinking laid heavy on his voice when he spoke.

"Ever serve?"

It took me a moment to comprehend. "No, sir, never did. Too young for Vietnam."

"Not many of us left," he noted.

"From World War Two? You're right."

"You a reporter? Your friend speaks highly of you."

I just nodded. "He said you had a story to tell." I was hoping he would talk without too much coaxing.

"Before I die, the truth needs to be told. Although I doubt it matters after all these years," he said, his voice trailing off.

For a moment, I thought his mind had wandered off. He turned to the adjacent table to show me a black-and-white photograph of himself during the war, looking sharp in his well-fitted uniform.

"Mud!" he exclaimed.

"Excuse me?"

"What I remember the most. All that damn mud. Red clay, slippery as all hell. I don't know which was worse—Okinawa or Oak Ridge."

I was hoping ever more devoutly that his mind was clear. I didn't want to have to extricate myself if he was past the point of no return.

"I'm talking now. Hell, it's been 75 years. I'm terminal, in hospice. What are they going to do to me? Throw me in jail? A lot of folks should be thankful. Might not be here if it weren't for that briefcase. Or what was in that briefcase."

I leaned forward in my chair and flipped open my notebook. I switched on the recorder.

"The story centers around a briefcase," I said in the guise of a question.

"Centers on a briefcase."

"Come again?"

"Centers on. Centers around is nonsense. Nothing can center around anything else. Just good common sense." He paused. "It was the worst-kept secret at CEW, at least among the intelligence agencies. Even the local FBI office figured it out by the spring of 1945. The shipments went without a hitch until that one day in April when the shit hit the fan. But they covered it all up. Covered it up good. All's well that ends well, huh?"

"Yes sir." I had no idea what he was talking about or what I was getting into. I completely forgot about the bottle of whiskey in my pocket. I took copious notes. The old man kept talking. The digital device kept recording. What he told me was one of the biggest cover-ups of World War Two.

DISPATCHES FROM THE FRONT
March-April 1945

In the US, when you talked about the war, you meant the war with Japan. War production workers in and around Knoxville escaped the humdrum of their daily lives and enjoyed the benefits of air-conditioned comfort at the Tennessee Theater or Bijou Theater on Gay Street. Monday nights the workers were bussed from the village at Clinton Engineer Works (CEW) to downtown Knoxville. Every movie shown during the war featured black-and-white Movietone Newsreels on wartime events, set against martial music and a dramatic narrator. Lowell Thomas was the best. What you would have heard in the spring of 1945:

Movietone News

March 10, 1945 — "Operation Meetinghouse launched 270 B-29 Superfortresses from Tinian, Guam, and Saipan. The bombers dropped at low altitude 1,665 tons of incendiary bombs on Tokyo, Japan, creating a huge intense firestorm that obliviated sixteen square miles of the city, left one million residents homeless, and killed 110,000 people. It was the single deadliest air raid in human history."

Movietone News

April 18, 1945 — "Imperial Army forces on the island of Okinawa, 340 miles south of Japan, attacked for the third consecutive night two US Army divisions, and were repulsed after heavy close fighting. A US counteroffensive resulted in the loss of 22 tanks. The Japanese use native Okinawans as human shields, conduct nighttime raids, and refuse to surrender, forcing the use of flamethrowers, napalm, and high explosives to root them out of their extensive network of underground tunnels. The heavy rains and muddy conditions make military logistics a nightmare. Combat fatigue is a rising concern amongst the US Marines and Army soldiers. Meanwhile, Japanese kamikaze pilots are inflicting their own style of terror by deliberately crashing their airplanes into US warships, including aircraft carriers. Allied officials fear the taking of Okinawa, which is inevitable, will result in 50,000 US casualties, the annihilation of the 80,000-man Jap garrison, plus more than 100,000 native Okinawans killed."

THE GENERAL AND THE CHIEF ENGINEER
Sat., April 1, 1945, 10:00 am Eastern Wartime

The administration building atop a prominent hill at Clinton Engineer Works (CEW) is known as The Castle. The king of the Castle, and leader of the entire Manhattan Project, is referred to respectfully as The General. When the General speaks, everyone listens. This is not solely due to his rank and no-nonsense attitude but also his record—he has just finished supervising the construction of the Pentagon in Washington, DC, the largest building in the world. He is a ranking officer in the U.S. Army Corps of Engineers, known more as a doer than a thinker, although he is highly intelligent and knows how to handle people. The son of an Army chaplain and fourth in his class at the West Point. The General eats well and carries a lot of bulk, but he is not obese. Too much inner energy and nerves keep his weight in check. He has short, wavy hair, a small mustache, and sunken but expressive eyes.

He does not drink and he doesn't smoke cigarettes or cigars, somewhat unusual for a man in his situation. Instead, he adores sweets, especially hard candy.

The General is used to getting what he wants, although due to his experience and knowledge he has been denied an in-theater combat command. He is too valuable. What he wants is to beat the Germans, more forthrightly the Nazis, in producing an atomic bomb. The thought of Herr Hitler in control of an atomic weapon keeps the General up at night. The sole purpose at CEW at this point in the war is to produce enough enriched uranium to produce at least three bombs. Nobody knows exactly how much is needed.

The project is without precedent and supremely urgent. Research, development, construction, and operation all have to be started and carried on simultaneously without appreciable prior knowledge.

The General, and by assimilation his subordinates, operates on the "always overriding necessity for speed." He is decisive and confident, but he likes to hedge his bets. He listens to those subordinates he trusts who are duly qualified to express an opinion. He does not suffer fools gladly, but he respects people of intelligence and integrity who stand up to him.

Inside the security perimeter of CEW uranium is referred to as tube-alloy or oralloy, and the bomb is the gadget. Only a dozen officials know the whole story of CEW and fewer still of the Manhattan Project. Workers and technicians are kept in the dark, given only the information they need to do their jobs. Even most of the scientists are tasked with specific duties and missions without knowing the end product.

The General and his second-in-command at CEW, the Chief Engineer (a colonel), have called a "come to Jesus" meeting at the Castle to check on the progress of refining raw uranium ore into bomb-grade U-235 isotope. Trainload after trainload of freight cars have rolled into the 58-square-mile reservation over the past two years and nothing is rolling out. A fresh, new hard look at the process is needed by his men, the General has concluded.

Before the meeting, the Chief Engineer briefs one of the majors, a newcomer to the staff, about the General. "He is most demanding, abrasive, and sarcastic. He disregards all normal organizational channels. He is extremely intelligent. He has the guts to make difficult, timely decisions. He is the most egotistical man I know. He knows he is right and sticks by his decisions. He is the biggest SOB I have ever worked for," the Chief Engineer says, looking the major in the eye, "but I wouldn't want to work for anyone else."

The General, serving at the pleasure of the President, makes the hard decisions and the Chief Engineer makes sure they are carried out.

The General surveys the half dozen army officials in the wooden-floor conference room, paces the floor, strokes his chin. Without expression, he looks each man in the eye for several long moments, moving from one to the next, saying nothing. Each man is put on edge; nobody dares speak. Only then he speaks. "First the good news. It is highly unlikely at this point that the Nazis are going to produce a nuclear weapon. The reason I know the Germans don't have an atomic bomb, is that if they did, they would have used it by now. However, I must admit, Hitler has chemical weapons and hasn't used them. Probably because he himself was gassed in the Great War."

The General paced some more, then stopped to lean over his desk, placing his weight onto his outstretched palms. "The bad news. We still aren't producing enough enriched uranium. Isn't that so?" he stated, more as an demand for explanation than a question.

Nobody knew the answer for sure yet, but CEW scientists estimated that about 200 pounds of Oralloy (enriched uranium U-235) would be needed to test and manufacture the "Little Boy" atomic bomb.

The bird colonel spoke up first. "Yes, sir. My people assure me that we are at full capacity at Y-12. All the calutrons are geared up and operating at full speed."

"Good, but not good enough," the General grumbled.

"We are building new calutrons with multiple source beams as we speak."

One of the lieutenant colonels added, "Gaseous diffusion has increased its level of enrichment, Slowly yes, but surely. We are feeding Y-12 as fast as we can."

"Not good enough. The boys at Los Alamos have increased their requirements. We've got to get this job done, gentlemen," he said, banging his fist on the table for emphasis.

"Well, what I have been recommending," said the Chief Engineer, "is that we use the end product from thermal to supplement the feeders at gaseous diffusion."

"Won't work," stated the lieutenant colonel. "Like I said, we're already at full capacity."

"What if we fed thermal straight into Y-12, would that work?"

The bird colonel replied, "It might. I'm certainly not going to tell you it won't."

"Then don't," replied the General. "Let's get it done. Make it work. Let me know what you need, I'll get it to you pronto. We have the resources; what you don't have is a lot of time. I want production reports by 1700 tomorrow."

"It's as if we've produced a marble, but we need to fill a bathtub full of marbles."

"Production is ramping up for sure. If you remember, we had only produced a little over 17 pounds of U-235 as of last December. The question remains, can we produce enough for Los Alamos by this September?"

"Gentlemen, I don't need to remind you of the urgency of our mission. The outcome of the war depends on it. The Germans are done; it's only a matter of time before the Russians surround Berlin and capture Hitler. You know what's going on in the Pacific. The battle for Okinawa continues. The Japs are dug in like Tennessee ticks and nothing short of high explosives, gas, and flamethrowers are rooting them out. They don't surrender. My sources tell me the Marines stand to sustain close to 70,000 casualties. Tens of thousands of civilians have committed suicide, that's how badly the Japs have indoctrinated them against us. Kamikaze planes are taking out battle cruisers, aircraft carriers. And this is just the beginning, gentlemen.

Intelligence indicates that the Imperial Air Force is holding back fighters for the defense of their homeland. Japanese civilians are being armed with crude weapons to fight our boys on the ground, in the streets."

The General paused for effect, circling the table, glancing at the floor (floorboards creaking), looking troubled. "Operation Olympic, the beginning stage of Operation Downfall, is predicting eleven divisions of Japs on the southernmost island alone. Once the actual invasion begins, hundreds of thousands of American boys are going to be killed and wounded. Rumor has it there's a warehouse in DC with five hundred thousand Purple Heart medals ready for use, not to mention the body bags. Millions of Japanese will perish, if not in battle then by starvation. The carnage will be hard to imagine. Right now, Jap cities are being burned to cinders by low-flying B-29s. Their military brass and the Emperor show no sign of backing down; they have to save face at all costs. Gentlemen, the American people are sick and tired of war. We may be looking at, conservatively, another three years of war."

The General rooted through some dispatches in the tray on his desk and scanned the one he was looking for. "Under the command of General Lemay, in one night alone, three hundred B-29 bombers dropped 500,000 cylinders of napalm and incendiaries on Tokyo. A 40-square-kilometer firestorm killed over 100,000 and maimed another million."

"I don't mean to be frivolous, I don't drink, but eight bottles of Scotch are riding on this project. Gentlemen, we have got to end this damn war."

COMPARTMENTALIZATION

For all most people knew about it, the Clinton Engineer Works was a massive restricted-security U.S. war production facility just like the nearby Holston Ordnance Works (the largest explosives plant in the world) or the dozens of small businesses around town producing munitions or uniforms or army vehicles. The only difference was that nobody knew exactly what the government was doing at CEW and to what purpose.

Security and secrecy were of the utmost importance. The entire CEW reservation not bounded by water was secured with guard towers and a perimeter fence topped with razor wire. Military policemen on horseback or in Jeeps constantly surveilled the fencing for breaches and suspicious activity. Access was strictly controlled at seven security gates manned by armed guards. Airspace over CEW was restricted; the facility itself did not have a dedicated airfield or train station. Power utilities were buried underground to avoid sabotage. The facility did not exist on maps.

All employees were required to wear photo ID badges at all times, except inside their own homes.

Only those with the need to know—and those were few—knew the whole story. Every activity was based on compartmentalization. Technicians were told only what they needed to know to do their jobs. "Stick to your knitting" was a favorite expression of the General along with "Do your job." The General's aide in charge of project security created the Counter Intelligence Corps. The CIC consisted of agents who spied on everyone within the reservation, and even outside its boundaries. CIC agents posed as bus drivers, bartenders, and waiters to see who was talking too much. Those who talked out-of-line or even those who asked too many questions quickly found themselves out of a good-paying job and banned from the reservation. Phone lines were tapped and all mail—incoming and outgoing—was examined and censored. There were films and lectures on security, along with the distribution of posters, handbills, circulars, notices, and leaflets. Large billboards throughout the reservation warned workers to "Zip Your Lip" and declared that "Silence Means Security." Most all workers got the message and kept CEW business to themselves. Besides, people didn't know much of importance in the first place.

Cover stories were planted amongst the local press. Wild rumors, if not about atomic energy, were encouraged. The authors of any story printed in a newspaper or magazine that even hinted at the purpose of the Manhattan Project or the nature of affairs at CEW were immediately investigated by intelligence agents. Usually their stories stemmed from pre-war research or pure speculation.

Even the official Corps of Engineers photographer at CEW, a young man who took thousands of photos of the production plants, the workers, the village, and all else, did not know the specific purpose of CEW.

The *Oak Ridge Journal,* the newspaper of CEW, expounded on the prevailing conditions: "Yes, we know it's muddy... Coal has not been delivered... The grocer runs out of butter and milk... Your laundry gets lost... The post office is too small... There are not enough bowling alleys... Your house leaks... The water was cold... The telephones are always busy... The dance hall is crowded... The guest house is full... Employees are inexperienced... The roads are dusty... You would have planned it differently."

THE CEW WHITE PAPER

At the request of the General, the Chief Engineer prepared a detailed white paper or factsheet that the General could use on his upcoming trip to DC. Army Chief of Staff George C. Marshall needed to be kept up-to-date on the project and Vice-President Harry Truman, in office only a couple of months, needed to know the details in case anything happened to President Roosevelt. Interesting to know, but if anything happened to the General (he always traveled by train and packed a pistol on his person), his secretary, known as Major or her initials JOL, had been briefed regularly on all the details of the project.

The Factsheet (Top Secret):

At the urging of Albert Einstein, President Roosevelt authorized the Manhattan Project in a race to beat the German scientists in the making of an atomic bomb. The Germans had a head start of at least 18 months. Einstein had stated, in part, "the element uranium may be turned into a new and important source of energy in the immediate future…it may become possible to set up a nuclear chain reaction in a large mass of uranium, by which vast amounts of power and large quantities of new radium-like elements would be generated…This new phenomenon would also lead to the construction of bombs…"

In November 1941, Roosevelt was informed by scientists that building a uranium bomb was feasible. Ten days later, the Japanese attacked Pearl Harbor and, subsequently, Hitler declared war on the United States. By August 1942, the Manhattan Project had been created by the U.S. Army Corps of Engineers.

Uranium-235 is the rare isotope of uranium-238, which is found abundantly in nature (less than one percent of natural uranium is isotope 235). In order to make an atomic bomb, effective ways of enriching raw uranium ore and producing uranium-235 had to be developed.

The General authorized the immediate purchase of 1,250 tons of high-grade uranium ore. The Belgian firm Union Minière had shipped the ore to the United States in 1940 from its Belgian Congo mine in order to remove it from Germany's reach. It had been sitting for two years out in the open in 2,000 steel drums on Staten Island. The other main source of uranium ore (called pitchblende) was Canada.

Los Alamos, New Mexico was chosen as the site for the fabrication of the atomic bomb, which was known as "the gadget." Bear Creek Valley in East Tennessee, bordered on the north by Black Oak Ridge and on the other three sides by the Clinch River, was chosen as Site X, for the production of enriched uranium. It was known as the Clinton Engineer Works (Clinton was a nearby small town). There was plenty of electricity available from Tennessee Valley Authority (TVA) hydroelectric plants, plenty of fresh water, convenient railroad facilities, and an abundant workforce in nearby Knoxville (pop. 120,000). CEW encompassed 60,000 acres of wooded hills and valleys, 17 miles long and seven miles wide.

At one point, the operations at CEW consumed more than 16 percent of the electricity produced by TVA, comparable to the power consumption of New York City. On the other side of Knoxville, the ALCOA (Aluminum Company of America) plant was also devouring vast amounts of energy to produce aircraft-grade aluminum.

STRANGE PHENOMENON

To hedge their bets, the officials of the Manhattan Project use several processes to enrich uranium, two of them dominant.

The electromagnetic separation process uses a customized mass spectrometer known as a calutron (CALifornia University cycloTRON), which requires use of the world's most powerful magnets. In basic terms, the calutrons vaporize and electrically charge the uranium atoms or ions, which are then pulled around a semi-circular track by powerful magnets. Due to their difference in weight, the two isotopes of uranium land at different spots on the receiver plates, where they accumulate and are then collected. Shaped like the letter "D," the calutrons are arranged side-by-side in an oval resembling a "racetrack." Although theoretically sound, the day-to-day operation of the calutrons has proven to be quite vexing.

There are nine calutron buildings—five Alpha and four Beta. The Alpha machines enrich the uranium by about 15 percent, then the Betas enrich it to the level of weapons-grade material. The formal start of mass operations was Jan. 27, 1944. Companies involved include Westinghouse, General Electric, Allis-Chalmers, Stone & Webster Engineering, and Tennessee Eastman.

The Y-12 plant houses 1,152 calutrons in nine major buildings that cover an area equal to 20 football fields. The plant comprises a total of 268 buildings at a cost of $500 million (15 times the original estimate). Within one four-week period, 63 rail cars of concrete blocks were unloaded here. In eleven weeks, 1,585 rail cars of lumber arrived. One hundred and twenty-eight carloads of electrical equipment arrived in a two-week period. Most of these materials had to be warehoused before being used for construction.

When first turned on, the electro-magnets in the calutrons, weighing 20 tons each, pulled nails out of the walls and wreaked havoc on metallic objects. Strange magnetic phenomena were observed. Workers on the catwalk above the powerful magnets could feel the tug of the magnetic field on the nails in their shoes. The metal innards of watches would be smashed together by the magnetic fields. Workers had to use non-ferrous tools. One worker carrying an iron plate got too close and was pinned between the heavy plate and the magnets. Told to shut off the magnets, the supervisor replied, "The war is killing 300 people an hour. If we shut down the magnet, it will take days to get re-stabilized and get production back up again, and that's hundreds of lives. I'm not going to do that. You're going to have to pry him off with two-by-fours." Eventually, the trapped worker was freed without serious injury.

Tennessee Eastman hired and trained young women just out of high school to operate the calutrons. Sitting on stools in front of tall control panels, the "cubicle operators" would patiently monitor the controls and adjust rheostat knobs to run the calutrons efficiently. Eventually, some operators could control up to four cubicles at one time.

Due to the wartime shortage of copper, silver was used as the electrical conductors for the calutron magnets. Accordingly, 14,700 tons of silver valued at $300 million was borrowed from the U.S. Treasury at West Point. The silver bars were shipped to New Jersey to be fashioned into billets and then shipped to a copper plant to be rolled into three-inch-wide strips, less than an inch thick and 40 feet long. Then the strips went to Allis-Chalmers in Milwaukee, where they were wound around giant steel spools, insulated with wood, and shipped to CEW.

The other major process is gaseous diffusion, housed in the world's largest building at the far western end of the reservation. The K-25 structure measures 1,000 feet wide and half-a-mile long and covers 44 acres. K-25 houses thousands of diffusers in which highly corrosive uranium hexafluoride gas is pushed through barriers with microscopic openings. Producing these micro-fine barriers was problematic, and the process wasn't proven until March 1945. The process of pushing gas through barriers had to be reproduced many, many times to be effective. The pores of the barrier had to be less than one millionth of an inch, uniform in size, could not become plugged, and had to be rugged enough to withstand high-pressure uranium hexafluoride gas. In all, the plant uses 3,122 diffusers containing 5.2 million barrier tubes measuring 6,659 miles in length. In addition, the corrosive gas attacks the grease in the seals; therefore, new gas-tight pump seals had to be created. The material used for the seals is known as Teflon. The plant was highly automated but still required 9,000 workers employed in three shifts.

GREEN SALT

Fifty kilograms (about 110 pounds) of U-235 were collected during the first year of CEW operations. The first shipment of enriched uranium-235 (seven ounces at 12 percent enrichment) was delivered to the scientists and fabricators at Los Alamos in March 1944. Air travel was deemed too risky. The precious enriched uranium would be transported from CEW to Los Alamos via Chicago by teams of armed plainclothes couriers riding passenger trains. The couriers, military policemen in reality, do not know what is contained in the briefcase, only that it is critically vital to the war effort. They have pledged their lives to safeguard the briefcase and its contents.

Two billion dollars worth of infrastructure, tons of raw material, hundreds of thousands of man-hours, heart attacks and divorces, massive amounts of electricity, and cutting edge engineering have been expended to produce the uranium tetrafluoride ("green salt") inside the briefcase, which is critical to the successful prosecution of the war.

Despite attempts to infiltrate the German program to build the bomb, the US knows little about their program and their progress. In one aspect, however, the Germans face as much trouble enriching uranium as the Americans. Instead of using carbon as a moderator for a nuclear reactor, the Germans use heavy water, D_2O or deuterium oxide. Only two-hundredths of a percent of water is heavy water. Five tons of heavy water would be needed for a reactor. Using electrolysis as the enrichment process, 40 grams of heavy water can be produced for each ton of water. To produce enough heavy water for a reactor, the Germans would have to process 113,398 tons of regular water.

U-BOAT MISSION
Mon., April 3, 1945, 9:00 am Central European Summertime

In the waning days of the European war, an impressive ceremony, set against the backdrop of the screes of diving seagulls and the clanking of halyards against metal poles, permeates the atmosphere at the German Unterseebooten naval base at Bergen deep within a foggy, frigid Norwegian fjord. A small colony of black-and-white mews, wailing and squawking, hovered in the steady sea breeze, bobbing up and down as if war kites. Every now and then a large Dalmatian pelican would plunge-dive into the saltwater, only to rise up with its massive wings flapping slowly, a sardine scooped into its impressive pouch.

A giant red Kriegsmarine flag with swastika hangs over the entrance to demolished Pen No. 3, hit six months previously by a British tallboy bunker buster. In the adjacent pen at the Bruno bunker, crews have been working feverishly to outfit and provision the latest in submersible technology, the U-3008 Type XXI Electroboat, a submarine which can journey underwater much longer and farther than earlier types. The crew of 60 men has loaded the boat with all kinds of foodstuffs and equipment. There are two bathrooms or heads on the boat, but one will not be used until all the food stored in it, including many loaves of Kommissbrot (hard black bread), has been consumed. There is much more room available than normal because the U-boat will carry no torpedoes. The upcoming mission is not to sink shipping; the boat can travel faster with a lighter load. The boat also carries only an aft deck gun due to its mission and its highly unusual configuration.

The head engineer has lubricated and fine-tuned the diesel engines and their myriad moving parts. Diesel fuel has been loaded. The batteries have been charged. Fresh water has been pumped onboard. Now the long, sleek boat is out of its pen and moored to the concrete pier outside.

The crews, the high officials, and the curious onlookers who have been ravaged by years of war know that the end is near. However, they are anxious to christen this last desperate mission in the name of vengeance against their most steadfast enemy. No, not the Russians nor the British, however forcefully they have fought and gained the advantage. The overriding belief is that the Third Reich and its ambitions would have succeeded had it not been for the United States of America. First, the US supplied the Brits and then the Russians, delivering to them precious oil

and metals and the weapons of war—thousands of fighters, medium
bombers, tanks, and trucks. Herr Hitler underestimated the Yanks, thought
them to be soft and greedy, part of an perceived Negro/ Jewish perversion
of civilization. Then came Pearl Harbor, which provoked the USA into
seriousness.

Perhaps a scholar in this Nordic crowd might think back on Benjamin
Franklin at the beginning of the American Revolution, who noted, "Like
the wise and cautious rattlesnake, the American spirit is both vigilant and
patient, prepared to strike only when the defense of its cherished liberties
demands it."

America also was a nation of mechanics, champions of mass
production and assembly lines. The over-engineered Tiger, the finest tank
produced during the war, did not bring victory to the Nazis. It was the
relatively primitive M4A4 tank (later known as the Sherman), fifty
thousand in number, that overwhelmed the Wehrmacht.

But it was the ultimate failure of the Battle of the Atlantic that has
embittered most of the Unterseeboaten officers and crew members.
Americans built more transport ships than the Germans could build
submarines to sink them. At this point in the war, the submarine pens on
the Bay of Biscay in France have been overrun by the Allies and are no
longer usable.

Last August, the RAF began using Tallboy 6,000-pound delayed-
explosion, earth-penetrating bombs and the massive 22,000-pound "Grand
Slam" bombs which exploded deep underground, producing an
"earthquake" effect, sending shock waves through the ground and causing
damage some distance from the actual blast. The Tallboy and Grand Slam
bombs gave the Allies a weapon that could not penetrate the entire
thickness of a submarine pen roof, but its blast could still cause a collapse
or create a hole in the overhead protection. With its huge bomb bay, the
Avro Lancaster was the only aircraft in the world capable of dropping the
giant bombs.

The Oberbefehlshaber der Kriegsmarine himself, Grossadmiral Karl
Donitz, the rumored successor to der Fuhrer himself, stands erect on the
pier jutting from the massive concrete pens protecting the war's most
deadly naval weapons. He is middle-aged, with piercing eyes and a pinched
face that makes his cap appear much too big.

The Gross Admiral, a true believer, fervent party member and follower
of der Fuhrer, wants revenge and in time for Adolf Hitler's 56th birthday

celebration on April 20th. That is the mission of Feldzug Ultimativ
Vergeltung (Operation Ultimate Vengeance).

Donitz has lost both of his sons in combat. He considers the crew of
U-3008 as his sons, warriors against the British and Americans. He is
especially proud of the commander, Fregattenkapitan Karl-Friedrich
Scholtz, and expects much of him.

The leader of three wartime patrols, FKpt Scholtz, a young, handsome
man, is responsible for sending 28 Allied ships displacing 176,800 tons to
the bottom of the sea. Clean-shaven and wrapped in a warm, gray leather
coat, he proudly wears the Knights Cross with Oak Leaves and Crossed
Swords and the U-boat War Badge with Diamonds.

He is the ideal commander for U-3008, a new Type XXI Electroboat;
he wrote the battle instructions for the new weapon and helped train the
crew during crash sea trials. He receives the warm handshake of the
Grossadmiral, who places a opened, gloved hand affectionately on the side
of his face.

"We know that you and your crew will serve the Reich well," he tells
the commander. Although he might harbor such thoughts in the back of his
mind, little does the Gross Admiral know that he himself will assume the
duties as the Third Reich's leader in a matter of weeks.

The captain stands ramrod straight, staring straight ahead. "Absolutely,
sir. We are ready." He knows his chances of returning to his native land are
slim.

Donitz waves his gold-plated and velvet covered baton enthusiastically.
The baton, adorned with dozens of eagles, anchors, and iron crosses, was
presented to him personally by Hitler.

Most everyone at the ceremony knows that the U-3008 is being sent on
a desperate suicide mission. In the past few years, 648 U-boats have been
lost, 429 with no survivors. Of these, 215 were lost on their first patrol. For
security reasons, the U-3008 will be crossing the Atlantic in radio silence.
The new Electroboats are the first true submarines, capable of making up to
14 knots submerged for up to ten hours. It is equipped with improved
underwater listening devices, sonar and radar, and a Schnorkel breathing
device. The craft uses silent electric motors and carries three times the
battery capacity of a conventional U-boat.

At the silent submerged cruising speed, the Type XXI has to schnorkel
for only three hours a day to keep the batteries charged. This speed of five
knots with a range of 365 miles means that it will pass the dangerous

waters between Norway and Iceland in five days, schnorkeling briefly only five times.

The brass band on the pier launches into Erzherzog-Albrecht-Marsch as the behemoth slides off the pier and glides beside the reviewers. The crew, wearing their Kreigsmarine caps, stand at attention along the rear deck as the Grossadmiral slowly nods in approval. Normally a stoic man, Donitz can't help but shake his fist in the air and then give a full Heil Hitler salute. He is proud of these men and appreciates their commitment despite the odds. After the ship leaves, Donitz will be whisked back to the airstrip, where a Fw300 Condor will take him to headquarters at Wilhemshaven, and then onward to Berlin, if possible. Donitz is committed to the Third Reich and Herr Hitler, but he is practical enough to know that the end is near. If only U-3008 can strike one last final blow against the decadent Americans.

FKpt Scholtz makes last-minute inquiries of his First Wachoffizier and Leitender Ingenieur, making sure all the proper provisions of certain quantities are aboard and that all mechanical and engineering systems are operating and functional, respectively. The two high officers answer affirmatively. The commander barks the equivalent of "Let's go!" and follows his officers onto the gangplank and waits for the crew to board the ship.

The new type of boat carries no front deck gun; the men cannot stand there because the deck in front of the conning tower supports a slender ramp and a large cylindrical waterproof container. Inside sits a special version of the V-1 cruise missile commonly known as the buzz bomb. Londoners have become acquainted with this vengeance weapon, which carries 1,870 pounds of Trialen explosive in its warhead. The buzz bomb is propelled by a pulse-jet engine. The wings of the V-1 are neatly folded inside the tubular container.

This underwater Wunderwaffen, of which no prototype was built due to urgency, carries no "eels" in the forward torpedo room. Instead, this cramped area has been fitted with a chemical-operated steam generator or Dampferzeuger, which will launch the V-1 forward along its elevated ramp once the boat is on the surface and pointed towards its target.

The crew of the U-3008 includes technicians trained in the workings of the Dampferzeuger, the assembly of the ramp, the loading of the warhead, and the other preparations needed for launch.

The concept, in general, had already been realized by the Japanese, who had produced a massive submarine with watertight chamber containing an airplane with folded wings and floats.

As the sleek German craft breaks from the pier and cuts through the calm seas the band plays ever louder. The Grossadmiral is already in his staff car and on the move. Although enthusiastic about the mission, Grossadmiral Donitz gives the crew at best a 50-50 chance of success.

Soon the submarine base is far behind and no longer visible. In command atop the conning tower, FKpt Scholtz guides the massive vessel out of the narrow fjord and into the North Sea, where he will have to negotiate the Rosengarten (Allied minefields).

THE DOCTOR AND THE CUBICLE GIRL
Mon., April 3, 1945, 9:00 am Eastern Wartime

Her hair is short and blond, a cute face, button nose with freckles. Her eyes are blue. She's tall and scrawny, a girlish figure. Although in her early twenties, still awkward as a teenager. She usually wears sundresses which accentuate her subtle curves. She has a slender neck and a gold-chain necklace. When sitting and concentrating on something, such as listening to the good doctor, she would place the chain in her mouth and gently nibble on it, just one of her many habits and idiosyncrasies he adored. She could be a tomboy, the girl next door. She is nearly half his age, but she is mature for her age. She giggles and acts shy sometimes but she doesn't play games like other girls her age, and she doesn't flirt only to tease. She wants to know all about him and his medical work. She's bewitched and bewildered that someone is infatuated with her.

He's smitten. It's a good thing the young lady couldn't read his mind. He's a gentleman, but he's also a man. A married man, but he didn't care. His wife was away, working in the war industry in another state. He was a professional and his wife was a blue-collar worker. Opposites attract, they say. He was alone and lonely, and then she came along and made him forget about a lot of things. She was all he could think about—was she a blessing or a curse?

Billie Jean Holloway worked as a calutron girl at CEW and lived in the village in a dormitory for unmarried women, behind the security gates of the reservation. She was from nearby Clinton, the seat of Anderson County. Her father was a merchant of modest means, her mother a good Christian woman. She was the oldest of seven children.

Billie Jean was paid a decent wage for her work. She gave most of her earnings to her family. She didn't know much about her job except that it was vital to the war effort and getting the soldier-boys back home. Her small space at the dorm was modest, privacy almost non-existent. But the meals were decent and there were lots of similar guys and gals to have fun with. As long as you did not discuss your job or CEW.

Billie Jean was one of many young women employed to monitor the production of the calutron machines. What she didn't know was that the calutrons were sophisticated devices that used huge magnets and enormous amounts of electrical energy to enrich uranium so that it could be used in a bomb. The inner workings of the calutron, which separated the valuable

U-235 uranium isotope from the much more common and heavier U-238 isotope, was hidden from view. The calutrons, more than 1,100 of them, ran around the clock with three shifts of young women sitting on stools at consoles displaying an array of dials, switches, and knobs.

Billie Jean's job as a cubicle girl was to monitor the gauges on the instrument panel of the machine and adjust dials so that the needles registered within an acceptable range of measurement. This was not difficult to understand but much more difficult to master. For one thing, the operator had to stay focused over relatively lengthy periods of time; she could not leave her post. She sat in a brightly lit high-ceilinged hallway in the Y-12 plant along with dozens of other cubicle girls. Every so often, she met in an interview room with a supervisor, who evaluated her performance. She got so good at her job she could monitor two sets of controls at one time.

For example, she knew nothing of physics or science, but she knew that if you got your D voltage up and your E voltage down, then Product would hit the birdcage in the box at the top of the unit, and if that happened, you'd get the amount of Excess you wanted.

The machines, however, couldn't produce results fast enough or large enough, so eventually the technicians consulted with the supervisors and blamed the lack of production on the cubicle girls. After all, these young women were right out of high school and although they were literate, they knew very little about science or technology. Perhaps they just weren't serious about their jobs.

Tennessee Eastman Company agreed to a one-week competition between male engineers controlling the cubicles on one side of the aisle and the young ladies on the other. The females won the contest hands down. The engineers couldn't leave the controls alone, constantly diddling with them. The women were much more patient. Every now and then an engineer would claim to get more production out of the machine, but then it would take hours to recalibrate the controls and get the machines running at normal speed.

Billie Jean couldn't help but wonder, since they didn't tell her anything, whether her job was just some giant government research experiment to see how humans could sit still and monitor dials and gauges. What possible purpose would that research serve? She didn't know. But it was a good-paying job which wasn't very difficult. So she would carry on and keep her mouth shut.

As a cubicle girl, she wore an ID badge and a radiation dosimeter shaped like a fountain pen. Nobody knew exactly how much radiation was harmful and exactly how it affected the human body. Every week Billie Jean met with a doctor to screen her for radiation and make an assessment of her well-being and mental attitude. Over time, Billie Jean became attracted to her doctor, an older man who seemed quite charming and interested in her.

As a professional, Dr. Martin "Marty" Hamblen led a double life, working some days at the nearby university medical school and others at CEW as a medical physician specializing in radiology. When working at CEW, his office was located at the Castle, although much of the time he was making the rounds. Much of his work was screening employees for radiation exposure and other occupational conditions and hazards. He used a Geiger counter, a small battery-operated device with gauges and meters and a detection probe. Every now and then he was called upon to take a train trip to Chicago and back, dressed in civilian clothes and carrying his Geiger counter in a suitcase. There were couriers on the train carrying materials that may or may not be radioactive. So far, he had made four such round trips with no incidents other than boredom, bad meals, and extreme physical yearnings.

There were trips by the couriers when he was not required to travel with them—he speculated that such trips might be decoys, the couriers not carrying any materials in their suitcase.

He worked part-time in Knoxville at the University of Tennessee (the college on the hill). Many classes had been curtailed during the war, students enlisted in the services, and the university assumed various roles in the effort to win the war. He resided in the fashionable Fort Sanders district, the site of an old Civil War fortress eighty years before. His office was on The Hill in the main administration building although the labs were situated beneath the stands of the football stadium. There were no college football games during the war. The football coach, Robert Neyland, was a general in the US Army Corps of Engineers, stationed in India and handling logistics for Stilwell's troops in China. He was a football genius on defense. In 1939, his Tennessee Volunteers went undefeated, their opponents failing to score a single point against them.

RISKY BUSINESS
Wed., April 5, 1945, 10:00 am Eastern Wartime

Doc Hamblen confided in Billie Jean that his wife was cheating on him. That might be true, but the doctor had no evidence or proof of it. There were few places that the doctor and Billie Jean could safely rendezvous for their trysts. The risk of being discovered, along with the difference in their ages, heightened the heat of their passion. That the doctor was married seemed to matter little in their calculations. His was just one of many marriages ruined by the war. Both of them felt guilty about what they were doing together but nowhere near guilty enough to stop.

Billie Jean and the other young women residing in the dormitories and barracks enjoyed little privacy. Most everyone was privy to their comings and goings. Although there were leisure activities in which to participate, such as bowling or the movies or sing-alongs, there were few places where two people could be alone, intimately, and enjoy each other's company.

Doc Hamblen devised a devious plan to allow them more time together. Following one of the routine examinations at CEW, the doctor recommended that Billie Jean be dismissed for the simple reason that she was pregnant and that exposure from the calutrons might be harmful to her pregnancy. The supervisor readily agreed, and told Billie Jean that her services would no longer be needed. He did not give her the reason. He took her badge away. There was a list of young women waiting to replace her. She could no longer reside in the dormitory, and although the supervisor was courteous, he advised her that she no longer had access to the reservation. The termination of her services was duly noted by the CIC, along with all the other hirings, firings, transfers, and re-assignments. For several days, a CIC operative shadowed her to observe her activities. As she removed her belongings from the dorm, escorted by a security guard, she was met by Doc Hamblen outside in his sedan. As they left the reservation, he told her she had been let go because she asked too many questions, others had questioned her loyalties, and she could not account for extended periods of time not spent at the dormitory. He assured her that she was getting a bum rap, probably from jealous girlfriends or vindictive supervisors.

He drove her into Knoxville and helped her move her scant belongings into his bungalow. He also informed her that he would like her to work as his assistant at the university. She readily accepted, not knowing what her duties would be. And Doc Hamblen was not sure about his strategy or tactics if and when his wife came home.

It was all risky business, but that's the way he liked it. She was eager to please; she told him she preferred older men. Probably because she was a daddy's girl. Not that she was all that experienced, she didn't have to be. Her skin was so clear and soft and warm. And despite being skinny, she was a furnace, a human hot-water bottle. They thoroughly enjoyed all the fooling around, the groping, the undressing, her displays of modesty, wrapping their arms and legs around each other. The anticipation was more than they could stand. She would let him do whatever he wanted, then roll him over on his back, climb on top, guide his erection into herself, and rock, sway, pitch and roll herself to the point of passing out. She made sounds she couldn't believe she was capable of uttering. Lord knows, she lost all sense of modesty and self-consciousness by that point. He possessed quite a bit of endurance for his age, he didn't know why or how and didn't really care. Their mutual passion seemed to blot out other considerations, and they weren't careful about taking precautions.

It was all rather wild and untamed, and each felt some regret, but the joy and pleasure was worth the guilt.

Doc Hamblen did feel a nibble of remorse for his adultery; his wife had done nothing to deserve it except for perhaps not paying him enough attention. It was wartime and there was a lot of that going around. He didn't feel quite right about the situation, and he felt even worse because he could not help himself. This young woman, so soft and warm and sensuous, hung on his every word as if he were a minor deity. She liked the hair on his chest, his cute dimple. She did not mention his receding hairline. She admitted to having had a few other flings but nothing serious, just immature boys her own age, copping a feel more than anything else. She never asked about his wife and she never even hinted at any desire to replace her, at least not legally. What began to gnaw at the good doctor, despite himself, was that he could not foresee the outcome of their tryst. To her it had to be more than just great sex with an older man. There were throngs of older men, married or not, in the service or not, swarming out there on the home front.

Their co-habitation had to be temporary. He needed to set her up with an apartment in town. After all, her parents lived in the vicinity, and Knoxville was a small town. In the event, she found a small room to rent in the district, not far from his place. It wasn't much, but she spent most of her time at the bungalow anyway.

THE CIC IS EVERYWHERE
Wed., April 5, 1945, 9:00 am Eastern Wartime

It could be that bartender downtown or the matronly women sitting behind you at the theater. Perhaps one of your co-workers or a roommate at the dormitory. Could be anyone; most everyone was suspect.

The CIC undercover agents work everywhere, posing as civilians driving buses and trucks, bartending, clerking at stores, running errands at office buildings, ushering at the theater, waiting on restaurant tables, and as customers at nightclubs and taverns. In addition, there are scores of CEW employees eager to bear witness (sometimes falsely) against fellow workers. Then there are the uniformed US Army military police, the civilian police force in the village, and law enforcement officers outside the reservation, such as sheriff's deputies, municipal policemen, and the state and federal bureaus of investigation. CIC agents trailed Billie Jean for several days, noting her work at the university and her cohabitation at Doc Hamblen's. She did not visit any doctors or physicians. She made no purchases at the drugstore. She did not stop smoking cigarettes, a habit she picked up from her friends in the village. She was not showing. She sure didn't act as if she was pregnant. If it was so, it was probably the doctor who did the deed. The CIC decided to place a tail on the doctor himself and examine his bank records to detect any signs of blackmail against him. Nothing of concern showed up.

Unbeknownst to CIC or other intelligence authorities, a Soviet agent managed to infiltrate CEW, obtain a security clearance, work as a health physics officer, and provide the Soviets with information on building their own atomic bomb. (The Russians exploded their first atomic bomb four years after the end of World War Two but far sooner than the US had anticipated.) The agent was Vladimir Davidovich Asimov, code name Delmar, who worked in the Special Engineer Detachment at CEW but took orders from the Soviet Main Intelligence Directorate (GRU). He had been born in the United States of emigre Jewish Russians, joined the Communist Party and moved to the USSR to work on a collective farm only to be recruited by the GRU. Back in the US, he attended Columbia University and became deputy commander of the local GRU cell, which operated under the cover of Raven Electric Co., a supplier for General Electric. Asimov was drafted into the US Army in 1942 and attended the Army Specialized Training Program. He studied electrical engineering at City

College of New York. At CEW he had top-secret security clearance and relatively open access to the reservation, monitoring radiation levels at the production plants. He transferred secrets to his handler, codename Clyde, which reached Moscow via coded dispatches, couriers, and the Soviet Embassy. Based on his findings, the Soviets abandoned their pursuit of an enriched-uranium bomb in favor of producing an atomic bomb using plutonium.

The CIC currently possessed a valuable Russian asset who resided in Knoxville and worked at the university. At first, this individual worked solely for his Soviet handler, but he turned out to be less than a true believer. He had become accustomed to living in the States and responded to payments of cash and assurances (such as can be made) that he would not be deported back to the USSR. He was a double agent, posing as a Soviet spy while working for CIC. So far, he had proved to be reliable and valuable.

NIGHT SWEATS
Wed., April 5, 1945, 2:00 am Eastern Wartime

Master Sergeant John Lee Pettigrew confided in the lieutenant, his roommate, about his nightmares. He had to talk to somebody. The lieutenant promised not to share his buddy's ordeals with anyone. Conversely, a heartfelt chat with the unit chaplain or psychologist would be a one-way ticket to the nervous hospital, probably with a Section-8.

Sarge wasn't sleeping well, despite taking the goof balls he had scored over in Happy Valley, the construction worker town just outside Dogpatch. He tossed and turned on his army cot. Good thing the lieutenant slept like a log, snoring up a storm.

Sarge felt as if he were living a constant dilemma, attempting to maintain an unflappable exterior or façade while trying to somehow fix himself inside. Could he do both at the same time for any length of time—that was the question.

Darkness was falling quickly. The landscape smelled damp and fetid. Mud everywhere. Bright red flares lit up the sky, throwing ghastly shadows over the South Pacific wasteland. Japanese corpses rotted in various stages of decay and putridness. Debris littered the landscape amid piles of expended brass shells. Expended paper turned to pulp. He smelled like a goat, but he had become acclimated to that stench a long time ago. Two men occupied each foxhole. One kept guard, trying desperately to stay awake, while the other tried to sleep, hunched over and squatting. Personal hygiene did not exist anymore. The soldiers suffered from trench foot and rashes and infections.

The screams and the cries of the wounded, many pleading for water or begging for their mothers, rent the air. Whistles and Nippon bugles sounded another frontal assault. "Yankees, you die tonight," the Japs shouted at them in English. Hopefully the grunts had enough ammo to mow them all down before resorting to hand-to-hand combat. Mortar shells began to thump and then whistle down inside their perimeter, throwing great clumps of mud and shrapnel. He saw the ferocious screaming faces of the Japs coming at him, grotesquely out of proportion to their bodies. He couldn't locate any of his buddies. He was alone and nearly surrounded. He yelled for the password, which was lilliputian (the Japs couldn't pronounce it correctly). A Jap jumped into the foxhole and they just stared at each other for several long moments. Then they grappled desperately in that cramped mudhole. There wasn't enough space to use a knife. The G.I. managed to get both hands around his foe's neck and squeezed as hard as he could until eventually the Jap went still.

Then the body in the foxhole transformed into a huge winged beast with bright orange eyes and horns, an apparition.

An involuntary body spasm woke him suddenly, in a cold sweat and eyes wide open. He thought, my God, what the hell? How long do I have to put up with this? I can't go long without some quality sleep.

This is what Master Sergeant John Lee Pettigrew actually admitted to the psychologist:

"At first, you're afraid of getting shot and killed or wounded in a grievous way, like shot in the gut—a slow, painful death. Then after a while you don't worry too much about getting killed. You figure your number is up, that's it. I mean what are the odds of surviving this horror show? So after a while you operate as if you're already dead or marked for death. Death would be a sweet relief. You pray for that million-dollar wound that will get you home and out of this mess. What you really are terrified of, actually two things—letting down your buddies, sleeping on guard duty, getting them killed through your own negligence. And the other is that you are terrified of losing your mind, losing control of your senses. That seems cowardly and yet it somehow seems inevitable, given the circumstances. And it could happen right away. I've seen it happen, several times. The lucky ones, I guess, just go into a catatonic trance from which there is no escape. Others go wild and crazy and end up getting killed one way or the other. But if you can somehow successfully adjust so that the killing and the privations don't matter or affect you, what have you become?

"I was lucky beyond belief. I got the million-dollar wound. Shrapnel in my foot. Enough to get me shipped back home. But not bad enough to leave me permanently disabled. The worst part was having to prove I didn't shoot myself in the foot. That was the suspicion. Guys who knew me, trusted me, couldn't believe it, yet there was still that suspicion. The medics knew better. They couldn't find the piece of shrapnel that did the damage, but the wound obviously wasn't from a self-inflicted bullet. Sometimes I feel ashamed. If I had known the consequences, maybe I would have tried to section-eight. But I didn't."

THE COURIERS
Wed., April 5, 1945, 6:00 am Eastern Wartime

On this bright and beautiful April morning, the mist arose from the valley in the East Tennessee mountains just as it had for the past 400 million years. Adding to this primeval fog were the coal and wood-burning plumes from hundreds of huts, shanties, barracks, and other expedient buildings in the village nestled in the northeast quadrant of the top-secret military reservation. Other smoke and steam effluent wafted into the air from the gigantic industrial complexes situated down and along the other valleys. The valleys (seven in number) and ridges run southwest to northeast. The village of workers is in the northeast corner of the reservation, with the war factories situated to the west in the various valleys. Only a handful of officials know that the final product produced here is enriched uranium suitable for an atomic bomb. The uranium tetrafluoride, the rare U-235 isotope, is known as green salt because that's what it looks like. The technicians and other workers know only what they need to know. They are told not to talk about their work to anyone. Spies and snitches circulate among them, and anyone who asks too many questions will be summarily expelled from the reservation.

Folks in the nearby towns of Clinton and Knoxville are left to ponder endlessly as to the purpose of the super-secret CEW, especially since trainloads of material constantly enter the reservation, but no end product seems to come out of it.

The atomic bomb, known as the gadget, is being built on another secret military reservation in Los Alamos, New Mexico. The bomb requires relatively minute quantities of enriched uranium, which is good because the folks at CEW are having to move heaven and hell, cost no concern, to produce enough of it. The world has been at war for five years, the U.S. more than three years. At this point, Hitler's Third Reich is about to fall, the Allies approaching Berlin from the west, the Soviets from the east. However, in the United States, "the war" is the conflict with the Japanese Empire, begun with the attack on Pearl Harbor in December 1941. It is becoming more and more apparent that the atomic bomb will be needed to persuade the Japanese to surrender.

On this morning in the center of the village, two military policemen awake before dawn in their cozy Quonset hut with the plywood floor and black iron heater and prepare for a special mission. A multi-day railroad train trip to Chicago and back.

Sarge, the younger man, sitting on the edge of his cot, fondles the Remington-Rand 1911 .45-caliber semi-automatic pistol, inspecting it from several angles. The weapon had seen him through several horrific campaigns in the South Pacific. The stainless steel sheen had been worn dull with usage over the years.

"Another day in Dogpatch," grumbled Master Sergeant John Lee Pettigrew. He shook a cigarette from a pack of Camels, stuck it in his lips, and lit it with his Zippo lighter, snapping it shut.

"Except today we go to Chicago," replied First Lieutenant Earnest Ledbetter, who preferred Lucky Strikes. "You cleaned Rita last night and once again this morning. Leave her alone. You'll end up shooting yourself," chortled the senior officer. He immediately regretted the remark, recalling that his partner had received his "million-dollar wound" in the foot, and not with Rita. Sarge was a mite edgy talking about his wound, seeing as how he had to endure the interrogations required to ensure that he hadn't shot himself in the foot to get a ticket home. The wound had been from shrapnel, uncommon for foot wounds but legitimate nonetheless.

"Yes, sir. Just giving her some attention," said Sarge with a nod. "Did you know that every night before combat Rickenbacker polished each cartridge so his machine guns wouldn't jam." He racked a cartridge into the chamber and slowly, carefully lowered the hammer. Normally he would slide the weapon into its form-fitting holster on his web belt but today is different. He shoulder-holstered it under his left arm and checked his vest for extra magazines.

"I'm getting the feeling you need some good old-fashioned R&R," the lieutenant suggested. He inspected the hollow-point rounds in his Army Special, slapped the cylinder shut, spun it, and stuffed it inside his jacket. His weapon was a Colt M1917 revolver using .45 ACP rounds with a full moon clip. Semi-automatic pistols can store and fire more rounds than a revolver, but a revolver is more reliable. The semi-automatics tend to jam and misfire if not used and maintained properly. The lieutenant rubbed the belly of his Billiken doll for good luck, just as he did every morning.

"Yes sir. You're very perceptive. That's why you outrank me," replied Sarge with a smile.

The lieutenant and the sergeant continued to dress for their assignment. Instead of their Army military police uniforms and helmets, both donned civilian clothes, dark wool suits and narrow neckties. Sharply creased trousers and highly polished brown wingtips. Rakishly tilted fedoras.

The lieutenant was a much different man than the sergeant, better educated, better manners, more erudite. He hailed from the Main Line of Philadelphia, the latest in a long family line of servicemen dating back to the Revolution. He had left the University of Pennsylvania to attend officer's school and earned his first-lieutenant O-2 bar quickly. He was 32 years old, an "old man" in a young man's army.

Sarge came from a hardscrabble family rooted not too far away in Cocke County, Tennessee. Descendants of those hardy Scots-Irish who emigrated to the Susquehanna Valley to serve as a buffer between the Indian tribes and the German farmers and Quaker gentry. Battling Indians in exchange for a few acres of land meant nothing to folks used to battling English lords and Irish landlords. Poor but proud, the borderlands men were known for fighting and fucking, with a generous dose of drinking and a pious religious nature to boot. Fiercely loyal to their clans, the folk did not believe in building fine mansions (the Royalists would burn them down anyway) and obtaining a fine education (to what ends?). His great-grandfather had been an overmountain man who fought under Colonel John Sevier at King's Mountain. Sarge's father was fierce and strict, likely to abuse his wife and children when soused by cheap whiskey, but a decent man when sober. His mother was worn with bearing seven children, took ill and died when he was six. Logging for the timber company built Sarge into a physical specimen, but he saw no future in the work. At age 18, he joined the US Army, before the war but while the winds were blowing in that direction. He ended up with the 26th Division, fighting in near proximity with the Marines on Guadalcanal. The horrid conditions, the fierce fighting, the barbaric tactics of the Japs—Sarge had seen it all with his own eyes.

Despite their differences, LT had grown fond of Sarge and had begun to consider him as his bodyguard, and even as a friend. He hated to admit it, but Sarge was more worldly wise, had seen actual combat under the most brutal conditions. Sarge did not suffer from undue sensitivity or what could be called nuance. In other words, in many ways, Sarge was more suited to confront reality for what it was (not what it wasn't) and deal with it.

The two men were beginning to function as a team, anticipating each other's moves. LT had to keep reminding himself not to get too close. Chain of command had to be maintained. Their lives might depend upon it.

"What's the forecast today, Sarge?"

"Lots of mud, just like every other day, LT."

"Seriously."

"Bright sunshine. A beautiful April day."

"Let's get some coffee and get outta here."

"Yessir," Sarge said, looking strangely out of sorts in his baggy civilian clothes.

Sarge was beginning to regard LT as a man of integrity and fairness. Perhaps a bit too soft, none of the killer instinct. Towards that notion, Sarge almost felt like a younger brother, not as educated as his superior, but rooted more in the humdrum business of daily self-preservation. In a way, Sarge was beginning to feel as if LT's future depended upon his alertness and his ability to spring into action. As if he were his bodyguard.

Seated on their cots, they pulled high-top rubber boots over their shoes. Everyone at CEW wore mud-stained trousers and mud-covered shoes—a sure tip-off as to their place of origin. Salesmen might wear worn shoes but not mud-covered ones. Sarge grabbed his rigid cloth suitcase filled with extra clothing, tactical gear, some grub, and more ammo.

The lieutenant had been paying particular attention to Sarge ever since the session with the Army psychologist. Sarge was displaying some erratic behavior, including sleepless nights, nightmares, and some might say paranoid delusions. One night on mounted patrol along the perimeter of the reservation he fired a couple of rounds at a rustling in the trees. A giant horned owl, wingspan of six feet, flew straight at him, talons extended, bright yellow eyes. The horse spooked, of course, and threw Sarge to the ground. Sarge was unhurt except for a few bruises, but he had been acting spooked ever since.

Sarge had been under a lot of stress lately, some of it his own accord. LT wasn't going to mention it to the psychologist, but Sarge brought the matter up first. LT trusted Sarge with his life. Sarge was a veteran of the Pacific war, having fought the Japanese on the island of Guadalcanal. For his efforts, he earned a Silver Star and multiple shrapnel wounds. He spent some time in a recovery ward in-theater, then rehab at Pearl. There was nothing waiting for him back in the states. No wife or family, not even an girlfriend. Women were attracted to him, but he had a way with women which did not result in lasting relationships. He insisted on re-enlisting and taking advanced training, getting back into shape. The chain-smoking psychologist told LT to stay alert and report any suspicious activity.

Once down the stairs of their hut, Sarge stopped short and ran back inside. He came back, showing a coin in his hand. "Forgot my lucky coin."

"Does that thing really bring you good luck?"

"Won't find out until I forget to carry it," he cracked wise, dropping it into his pocket. The coin was a 1923 Peace silver dollar, the last silver dollar minted in the US. Lady Liberty on the obverse was patterned after the Statue of Liberty; the eagle on the reverse clutched an olive branch in remembrance of the Great War, the war to end all wars.

The two plainclothesmen ambled over to the MP headquarters, an unpainted wooden structure, signed in and headed directly to the small canteen inside. LT chose an apple danish; Sarge grabbed a couple of chocolate-covered doughnuts. It would be their only meal until they ate on the train.

"You guys doing all right today?" asked the major, studying the two. "Ready to get outta here?" he added, grinning. "Well, if you have stuffed your faces adequately, let's head on over to the Golden Room."

The trio boarded a Jeep, Sarge sitting in the back, and drove over to Captain Lloyd Zimmer's office, where the prepared package was waiting for transport. The reinforced briefcase was carefully designed to hold the priceless package inside, yet still look like the average salesman's briefcase. The previous evening, over in Room 22 of Building 9733-1, technicians accepted the "green salt" collection from the production managers and used a mortar and pestle coated with 24-carat gold to grind it into a fine powder. Special precautions and after-measures were followed to make sure none of the precious material was lost or wasted, not a grain. The green salt was then poured into two small cylinders made of gold-plated nickel. The containers were secured and then fitted into the holders inside the briefcase, which was lined with cadmium, a sheathing similar to lead but not quite as heavy. Still, the briefcase weighed thirty-one pounds when finally assembled.

Officially, the green salt inside the briefcase was known as Oralloy. The couriers, however, had no idea what was inside the briefcase.

"Gentlemen, are you ready?" Capt. Zimmer inquired. The acquisition of the package always assumed the formality of a solemn ceremony. The MPs were not told what was inside the leather briefcase, which was not to be opened uner any circumstances. If anyone asked, they were salesmen selling fasteners to government contractors.

The captain handed a thick envelope to the lieutenant, who then handed it over to the sergeant. Sitting down on a bench, the lieutenant waited as the briefcase was secured to his arm with a leather strap.

"Need I remind you again of the importance of your mission?" the captain stated sternly. "You two are to guard this briefcase with your lives. The contents of this briefcase are extremely vital to the successful prosecution of the war. Is that understood?"

"Yessir," the two military policemen responded simultaneously.

"Be alert, be vigilant, act like civilians, and come back safely," he concluded.

The MPs saluted him briskly and stepped outside.

Right outside the headquarters was a Chevy sedan waiting for them with an MP driver and armed escort. The vehicle was unmarked and bore Tennessee plates. The two couriers got into the spacious backseat.

"Let's go," ordered the lieutenant, checking his watch. It was precisely 2:00 pm.

The sedan headed away from the Y-12 complex of buildings and through the Tennessee countryside toward the Solway Bridge security gate.

The security check at the gate took several minutes and then they were en route, cruising over the Clinch River on the Solway bridge and driving along the two-lane Knoxville Turnpike. They passed pastureland and a few farmers furrowing their fields and planting their tobacco or corn. Soon they were inside the city limits on Kingston Pike, which then becomes Cumberland Avenue as they drove along the northern boundary of the University of Tennessee with its brick administration building high atop a hill blanketed with yellow-orange wildflowers. The fragrance of blooming dogwoods wafted through the air and the barking of a hound sounding like a mournful wail.

In the backseat, the two couriers carefully removed their muddy booties. The remnants of an earthen Civil War fort could still be discerned on the high ground between the university and the downtown district. The Fort Sanders neighborhood, built around and somewhat over the old works, boasted many stately Victorian mansions, including the twin stone pillars marking the residence of author James Agee.

"Let us now praise famous men," mumbled Sarge to nobody in particular. LT just smirked.

It didn't take long until they swung into the entrance drive of the Louisville & Nashville terminal, an ornate red brick building in the Empire style. Each of the double entrance window-doors and four flanking stained-glass windows bore the fancy L&N logo in script. The escort vehicle veered away from the terminal without entering the driveway.

As with most train terminals built in the early 1900s, the main room was cavernous, constructed of marble which amplified footfalls and the echoes of the passengers. The rows of wooden benches were mostly vacant, a few occupied by couples and small groups of servicemen in uniform.

The front-seat MP passenger walked to the ticket window and retrieved their tickets.

"All set," he said, handing them over. "The *Southland*, 3:00 pm. We'll wait outside until y'all leave."

The couriers sat together on a bench. They carefully surveyed the waiting room for anyone looking suspicious. All seemed routine. Sarge pulled two paperbacks out of his suitcase and gave one to LT. They both got comfortable and began to read, occasionally glancing up to survey the room for any strange characters. Unbeknownst to either one of them, they were being watched by various individuals inside the station. And this was not the first time.

LT's book involved the history of England; Sarge's the pulp fiction account of gangsters and molls. Every once in a while, Sarge would chuckle and shake his head.

The *Southland Express* was scheduled to depart at three o'clock. At precisely 2:30 p.m., the couriers stowed the books and headed to the platform, where the sleek train already stood. The locomotive resembled an Art Deco masterpiece of grace and power. This streamlined train ran on diesel fuel and electric motors, a great improvement over the acrid smoke-belching, coal-burning locomotives of old, many still commonly in use.

The streamliner consisted of two locomotives, a freight car, three Pullman sleepers, three cars with private cabins, a dining car, a crew car, baggage car, and caboose. The *Southland Express* had scheduled stops at Lexington, Kentucky; Cincinnati, Ohio, and Indianapolis, Indiana, before pulling into Dearborn Station in Chicago. The train had already traveled eight hundred miles north from Miami, Florida.

The two "salesmen" boarded the train at the beckoning of a porter. If anyone asked, they were in the business of selling various fasteners to war industries. They made their way to a reserved cabin in the last passenger car. The dining car was right behind them. LT and Sarge sat opposite each other, LT settling the briefcase snugly next to him and Sarge lifting his legs up and stretching them on the opposite seat. It would be a long and restful train ride if all went well, first through Kentucky, then Indiana, and finally Dearborn Station in Chicago the next morning.

The lieutenant tore open the envelope and read the papers inside intently, memorizing the photos and codewords. He handed them to Sarge, who did the same. Sarge then inserted the papers into a special fortified pouch and sealed it. The pouch slowly became hot to the touch. He took out his sidearm and hefted it, examined it, and replaced it in the shoulder harness. The lieutenant shook his head and chuckled.

"I'm going to catch a nap," said LT.

"Okay. We'll change off every two hours."

THE SOUTHLAND EXPRESS
Wed., April 5, 1945, 3:00 pm Central Wartime

Outside, the porter announced their departure. The train was now leaving the station with subtle vibrations, the noisy banging of cars coupling tight, and squeaky rails. Soon they were clattering along the rails, heading northwestward toward Kentucky. They watched the wooded countryside dash by the window, occasionally interrupted when the train negotiated a high trestle over a sleepy creek or a dark tunnel through the foothills. Eventually, LT pulled the shade down and fell asleep quickly while Sarge strained to stay awake. He kept his right hand near his Colt 1911, the hammer now pulled back. If he had learned anything about military policing it was not to assume anything.

A gentle knocking fell upon their door. Both men stiffened, LT awake. Sarge had his gun out.

"Yes?" LT said.

"Porter, sir."

LT recognized the voice. He opened the door carefully and partially.

The porter announced that the bar was now open and that service would begin in the dining car at 6:00 pm.

"Thank you."

Sarge dreamed about getting a drink but dismissed that notion. One drink couldn't hurt, he thought, except that LT would smell the booze on his breath and then the gig would be over once they got back to Dogpatch. Oh well, maybe once they got to Chicago and passed off the package.

"What did you bring to eat?"

Sarge reached into his suitcase and withdrew a couple of wrapped sandwiches and some peanuts.

"Living large," exclaimed LT.

That's just what I want to do when we get to the big city, Sarge was thinking.

Time passed haltingly yet surely. The stops at Lexington, Cincinnati, and Indianapolis were uneventful. It would be sunrise soon. Not much to see out the window in Indiana. The motion and clacking of the train was rhythmic and soothing. The L&N line wasn't known as "The Old Reliable" for nothing.

The soft light of dawn just before sunrise lit the landscape. The train began to slide past shanty towns and huge metal dumps and industrial parks of arc-welding and wartime fabrications. The *Southland Express* slithered through yards of alternate tracking and trains parked on sidings until it approached the huge brick clock tower marking Dearborn Station. Massive and ornate.

"Richardson Romanesque," LT declared. "All these turn-of-the-century railroad stations are that style."

Once the train stopped and settled, LT and Sarge waited for all the other passengers to disembark. Then they donned their fedoras and tried to act like businessmen. The platform was nearly deserted. The porter bid them farewell. LT could not recall the porter having been on any previous run. There were men standing beside the front of the train. Others near the station itself. All of them looked suspicious, mostly because they were not.

LT and Sarge made their way into the station and walked directly to Room A20, as always. They closed the door and took seats at the big sturdy table in the small windowless room.

Momentarily, two "salesmen" entered the room, two others standing just outside the door. They fit the profiles. They presented credentials. They knew the code words. One of them stated, "No guts."

LT replied, "No glory."

Each of the four men broke into a grin.

"Any problems?" one of the others asked.

"None whatsoever."

One of the men unwrapped the briefcase from LT's arm and then strapped it onto the arm of his colleague. He tested it. Nice and secure. He hefted it to feel the weight.

"Have a good trip, wherever you're going."

The lead man tipped his hat and they all exited the room.

Unknown to LT and Sarge, the other salesmen were boarding the *Santa Fe Chief* and would disembark the next afternoon at a God-forsaken depot in the desert known as Lamy. From there the briefcase would be escorted to its final destination, a secret army lab in the desert—Los Alamos, New Mexico, aka Project Y.

The lieutenant made the affirmation call from the end booth along the wall in the station. "Package delivered," was all he told Capt. Zimmer.

LT had his suspicions regarding the integrity of their mission. He suspected that some if not all of their trips were decoys. The briefcases they were guarding with their lives could be filled with Knoxville telephone books as far as they knew. But, as in combat, they had a job to do, and success was getting the job done. "Ours is not to reason why."

They are ordered to haul the briefcase from Knoxville to Chicago and to guard and protect it with their lives, if necessary. What if their trips were some sort of operation designed to draw out enemy agents. On the train; in the depot. They were just the bait. Or what if these trips were just an exercise to test them and their loyalty? Maybe the high officials are trying out different scenarios to transport valuable items to Chicago, and they haven't sent anything of value yet. The CIC agents are everywhere. What if, what if...

"We have done our job," Sarge said to LT. "We have a couple hours until the return train. Let's go get wasted."

"Probably not a good idea," replied the lieutenant.

"What the hell? What's it gonna hurt? I'm about to go crazy if I don't get some action." He quickly reconsidered his remarks, "But you didn't hear that from me."

LT sighed. "What did you have in mind?"

"Earl talks about this place two blocks over. Second story of the Mertz Building. They treat servicemen real nice there, he says."

"We're salesmen, remember? We deal in fasteners."

"You're ordering me not to go?"

LT thought about what the psychologist had said. Relieving the stress could be beneficial. And Sarge might just go anyway. He didn't want to get into that type of predicament. Besides, Sarge would be sober by the time they got back to Knoxville. LT didn't have the heart, or the good sense, to say no.

"Go do your thing. But you better be back here in 90 minutes. If you're not, I'm leaving without you. And that would make you A-W-O-L." He mouthed the letters ominously.

SUPERMAN IN TRAINING
Wed., April 5, 1945, 10:00 am Central European Summertime

The instructor, Major Claus von Falkenstein, paced at the front of the classroom. He had drilled his students, and this one in particular, endlessly about all manner of Americana, including history, politics, the military, the war, customs, sports, mannerisms, even slang. His pupils probably knew more about the United States than most US citizens.

"Bill, let's begin with history. Tell me about the President of the United States."

"Yes, sir. The president is Franklin Delano Roosevelt, known affectionately as FDR. He was first elected in 1932, and then re-elected three times, lastly in 1944. He is a member of the wealthy class and is known for his homey fireside chats. He and Winston Churchill are good friends."

"What was the first thing he did as President?"

"He abolished Prohibition, which had been an amendment to the Constitution forbidding alcohol. He is a drinker himself."

"Good. He created an organization to put men to work on mostly rural projects."

"The CCC, Civilian Conservation Corps."

"The American soldier just awarded the Congressional Medal of Honor?"

"Audie Murphy, from Texas."

"Other than Europe, where are the Americans fighting now?"

"The island of Okinawa, in the Pacific, against the Japanese."

The instructor cleared his throat and thought for a moment. His ramrod stature was Prussian. His monocle reflected the overhead fluorescent lighting.

"How many states in the U.S.?"

"Forty-eight."

"The capital of Tennessee?"

"Nashville. The largest city is Memphis."

"How did Roosevelt bring electricity to Tennessee?"

"The TVA. Tennessee Valley Authority."

"What does FBI stand for and what are its agents called?"

"Federal Bureau of Investigation. G-men."

The instructor referred to papers on his desk and began shouting out questions quickly, attempting to trip up his student.

Bill responded quickly: Gone with the Wind. Rhett Butler to Scarlett O'Hara: "Frankly, my dear, I don't give a damn." Superman-Clark Kent, Glenn Miller, Miss America-Bess Myerson, Who's on First?-Who. Joe Louis (Brown Bomber) beat Max Schmeling in 1938. Jesse Owens won gold medals at 1936 Berlin Olympic Games.

"Sprechen zie Duetsch?"

"Nein!"

The instructor glared at the student, who immediately realized his mistake. One little miscue, that's all it would take.

"I suppose even the most ignorant American G.I. knows what the word nein means," the instructor admitted. "As long as you act like you belong, act like you know what you're doing, you can get away with just about anything," he said.

Von Falkenstein marched up to the student and demanded, "Your papers, please!"

The student nodded and produced an ID card from his blouse pocket.

"SS?" the instructor inquired.

The student didn't blink. He responded, "Selective Service. No, I enlisted."

"See any action, soldier?"

"No, sir. They are shipping me out to the Pacific."

"Very well," the instructor said, handing back the ID card.

"If it was up to me, I would train you forever, but the time has come. William Anderson—Bill—you are as ready as you'll ever be. I am extremely proud of you. You will do der Fuhrer proud.

"We have taught you all the skills you need to succeed. You are in fine physical shape, the epitome of the finest Aryan Ubermensch. You can climb ropes, walls, trees and jump long and high. You can run at full speed for several miles. You can lift tremendous weights, pull heavy vehicles. You are a master of the martial arts. You can quietly disarm and kill a man with two swift moves. You can endure the worst privations—hunger, thirst, sleep, and even torture to a great extent. You can eat things that would make a goat vomit. Endure odors, bright lights, pressure, and so on. You can parachute from low, fast-moving aircraft. You can drive a two-ton truck or a bulldozer, a light aircraft, and fire a howitzer.

"You are a survivor. You can be charming. You are smart and cunning. You can improvise. You can employ any conceivable weapon, make your own firearms, take guns apart and assemble them blindfolded. You are a competent sniper. You are an explosives expert. And you can work with edged instruments. Pick locks. Move with barely a sound. Like a shadow."

"Yes, sir. You have trained me hard."

THE EURASIAN EAGLE-OWL
Wed., April 5, 1945, 10:20 am Central European Summertime

"What is your code name, Bill Anderson?"

"Uhu. The eagle owl. The supreme predator." He pronounced the name as ooh-who. He handed the instructor a typewritten note:

"Uhu—The Eurasian eagle-owl is one of the largest species of owl, with a wingspan of up to six feet. This bird has distinctive ear tufts, mottled camouflage, and distinctive orange eyes. The eagle-owl is mostly a nocturnal predator. The Luftwaffe, in conjunction with Heinkel Flugzeugwerke, has developed the He129, nicknamed Uhu, a sophisticated night fighter. It was also the first operational military aircraft to be equipped with ejection seats and the first operational German aircraft with tricycle landing gear."

"Then go do your duty." The instructor saluted his protégé and then shook his hand heartily. The student known as Bill Anderson exited the classroom and prepared to make his way to war-torn Berlin.

Major von Falkenstein only then noticed that they were being watched by two others at the back of the room. The short, stocky man was Admiral Wilhelm Canaris, chief of Hitler's military intelligence, and the other was Colonel Erwin von Lahousen-Vivremont, head of Abwehr TT Division, that of espionage and covert affairs. Canaris had controlled German military intelligence since 1934. The scion of a noble Austrian family, Lahousen had orchestrated the staged provocation on the Polish border that launched World War Two in 1939, among other deadly escapades.

"Admiral, Colonel, nice of you to join us," the major greeted them.

"We have come for a status report on your protégé and the upcoming mission," Canaris said. "Let us not delude ourselves at this point; this is a mission of revenge, a personal gift for der Fuhrer upon his birthday. The Reich will doubtless survive as we retreat to the Great Redoubt in the Bavarian mountains and plan our counterattacks against worldwide Bolshevism."

The major was so overwhelmed by the admiral's enthusiasm that he stood rigid and pronounced, "Heil Hitler!" The other two high officials reciprocated with rigid salutes.

"Let us sit and hear your report," said the admiral, laying his hat on the table. The room reverberated with the sounds of chair legs chattering on the hard floor.

"Both of you will, of course, be receiving written reports later, under the highest classification."

Both of the high officials nodded silently. The major cleared his throat and began, referring on occasion to a folder of papers before him.

"Our subject has been exposed to a wide variety of tests, conditioning, development of skills, and deportment. He can swim 450 meters in ten minutes, do 80 push-ups in two minutes, run ten miles or swim two miles without stopping. He's an expert at the combat sidestroke. He has been exposed to intense pressure and stress, extreme temperatures, interrogation techniques, and lack of sleep, food, and water.

"Of course, we have to be careful not to be detrimental in our training; too much brutality might take its toll before we can launch the mission. We have very few suitable substitutes."

"How many substitutes?" asked Col. Lahousen.

"Very few."

"Continue, Major."

"He has undertaken survival training, outdoor craft, climbing and repelling, and, obviously, his experience in combat airborne operations. He is an expert at close-quarter combat and silent killing, and the handling of various Allied weaponry, including small arms, rifles, grenades, mortars, and Panzerschrecks, I mean bazookas, and the .50-caliber machine gun. He can drive an M4A4 tank, a deuce-and-a-half truck, and heavy earthmoving equipment, if need be. He can fix the engine in a Jeep. He is trained in usage of radio equipment and signaling. Also, a basic knowledge of first-aid. Of course, he is an excellent marksman."

"His background?"

"Parents are native Germans. He grew up in the United States. Cincinnati in the state of Ohio. As you have seen and heard he speaks like an American. He has no German accent. He is a superb specimen of Aryan manhood, an Ubermensch, if I may be permitted. He is the perfect undercover agent, infiltrator, and saboteur."

"And his political proclivities? His loyalty?"

"Impeccable. He is a loyal servant of der Fuhrer, more than willing to make the supreme sacrifice. He has an iron will, just like our leader. He will see the mission through. And just in case you're wondering, he has seen significant combat. He dropped into Crete with Karl Student and participated in the so-called Kondomari Reprisal. He participated in Operation Greif under Skorzeny during the Ardennes offensive, impersonating a US officer behind the lines. No fault of his own he was captured. He managed to escape before execution and worked his way back to our lines."

"Zehr gut! What about his contact in the States?"

"He is ready, willing, and able. All is set."

"Uhu is the the most complete Deutsche nationalist and agent of the Third Reich. As Nietzsche said, 'He has crossed over the bridge from the house on the lake to the mountains of unrest and solitude'."

Von Falkenstein settled down for a moment and stated, "Let's start at the beginning. His birth name is Hans Hammerschmidt. Heinrich and Helga Hammerschmidt married in 1919 in Leipzig. Heinrich was a baker and Helga helped in the local brewery. In 1920, they emigrated to the United States seeking a better life. But times were tough in Cincinnati. Heinrich could not keep a job and Helga worked as a washer woman. They became avid followers of Herr Hitler's new political party back in Germany. The couple had a boy child in 1923 named Hans and in 1925 another boy child named Heine. The older boy, Hans, age 11, was sent back to Germany in 1934 specifically to be developed as a special agent of the Third Reich, surpassing even the most ardent SS officer. Heinrich and Helga were investigated by the FBI for their activities in the Amerikan Bund and were deported back to Germany. At that time, Heine could not be located in the US by the authorities. Since then, he has become very useful to us in ways I'd rather not explain."

"Gut," replied the admiral. He glanced around the classroom. "I assume we are alone here?"

"Yessir. This room has been swept, this morning."

"Then go over the plan, and be concise."

THE NAZI PLAN
Wed., April 5, 1945, 10:35 am Central European Summertime

"Yessir. Once we get Uhu out of the country and overseas, he will parachute into the State of Tennessee, near the Clinton Engineer Works, at night. He will then be picked up by our agent via homing beacon and taken to the safe house, where he will be outfitted with a US Army serviceman's uniform and the appropriate papers. His gear will be loaded into the baggage car of the *Southland Express*. He will confront the couriers at the Knoxville train depot and inject the sedative via a pinprick. The military policeman junior in rank. Then on the train at the precise geographical landmark he will make his way to their private cabin, knock down the door, and quickly subdue the senior courier. The briefcase will be cut from the courier. Our man will retreat to the baggage car and don his backpack from a crate placed there that morning. He will open the briefcase and remove the package, which he will secure to his chest in a special bag or harness. He will also carry a lightweight tubular-metal frame that he will attach to the trailing edge of the railcar roof to steady himself. He will have a lightweight but strong loop of canvas-like material to lasso the hook underneath the aircraft, which will be flown above the railcar, traveling at the same speed. The aircraft is a seaplane with twin floats. He will then climb up onto the float structure and up into the cockpit.

At the Grand Gulf trestle in the State of Kentucky he will have approximately 30 seconds to grab the aircraft and be flown away."

"Why this location, this trestle?"

"The overall terrain is heavily wooded and hilly with many twisting curves. In fact, the trestle itself has a gentle curve, which will work to our advantage. The trestle is the only spot clear and open for the connection. The bridge has no superstructure, thus allowing the floatplane to engage with the train."

The admiral expressed his doubts by arching his brow.

"The pilot, passenger, and package will then fly nearly 500 miles to the East Coast to rendezvous with the Unterseeboaten. Specifically, near the Wright Brothers tower at Kill Devil Hills, in the state of North Carolina, at a place called the Outer Banks. The tower is a 60-foot-high monument with flashing light."

"What's the window for the rendezvous?"

"Five hours. At night, of course."

"Go on," replied the admiral, making a point of consulting his pocket watch.

"The men will paddle out to the U-boat and be boarded. During its subsequent underwater journey the package will be loaded into the warhead of the cruise missile."

"The buzz bomb."

"Yes, the jet-pulse missile. Upon surfacing, the missile and launching apparatus will be assembled on deck and the missile launched via the ramp on the forward deck. The objective, of course, is Wall Street, New York City."

"The result?"

"The blast above the city will disperse the radioactive U-235 over a wide radius, rendering the city uninhabitable for the foreseeable future."

"Excellent! Where is the launch point?"

The major referred to his papers. "Ya, here. The Romer Shoal Light, a sparkplug lighthouse in Lower New York Bay, 4.6 kilometers north of Sandy Hook, Jersey. The signal is flashing white twice every 15 seconds."

"What are the hazards in handling the package?"

"Manageable. The Kreigsmarine has taken precautions. They have perfected the techniques needed to facilitate the launch."

"It has been done successfully?"

"Yes. On a trial basis."

"I'm concerned about our man getting off the train successfully. He has trained for this?"

"If you can only imagine. This scenario is difficult to replicate without the possibility of losing our most valuable asset. He has practiced his routine, first on a stationary train, then on a moving train. Then, to replicate grabbing onto the aircraft we had him work with, uh, flying trapeze."

"As in a circus?"

"Something like that. It can be done. It will be done. Also, let me note that our operative in the States has perfected his flying skills over the actual train en route and assures us it can be accomplished."

"Well, for your sake and ours, I hope so," the admiral sighed, glancing at his associate. They donned their hats in unison, gave the HH salute, and promptly left the room.

Major von Falkenstein rubbed his chin and looked wistfully toward the ceiling. Uhu had been trained to the utmost to perform this dangerous mission. He was hard as a rock; sharp as a knife.

The mission depended upon so many things going right, plus the precise timing. The U-boat being undetected off the coast. If everything went smoothly, he could expect an advancement in rank, perhaps a meeting with der Fuhrer himself. If the mission failed, and he gave it less than a 50-50 chance, he would use his trusty Walther PPK.

THE FISTFIGHT
Thurs., April 6, 1945, 6:00 am Central Wartime

The moment Sarge disappeared out the stained-glass doors of the Chicago train station LT regretted not pulling rank on him. Would he really leave without Sarge if he didn't come back? I'm not one to make idle threats, he mused. This is going to be a long 90 minutes.

Sarge had left him in charge of the suitcase, the one with the odds and ends. Hungry, he walked to the Fred Harvey restaurant in the terminal. As he recalled, Harvey started the first restaurant chain, linked to the railroads, back in the late 1800s. He thought about the grilled calf's sweetbreads with mushrooms, but he ended up ordering the buttered spaghetti with chicken giblets and a cup of coffee. He paid the Harvey girl—quite fetching in her little apron outfit—with a dollar bill and told her to keep the change. Throughout the terminal workmen were hanging red-white-and-blue banners. FDR himself looked down upon the vast open space from a large portrait over the marble staircase. Might as well grab a *Tribune* and read about the war while waiting.

Ink-smudged fingers and 85 minutes later and still no Sarge.

"Damn it," LT cursed, glancing again at his watch. All of a sudden, a crescendo of heated words between what sounded like two men erupted from outside the entrance. Some kind of ruckus. The lieutenant grabbed Sarge's suitcase and tromped to the doorway. He swung open a door only to find Sarge sprawled out on the steps rubbing his jaw with a bloody hand. His suit was laid open. Blood trickled from the corner of his mouth. He was three sheets to the wind.

"What the hell," LT said, glancing around. The perps were nowhere in sight. No cops yet either.

LT grabbed Sarge by the upper arm and pressed a handkerchief to his face. He awkwardly buttoned Sarge's jacket so his sidearm and holster wouldn't show.

"Can you get up? We have a train to catch. You can have a nice, long train ride to sober up. By that time maybe I will have decided what to do with you. I just hope this little stunt was worth it."

Sarge was wobbly on his legs and unable to move his body in any coherent manner.

"Stand up, I'll help you. Wipe that blood off and let's get you on the train."

A porter emerged from the station, looking concerned. "What the heck happened to you?"

"He fell and hit his head."

"Uh-huh. I'll have some ice and a compress sent to your cabin."

"Thanks. Appreciate that."

Obviously, the porter was familiar with them. LT suspected at this point that half of the denizens at Dearborn wondered why two salesmen would took the *Southland Express* from Knoxville to Chicago and then turned right around to catch a train back to Knoxville.

LT and Sarge occupied a reserved cabin in the last car on the sleek train. Heading south out of Chicago. On this leg, they had no briefcase to safeguard with their lives. LT felt a little more relaxed, although he still had to figure out what to do about Sarge. He pulled down the shades on the windows.

The porter brought the ice compress and Sarge held it against his aching head. Sarge spread out on the bench seat after taking his shoes off. "Yeah, it was worth it alright. The whiskey's in my head and a gal named Angela, she was an angel all right." Then he fell asleep with a stupid smile on this face and didn't budge for the next eight hours. He moaned and groaned a lot though.

By the time they reached Knoxville, Sarge had sobered up but still looked like hell. His lip was swollen. He had some explaining to do.

Back at Dogpatch, the couriers were immediately debriefed by the major and two aides in a windowless room. Following the perfunctory checklist, LT asked the major, "Sir, will there come a time when we learn what's inside the briefcase?"

"Soon enough, lieutenant, soon enough." The major did not want them to know that he was clueless himself. He did know that if the couriers failed, it would be his ass in a sling. He chuckled, "Be careful what you wish for, lieutenant."

Turning to the sergeant, the major noted, "That's quite a bruise you got there on your face, Sergeant."

"He fell," offered the lieutenant.

"He fell. Uh-huh," said the major, unconvinced. "What's the other guy look like?" he wondered rhetorically.

One of the aides stated, "Well, if you guys have nothing else, I guess that's it."

"Sergeant, stay behind," the major ordered and then waved the two aides out of the room.

"Sergeant, you were recognized in Chicago at Madam Chang's so-called House of Delight on Dearborn. We have informants all over the place."

Sarge tried to look contrite. LT rolled his eyes.

"I don't know what happened and I don't want to know. I do know you had only a brief time between trains. Madam Chang's is only two blocks away. I guess you needed some R&R. Well, honestly, I hope you got some. I'm going to let it slide this one time."

The major arose and glared at the sergeant with dead-serious eyes. His voice rose. "Do you understand, sergeant?"

Sarge had already jumped to attention and hurried a salute. "Yes, sir."

"Dismissed."

The major held the lieutenant behind and shut the door. He sat on the edge of the desk, lit up a Lucky Strike, and offered one to the other man, who declined.

"I'm concerned," said the major.

"Just a rough spot he's going through."

"Can you straighten him out? He goes Asiatic on us it's both our hides."

"It'll be all right," the lieutenant assured, nodding. "I'll keep an eye on him."

"No more of this hoochie-coochie business."

"No sir!"

"Dismissed."

Little did either officer realize that they both had already decided one more courier duty for Sarge and that was it.

ANXIETY
Fri., April 7, 1945, 10:15 am Central Wartime

The major met with Captain Zimmer in his office in Building 9733-1. The small room was festooned with photos of the captain and military colleagues, some grip-and-grin shots with politicos, banners, and athletic trophies. A wooden desk and three chairs. The major sat in one of them, crossed his legs, and lit up a Lucky. The captain fit an unlit pipe between his teeth.

"Well, major, what do you think. Do we give them a real one or not? Do we pull them off courier duty altogether?"

The major pursed his lips thoughtfully.

"The lieutenant is a solid sort although he doesn't exert his authority. Not a Type A personality."

"The sergeant?"

"Something altogether different. I have my concerns, serious concerns. He's a Pacific combat veteran, you know. He's had nightmares. The stress of combat. Can't get it out of his head. On the other hand, I get the impression he is bored stiff with his MP duties. Nobody shooting at him. And life on the reservation. Pretty dull."

"What's your recommendation?"

"I think we give them at least one more courier mission."

"Okay. But I'm going to assign at least one more MP to the train. Just to make sure things don't go awry."

The major nodded in approval. "Well then." He slid the chair back and left the room.

Captain Zimmer took the pipe from his mouth and set it on the ashtray holder. He picked up the phone. "Get me military intelligence," he ordered.

BIG DAN THE HARDWARE MAN
Fri., April 7, 1945, 2:30 pm Eastern Wartime

Courier duty on train trips to Chicago and back were only a small part of the chores of CEW military police. Patrolling the perimeter of the reservation on horseback occupied much of their time. They also assisted with guard duties at the gates and dealing with the paperwork needed for resident and guest credentials. They maintained law and order amongst the reservation residents. Sometimes they were ordered into town on various chores.

On Friday, LT and Sarge drove a deuce-and-a-half truck into Knoxville to deliver raw materials to Cumberland Machine and bring back some finished work. They wore their MP uniforms, helmets, and sidearms. In the back bed, wooden crates with rope handles contained some rare tungsten metal, cylinders made of pure nickel, and a couple of bars of 24-carat gold straight from Fort Knox. Cumberland Machine was located in a storefront on State Street down by the river. The streetside portion of the building was a display floor for construction contractors, with the machine shop in the back and in the basement.

Mel the proprietor, who always wore a vest and visor, met the Army truck at the rear loading dock in a darkened alley. Emerging from the doorway to watch over the proceedings was none other than Big Dan the Hardware Man. Daniel Ross was a big man with sturdy build, blue eyes and a shock of blond hair. He was also the owner of Cumberland Machine and other shops, a chain of hardware stores, rental properties, real estate, and only God knows what else. His businesses held a lot of wartime contracts with the federal government.

A wizard at self-promotion, Big Dan likes to star in his radio commercials and experiments with stage appearances. He is a well-known character about town, although he is not a native.

"Didn't expect to meet Big Dan the Man today," LT crowed and put his hand out.

Big Dan shook his hand and then offered a sharp salute. "How's things on the reservation?"

"Same ole same ole."

"Can't talk, I understand. You got some good stuff for us today?"

"Yessir."

LT and Sarge grabbed the handles on each end of a small crate stenciled "HEAVY."

"You know what's in there, don't you?" Big Dan teased.

"I got a good idea," LT replied. "Something heavy."

"You know what we do with it?"

LT shook his head.

"Well, I'll tell you, seeing as how you guys are military police officers." Big Dan glanced over at Mel, who was busy checking the manifest on a clipboard. Without looking up, he gestured as if to say "you're the boss."

"We do a lot of electroplating here, you know, for electrical contractors and such. Even plating for mechanicals out at CEW. Anyway, we take the gold in them bars and electroplate it onto the surface of those cylinders in that other crate. Type One with a Knoop hardness of two hundred. The gold is plated onto the nickel cylinders to a thickness of one micron. The thickness of paper, like that manifest sheet, is about one hundred microns."

"Wow, that's thinner than a frog's whisker."

"We do precision work here. No idea whatsoever the purpose of those gold-plated nickel cylinders. Whatever they hold must be something precious. We've got a couple of plated ones for you to take back to CEW."

"The government must pay a lot for you to do that."

"I ain't smoking no five-and-dime cigar, sonny," said Big Dan, laughing.

A couple of workmen loaded the small wooden crate into the bed of the truck.

"Don't you go losing that, you hear? See you next time." Big Dan waved them off.

One of the workmen said to the other, "It's lunchtime, Stinky. Let's go get some grub."

While the MPs drove back to the reservation, Big Dan drove his shiny 1938 Packard convertible away from downtown and along Kingston Pike, admiring the dogwoods in bloom along the way. Knoxville was well-known for its abundance of dogwoods, azaleas, magnolias, forsythia, tulips, and other flowering species. The city celebrated with a Dogwood Festival each spring. The cultivation of the flowering trees intensified after a well-known big-city travel writer described Knoxville as the ugliest city in the USA.

Holston Hills was a fancy neighborhood, but Big Dan resides in a fine brick home in Sequoyah Hills right on the river. He and his wife, Doris, have two children, a boy and a girl. He has a pleasure cruiser parked at his dock. Knoxville is within easy driving distance of the Smoky Mountains National Park and the foothills are even closer. It's only twenty miles to his second home on the manmade lake at Top of the World, just off the Foothills Parkway.

One might ask how Big Dan could obtain the fuel necessary to operate such vehicles and an opulent lifestyle. Big Dan owns hardware stores, tool and dye shops, machine shops and fabricators, many of which are involved in lucrative wartime contracts with the government. Big Dan is careful that his products and services are top-notch. He is a patriotic American who supports the soldiers overseas. He buys war bonds and even helps with the bond drives. He also doesn't mind charging the government outrageous fees for work the government can't or won't do itself. He shares his wealth with the community, making lots of contributions toward the common good.

He also likes to contribute generously to the campaign funds of his favorite local politicians, and he is not shy about asking favors in return. Nothing outrageous, of course, all within the limits of common decency. He also likes to entertain at his lakeside retreat in the foothills. The lodge's liquor cabinets are stocked with the finest Tennessee whiskeys, Kentucky bourbon, and single-malt Scotch, along with fine wines and brandies. Cigars are plentiful; don't ask how he obtains them from foreign countries. Entertaining local politicians and local captains of industry also involves securing female "companionship" in a discreet manner. After all, Big Dan is not a common pimp. One of the favorite activities at the lodge is skinny dipping after the sun sets. The Polar Bear Club. At altitude, the clear waters are so cold one does not even feel the shock of entering.

Alcohol makes for loose lips and female companions can pry all kinds of information from their relaxed paramours.

THE KNUCKLEHEADS
Fri., April 7, 1945, 4:05 pm Eastern Wartime

Down the cargo platform at the L&N rail station, past the warehouse full of boxes of C-rations, along the treeline covered with coal soot, into a low-lying dank underbelly of a commercial building glowed the dim lamps of an establishment known only to its patrons as Pinky's. The original proprietor, a beefy fellow who would grill his thick steaks in a shovel over a coal fire, was long gone, the place now run by a nephew who waters down the drinks, spits tobacco on the floor behind the bar, and exhibits a nervous facial twitch. For all this, they call him Pops.

The clientele is strictly semi-skilled blue-collar, if they have any employment at all. Many have no visible means of support, financially or physically. Any college-age student who stumbled into this hole-in-the-wall with thoughts of a good time would be lucky to exit with merely a black eye and a poke in the chops. Delmonico's this is not. Not even servicemen are welcome unless they are related to a regular customer.

Impressive is the old wooden bar along one wall, forming a mantel over a large grimy mirror and holding souvenirs and mementoes of dubious providence. Old calendars share space with pin-up girls and an old portrait of Ambrose Burnside. Southern men these are through and through, many flinty ole Scots-Irish, but loyal to the Union even during the late great unpleasantness. A few old pensioners sit heads hung low at the bar, gripping their heavy glass mugs of low-alcohol, watered-down beer and staring at their blurry images in the mirror. The narrow room hangs heavy with cigarette and cigar smoke. Unspoken is the fact that any female lost enough to wander into the premises would be quickly but politely escorted outside. The police knew well of the place and leave it alone as much as possible.

Drinking alcohol during wartime is a peculiar pastime. Breweries are allowed to produce low-alcohol-content beer, the favored brand here being Barbarossa lager rated at three percent. Pre-war stocks of whiskey, brandy, and gin are just about to run out after years of war, but the locals could turn to moonshiners for their poison and use various fruit juices to chase the vile, unaged spirits. The best illegal distillations, particularly the red corn variety, are reserved for special buyers, such as the joints up in Chicago run by wise guys.

Barbarossa beer is brewed in Cincinnati by Red Top Brewing Co. at their Dayton Street plant. The beer is named for Frederick I, king of Germany and a Holy Roman emperor. According to legend, Barbarossa hides in a cave, biding his time and waiting for the ravens to stop flying so he can return to Germany in triumph. Frederick I has been rehabbed into a military hero. His legend is worshipped by Adolph Hitler, who named the 1941 German invasion of the Soviet Union, Operation Barbarossa, after him.

Stateside, war brings scarcity. Most every commodity is regulated by the Office of Price Administration. Gasoline and beef are rationed, as are sugar and tires. Monthly, citizens are issued books of coupons which could be exchanged for foodstuffs and fuel. If you are a war industry worker, you put the "B" sticker on your windshield and are allowed eight gallons of gasoline per week. Fresh fruits and veggies are not rationed, and neither are whiskey and cigarettes. Each person is allowed a half-pound of sugar per week and one pound of coffee every five weeks. Violations draw $10,000 fine or ten years in prison. Rationing led to bartering, and a black market for counterfeit ration books.

During the war, premium-tobacco cigarettes are reserved for the troops overseas and at post exchanges at military facilities. US civilians get the inferior brands such as Dukes and Leaf. A vigorous black market ensures that folks with cash, such as war industry workers, can procure cartons of the good smokes, diverted from shipment overseas. Cigarettes can also be bartered for other scarce goods.

Certain patrons of Pinky's are rumored to be involved in black marketing and even the counterfeiting of ration coupon books. Business is brisk and profits were plenty. There is a racket run out of the railroad terminal where boxes of whiskey (red corn whiskey) are shipped to Chicago in exchange for stolen goods or counterfeit ration books. Inebriates paid a premium for what is essentially unaged corn whiskey. In the Appalachians, as in Scotland, usquebaugh (whiskey), is the water of life.

Pinky's informal gang of knuckleheads, who have used every trick in the book to avoid the draft, call themselves the Cods (shorthand for Carnal Order of Derelicts). There are few rules and no by-laws, but a member could be busted out by an impromptu kangaroo court for lack of activity, bad-mouthing other members, and other indiscretions that reflect badly on the gang.

The clientele of the tavern included Zemo, Bodean, Chuckles, Coon

Dog, DB or Dreamboat, Stevie Bug, Jabordnic, FlimFlam, and Squirrel, some of them high-functioning and some not so much. Alcohol influences many of their activities; memories grow dim with age and usage. There are no happy hours for the Cods. Happy hour is for amateurs.

Pecker is the unofficial leader of the gang, but Hacksaw is the only one with a steady legitimate job. He is employed along with dozens of other guys by Ace Freight to load and unload railcars at the depot. It was manual labor but a good, steady job. Hacksaw kept his mouth shut and his eyes open. Lots of important people and important cargo moved through the L&N depot and he knew the comings and goings of them all. Information is valuable.

Seated around the worn green-felt table are Jabordnic the dealer, Pecker, Hacksaw, Large Donnie, and Bum. Steel beer cans, bottles of whiskey, and ashtrays crowded the table. They played with chips—a blue chip for a four-pack of cigarettes (normally issued with each K-ration).

Pecker smoked Chesterfields; Hacksaw preferred Lucky Strike; Large Donnie liked Old Gold; and Bum puffed on Camels.

The game was five-card draw, nothing wild. The five cards are dealt and the players perused their hands, calculating the odds, keeping a straight face, and scrutinizing the others.

"Give me one," demanded Pecker, who was holding four spades.

The others reacted to Pecker's request with savvy expressions. They didn't know what he had, but it was something fairly good.

Pecker's expression did not change as he looked at his new card, a three of diamonds.

"I'll take three," Hacksaw told the dealer. He kept two tens. He got a jack of hearts, an ace, and the ten of spades. He carefully grouped his three tens together in his hand.

"Give me four" groused Large Donnie, throwing his cards on the table.

"You can't get four, you idiot. Three's the limit," the dealer explained.

"What a four-flusher," growled Pecker.

"Okay, then give me three," he said indignantly. Large Donnie looked at his new hand. He still had nothing. His face betrayed his disappointment.

"Well, we know who's out of this round," chirped Pecker.

Bum indicated he would take one card. He seemed proud of himself, but he should've known better than to draw into an inside straight. Never works.

The dealer took three cards and then threw down with disgust. "Can't even deal myself decent cards!"

Pecker played it cool and threw one blue chip into the pot.

Hacksaw scrunched his mouth, then threw two blue chips into the pot. "Raise you one blue."

Large Donnie rolled his eyes and threw his cards onto the table. "I'm out, that's for sure."

Bum tried to look like he was pondering whether to call or raise, then threw his cards down.

"Nice bluff," Pecker noted with a grin. "Just you and me, pal," he said to Hacksaw.

Hacksaw was confident. He raised Pecker another blue chip.

Pecker openly grinned. "Well, okay then. I will raise you another two blue ones." He stared at his opponent intently as if to say, "Now what are you going to do?"

Hacksaw tried to resist his growing doubts. But he couldn't. He had three tens but Pecker surely had better. He could be bluffing, of course, but it would cost him to find out.

"Shit, I'm out," Hacksaw finally conceded. "What you got?"

"Hell, I don't have to show you and I'm not gonna." Pecker raked in the chips.

Hacksaw reached over the table and grabbed Pecker's cards. He realized he'd been bamboozled and got mad at his own lack of gumption. Pecker was literally a four-flusher.

"Any other place, that would get you killed. You know that?" Pecker stated.

"Whatever," Hacksaw moped, still gritting his teeth.

OPERATION BRILLIANT
Fri., April 7, 1945, 4:30 pm Eastern Wartime

Pecker looked at the dealer. "Take a hike, would ya? I want to talk to these knuckleheads."

Jabordnic gathered up his beer and cigs and left the table.

"Yeah, what?" Bum said, his mouth full of pretzel.

"Ain't no laughing matter," Pecker insisted. "And it's worth a lot of money. For all of us."

"He's right," said Hacksaw, quickly forgetting about the poker game.

Big Donnie stretched out his legs and played with his chips on the table.

Pecker began in earnest. "We been stealing right and left for a while now. Black market's been good to us. Dealing in bogus coupons, same thing. But this is big stuff and I mean big." Pecker nodded his head and he met the eyes of each Cod individually. "Tell 'em what you know," he said to Hacksaw, who was privy to the plot.

"Okay, this is the deal. Nobody knows for sure what's going on up there at the Army installation, right."

"CEW, the engineering works?" asked Bum.

"That's right, genius."

"Hell, I know," he replied.

"How do you know? What do you know?"

"I put two and two together. They're making uranium for a super bomb," he stated matter-of-factly.

"What? You don't know your ass from a hole in the ground. You read that stuff in *Popular Mechanics*." Only he pronounced popular as poplar. "Dumb ass."

"I didn't know he could read," Large Donnie giggled.

"Anyway," he said, smirking at Bum. "This is the deal. Ever so often these two Army guys show up at the depot dressed like civilians, suits and all. Military shine on their shoes. Burr haircuts. Who they trying to fool? One has a briefcase strapped to his arm. And the briefcase looks heavy by the way he's holding it. They're packing heat. They take the train to Chicago."

"So what?" said Big Donnie.

"So what is this, wise guy," said Pecker. "I got a guy on the inside; he's paid well. He can tell us when these guys are coming to the depot with their…cargo. Besides, they always travel on Wednesday, every other Wednesday and get on the *Southland Express*. My friends up in Chicago confirm this. Every other Thursday the two couriers arrive at the Dearborn station and exchange their briefcase with two other couriers who get on the *Santa Fe Chief*."

"What cargo?" Large Donnie and Bum asked together.

"Something extremely valuable to the Army, that's for sure."

"It's the uranium," Bum said.

"Are you nuts? Something like that they'd ship in a convoy or something."

"Then it must be gold," said Large Donnie.

"I thought of that. For one thing, gold would be too heavy to haul around in a briefcase. Besides, I know a guy down at Cumberland Machine. They make special gold-plated containers out of nickel for CEW. Not very many of them, a few dozen. The containers are in the briefcase. Why would they carry gold inside gold-plated containers?"

"Then what the hell is it?" insisted Bum.

"Isn't it obvious? Tons of raw material goes into the reservation and the only thing that comes out can fit in a briefcase?"

"Well?"

"It's diamonds, bonehead. They're making artificial diamonds. It's the only thing that makes any sense."

"Jewelry?"

Pecker shook his head in exasperation. "Diamonds are a broad's best friend, sure. But diamonds have all kinds of industrial uses, for cutting materials and such. Big wartime industrial uses."

"Huh" was all Bum could utter as they pondered the implications. Then he shoved another pretzel into his mouth.

"Let's take those diamonds for ourselves. Trade them on the black market. I know a guy in Chicago that could make it happen. Split four ways, of course."

"Of course," said Hacksaw, although he really thought he should get more.

"How?" said Bum.

"Here's how. I got it all planned," said Pecker, "but first I got something to show you."

Pecker went into the back room through a black-out curtain and came back with a box and a case.

"First of all, this beauty," he said, unsnapping the locks on the small black case. He pulled out a Model 1928 Thompson submachine gun and propped it upwards on his thigh. "Just like Dillinger," he said proudly. He reached into the case, pulled out a 100-round drum magazine and slide it into place. It took several attempts to get it to fasten properly. "Serious firepower," he declared. He held the firearm with the front and rear pistol grips and swept the room as if to exterminate his buddies.

"Holy shit," Bum said. "Where'd the hell you get that?"

"Let's just say I have connections." He handed the Thompson over to Large Donnie for inspection. "Be careful with that."

Pecker bent over to unlatch the elongated box and brought up a long metal tube. An M1A1 recoilless anti-tank rocket launcher. He hefted it onto his shoulder.

"Damnation, a bazooka!" Bum cried out. "We're gonna take out a tank?"

"Something like that," Pecker agreed. "I only got a couple rounds for this thing," he noted.

"You know how to use that thing?" Bum wanted to know.

"Of course, piece of cake. Load, aim, and shoot. Just don't stand behind it. Might ruin your day."

Pecker also brought out some used handguns, their serial numbers filed off and untraceable, and boxes of ammo. "Help yourselves, guys."

"Now gather round, you knuckleheads, and I'll lay out the plan. Everybody's got a part to play."

"We need a name," said Bum.

Annoyed at first, Pecker thought for a moment. "Let's call it Operation Brilliant."

JONNY AND BIG BIRD
Sat., April 8, 1945, 4:10 pm Eastern Wartime

Down south, the canyons are called gulfs and the lakes are reservoirs, deep man-made lakes. Reportedly, Kentucky has only three natural lakes and Tennessee just one, created by an 1815 earthquake that made the Mississippi River flow backwards.

The Grand Gulf Trestle over Laurel Hill Lake in Kentucky is a masterpiece of engineering, a quarter-mile-long narrow railway bed curving 150 feet above the waters of the manmade reservoir. The all-iron bridge consists of 24 load-bearing trestles, each composed of three sections of varying widths. As Abe Lincoln once said of a similar trestle, it looks like it was built out of cornstalks and beanpoles. The bridge has no superstructure, no beams above the railroad track. Built in record time back in the 1930s, the bridge helped link Knoxville with Lexington and parts farther north. The supports for the bridge also make for attractive fishing grounds in the reservoir.

Jonny Jefferson fishes these waters often, using only well-worn gear and an old wooden rowboat, pitched in the bow and squared at the stern, no motor. Even if he had the wherewithal to buy a small outboard motor he couldn't get the gas to run it. This late afternoon, Jonny was poling along the south bank at a gentle bend which allowed a full view of the massive Louisville & Nashville trestle. If you were crazy enough to walk out to the middle of the railroad tracks you'd probably get dizzy and fall off. The damn thing was tall enough, several locals had used it to do away with themselves, with no uncertainty as to the outcome.

In the bottom of the boat Jonny kept a squirming tow sack containing seven fair-sized snapping turtles he had yanked out from under tree roots along the bank with a curved piece of rebar. Damn good eating, that turtle meat, if you knew how to prepare it. Tastes better than chicken. Turtle soup was the best. Not bad eating for some devilish-looking creature dating back 40 million years with jaws powerful enough to snap fingers like twigs. Jonny would have some work that night butchering, but the work would be worth it. With its jaws clamped tight on a dowel, the turtle's head came off with a cleaver chop, and the shell pried open with a crowbar. His dogs liked the tails and the legs. Besides, what else did he have to do with his time, now that Gladys was gone?

Jonny rowed the boat back across to the north bank when he saw something so peculiar he doubted his own senses. The episode took probably fifteen to twenty seconds in all. He knew the *Southland Express* was coming through, heading north, right on schedule. He could hear the echoes of the horn before the sleek locomotive broke into view from the thick wooded terrain that bordered both sides of the trestle. At the time he was midstream, almost under the structure. Then, just as soon, he saw what looked like a huge bird or shadow flying over the train, matching its speed. Halfway across, he realized he was watching a small aircraft, bright yellow, fitted with landing floats, soaring just above the passenger train, about midway along the 12-car train, speeding along as if it were actually attached to the top of the train. Then, just as it reached the north bank, the aircraft veered suddenly to the right, gaining altitude and then soaring back in the direction it had come.

"What the hell?" Jonny muttered to himself, sitting back down. He had seen some big birds above the lake—vultures, red-tailed hawks, even some eagles—but this for sure took the cake. He pondered for a moment what he had just witnessed. He had taken a few swigs from the mason jar for sure, but it was too damn hot to drink enough to see "things." He learned that lesson a few years ago when he passed out in the boat and woke up two hours later eight miles downstream.

Jonny rowed over to the rusting dock, tied up, and made his way up to Johnson's Grocery, now known as Hardscrabble. Once a decent neighborhood store, the ramshackle storefront resembled nothing more than a depository of odds and ends and selling some essentials such as tobacco twists, jars of white dog, matches, some canned goods, pickled eggs and other foodstuffs for barter, used equipment, and live bait. The glass display case, which once contained boxes of various sweet treats and candy back in the day, was now cloudy and opaque from years of scratches. Of course, if you had connections and the right amount of cash, there was real merchandise in the back.

The proprietor, a fella named Roy whose nickname was Doolittle, sat on a wood frame chair leaned against the wall. There were a few good ole boys sitting behind the counter biding their time, away from their wives.

"Whatcha say, Jonny boy? Fish biting?"

"Not really, but I found myself some big ole snapping turtles."

"Still got all your fingers?" Roy asked, pulling at the loose skin on his throat.

"Reckon so."

"You hear much from your boy, Calvin?"

"Not much lately. I reckon they got him busy up there in Jersey."

"Jersey, huh? He did right good for himself, ya know. Proud him."

Jonny's son, Calvin, was a sharp kid, much more than his old man. He flew with the Tuskegee Airmen, the proud Negro pilots in the US Army Air Force. It had been a tough row to hoe, but he had the guts and determination to make the grade. Not to mention the skills needed to master a North American P-51 Mustang fighter plane. Calvin and his particular unit never made it overseas; the war was winding down too fast, at least in the ETO. So he ended up based in New Jersey, participating in maritime patrols and other "garrison" duties. He didn't pilot a Mustang, he flew a Republic P-47 Thunderbolt, a powerful ground-pounder they call the Jug.

"Did y'all see anything peculiar about the *Southland* just now?"

"I heard it. Didn't see it. Why?"

Jonny ducked his head a little and stroked his chin whiskers. "I need to tell ya something. Something I just saw."

"Oh yeah, and what's that?"

"The *Southland* rode the trestle a mite back, just on schedule. And I seen an airplane swoop down on it like a redtail hawk on a field mouse. Almost like it wanted to hitch a ride on the top of the train. But then it just flew off…and away."

Roy squinted and grimaced as if the gesture could discern Jonny's honesty. "Say what? You been drinking that bad hootch again?"

"No sir. Well maybe just a bit. But I done seen what I seen. Hain't making it up."

"Oh, I believe you, Jonny. Surely I do. Maybe it was a military thing or a stunt."

Jonny wasn't convinced that Roy was telling the truth now. Perhaps he oughta just let it rest. Maybe he had conjured it up in his head. Being out in the hot sun can produce some wild sights. Besides, what am I going to do with this information, report it to the sheriff? That'll be the day.

"Oh well, shit, guess I'll mosey on home," he finally said.

"You do that now. Get some rest."

Hell, I ain't sick, Jonny thought. And I got a lot of butchering to do.

The next day Jonny rowed out to the middle of the lake. He did not go fishing. He watched the *Southland Express* rumble along that high track, right on schedule, but no airplane. Not a thing. On Tuesday, however, he was back fishing. The train showed up on time. And so did the same aircraft, the one with floats. It bird-dogged that train and then swooped away out of sight.

"Shit!" Jonny Jefferson spat. And he threw the mason jar as far as he could into the lake.

ESCAPE FROM BERLIN
Sat., April 8, 1945, 11:00 am Central European Summertime

The ruins of Berlin smolder under relentless artillery attacks. Most of the buildings in the city core are burned out, windows open, roofs gone, standing like teetering masonry exoskeletons. Thousands are homeless and on the move, fleeing to the west to avoid the Soviets. The streets, filled with rubble, discarded weaponry and vehicles, are barely passable. The bodies of defeatist Germans and deserters hang from street lampposts with piano wire, warning signs attached to their clothing. "Ich bin ein Deserteur. I have declined to defend German women and children and therefore I have been hanged." The stolid air is filled with lingering clouds of dust and the stench of death. The fighting is block to block, house to house, hand to hand. One Wehrmacht machine-gunner says of the enemy, "They weren't human beings for us. It was a wall of attacking beasts who were trying to kill us. You yourself were no longer human."

Over at the Ministry of Aviation, a brutalist office building (the largest in Europe), torrents of official Third Reich papers are being propelled out the windows inside the courtyards, where they drift down like large snowflakes. Upright barrels of burning fuel are used to incinerate the incriminating papers.

As Soviet troops with motorized artillery, ISU-122 assault guns, and T-34 tanks move into the suburbs and closer, Adolf Hitler, secure in his underground bunker at the Reich Chancellery, has suffered a nervous breakdown after being informed by his generals that all is lost. Hitler's plans to hold fast in the Berlin Festung are entirely delusionary, just pipe-dreams on a paper map. Advised by his staff to leave Berlin (a special Fw300 Condor four-engine aircraft is on hold at Templehof Airport) and continue the struggle at the National Redoubt in Bavarian Alps, der Fuhrer insisted, "Either I win the Battle of Berlin or I die in Berlin." He then rages on about the deception by his generals and the failure of the German people to stand fast and uphold the Reich. The people have failed him and they will suffer the death they deserve.

Other high officials seek to flee the city before being captured by the Soviets and suffering a fate worse than death. The Berlin police have stationed an Ordnungspolizei armored car platoon at the Ehrenhoft courtyard, ready to carry high officials out of the city. Perhaps, now it is too late. Soviet troops are raping German females of all ages by the thousands; many women commit suicide rather than fall into the hands of the Bolsheviks.

Defenses in the southwest sector of the city collapse as the 1st Guards Tank Army pushes along the south bank of the Spree River to reach the Zitadelle. The 8th Guards Mechanized Corps breach the southeastern Zitadelle defenses, crossing the Landwehr Canal near the Wehrmacht headquarters west of the Potsdamer railway station. Two King Tiger tanks are parked in the plaza of the train station with clear lines of fire in several directions. The crew of King Tiger 314, commanded by SS-Unterscharfuhrer Georg Diers, is personally decorated by Hitler for their efforts to defend the Fuhrerbunker. They are credited with destroying 39 Soviet tanks in the city.

Nazi party officials and Waffen-SS officers break out from the Reich's Chancellery to cross the Weidendammer bridge towards Spandau to the north. Moving in the dark with mechanized vehicles, the group is assaulted by Soviet infantry near the Friedrichstrasse rail station. Only a few survivors, along with one King Tiger tank, manage to reach the Humboldthain park across the river.

Meanwhile, a shadowy figure in military fatigues jogs his way through the debris and ruins, past the Brandenburg Gate and up to a small aircraft idling at the east end of the emergency landing strip running through the Tiergarten. He wears a light backpack with a metal tube strapped to it. The wide Ost-West Achse is mostly clear, lit only by a burning Sturmgetschitz assault vehicle on its shoulder. The tandem-seat Fieseler Fi156 Storch (Stork), a tail-dragger, resembles a delicate insect or kite rather than a military airplane. The Storch, with its abnormally long fixed landing gear, is specifically designed to take off and land on short runways. It will have to today, because halfway through the Tiergarten the emergency strip is obstructed by the tall Victory Column in the middle of the Grosser Stern.

The shadowy figure slips into the rear seat and greets the pilot, the celebrated Hanna Reitsch, a daring test pilot decorated by der Fuhrer himself.

Reitsch is petite with blond hair and blue eyes. She holds the Iron Cross 1st Class for testing the dangerous Me163 Komet rocket interceptor. She crashed and spent five months recuperating in the hospital. She was the first woman to fly a jet aircraft. She wanted to convert the V-1 buzz bomb into a manned "suicide" missile, but the concept never materialized. Of late, she has spent three weeks on the Eastern Front flying a Storch from one Luftwaffe unit to another.

German women, unlike the Allies or Soviets, did not serve in the military or work in war industries, but the militaristic talents of a few German women could not be ignored. Reitsch is an ardent Nazi and admirer of Hitler, who used her exploits for great propaganda effect. She starred in the grandiose films made by Leni Riefenstahl.

Reitsch had arrived in Berlin via the Storch, along with her fiancé, General Robert Ritter von Greim, the commander of Luftwaffe forces on the shrinking Eastern Front. Greim had been summoned to the Fuhrerbunker, where Hitler would promote him to field marshal and head of the Luftwaffe, replacing Hermann Goering, who had been charged with treason. Greim was ordered to arrest Heinrich Himmler, leader of the SS (Schutzstaffel), who was trying to negotiate a surrender with the British and Americans. Greim and Reitsch would fly out of Berlin in an Arado Ar96 multi-seat advanced trainer on April 28th, but not before the famed aviatrix flew an international errand.

"So they call you Uhu," she yelled. "Eagle owl. Fasten your belt."

He buckled up but said nothing.

"Well, Uhu, here we go."

She pushed the throttle forward, arousing the roaring engine and vibrating the instrument panel as one. The noise in the cockpit was loud; talking was difficult. The Storch began rolling down the avenue. She would have preferred to scout the so-called runway for debris, but she had no time and it would have been dangerous. The moon was half full and lit the runway when it wasn't obscured by smoke. The plane quickly gained speed and bounded as the Victory Column, 220 feet high, loomed ever larger in the windshield. The spindly craft hopped several quick times on its fixed landing gear, then quickly vaulted into the air as Reitsch angled the plane clear of the obstruction. He felt as if he could reach out and touch the monument. They heard small-arms fire at them to no effect. He could see the massive German flak tower at the Berlin Zoo, tall as a 13-story building and bristling with 105mm anti-aircraft guns. Don't bother with us, he silently prayed. At this point in the battle for the city, the structure housed thousands of cowering civilians behind eight feet of concrete. Up ahead was the castle at Charlottenberg and the Potsdam suburbs. Glancing down at the inferno below, he realized that tomorrow the city, the jewel of Deutschland, would probably fall into the hands of the Communist Bolsheviks. The plane headed west over Allied lines, barely over treetop level. Then Reitsch steered it southward, toward their destination in Vichy-occupied western France.

Although the airplane bore the iron cross insignia on its wings and a swastika on the vertical stabilizer, it was unlikely to be recognized as a belligerent. A small craft with no visible weaponry, it closely resembled the observation aircraft used by the Allies.

The passenger in the back tried to position himself comfortably in the cramped and narrow seat. However, soon he was asleep, lulled by the loud humming and heat of the engine. The slightest turbulence rocked the lightweight plane but did not disturb his slumber.

At daybreak, they landed at the solitary airstrip in Limoges, in a countryside far from the fighting or the war's destruction. They stayed on the ground only long enough to refuel, relieve themselves, and grab a bite to eat. Also a thermos of hot coffee. She was challenged by a minor local official, who promptly complied with her every command after he had read the papers she handed him.

TRANSATLANTIC FLIGHT
Sun., April 9, 1945, 7:00 am Central European Summertime

Aloft once again, Uhu asked where they were going and her concise reply was Spain.

Approaching the border, they had to slowly gain altitude by bumping the throttle, enough to fly over the snow-capped Pyrenees, negotiating the 10,000-foot Pique d'Estats without supplemental oxygen. They did not linger because not only was the air thin at that altitude it was damn cold. But the mountain range was a beautiful sight in the clear air. Soon they were flying over Spain along the Mediterranean coastline. The aircraft flew smoothly at three thousand feet. He caught another nap.

Several hours later, Reitsch set the Storch down at the airport five miles west of Valencia on the coast of Spain where the weather was bright and clear. "This is as far as I go," said Reitsch as they taxied toward the largest hangar. They extricated themselves from the cramped cockpit and stretched their muscles. The local police chief and administrator waited for them.

"We greet you warmly as guests of the Generalissimo himself," the mayor chimed, paying particular attention to Ms. Reitsch. "In gratitude to your country's assistance in our own Nacionales Victory, and here I am referring to the magnificent flyers of the Legion Condor, Generalissimo Franco extends his greetings, his thanks, and his permission to allow this mission to proceed on Spanish soil." From the chief, the mayor procured two garish medals in cases and presented them to their guests, who politely accepted them. The four of them got into a large sedan, which made a long curving approach to the hangar, the largest structure in sight, and stopped. "They are waiting for you inside." As they got out of the car, the hangar doors, riding on metal wheels, began slowly parting with bangs and metallic squeals. Slowly emerging from the shadows within stood a huge, yet graceful four-engine bomber with a glazed nose and twin tails, the paint scheme being a black-green mottle pattern. The wingspan of 140 feet is wider than the hanger itself—the wingtips are accommodated by slots cut into the side walls. Painted over and barely visible is the black lion on yellow shield, the emblem of the esteemed Geschwader 26. Also painted over is the large swastika on the vertical tailplane.

Due to limited resources and other priorities, Nazi Germany has not managed to produce a practical heavy strategic bomber such as the Lancaster or Flying Fortress and yet here sits the magnificent

Messerschmitt Me264, fueled and ready to cross the Atlantic. The aircraft bears a striking resemblance to the American B-29 bomber, especially the fuselage. Greeting them is the German test pilot extraordinaire Karl Baur, a diminutive bespectacled man with receding hairline. He has tested virtually every German aircraft produced in the late 1930s and wartime, including thirty flights in the Amerika bomber. For this flight, however, the huge aircraft will not carry any ordnance or guns, only a crew of six and its special passenger. Once aloft, the craft could expect to travel at 380 mph and reach the American coast in about ten hours (elapsed clock time four hours). Baur will not be piloting this flight; he is too valuable to be expendable. Neither will Hanna Reitsch, who stood at attention and exclaimed to her elite passenger, "Um der Fuhrer Geburtstag zu feiern!"

He saluted back to her. "Heil Hitler!" Eagerly he unscrewed the cap on the end of a long aluminum tube he had carried on his person all the way from Berlin. He pulled out what appeared to be a piece of cloth wrapped in waxed paper. He allowed the paper to fall to the tarmac and unfurled the small flag entrusted to him by Hitler's close aide Martin Borman. It was the sacred Blutfahne, the blood banner preserved from the 1923 beer hall putsch in Munich. The banner bore the bloodstains of the fallen Nazi patriots. Back then, Hitler had tried to grab power by violence, but the insurrection failed and he landed in jail for nine months, time enough to write his manifesto *Mein Kampf*. The Blutfahne was saved and revered as a sacred icon of National Socialism ever since, shown at massive Nazi rallies. Now the banner would be safe from the Allies in neutral Spain until the Fourth Reich rose from the ashes.

The tractor on treads was now pulling the behemoth out of the hangar and onto the tarmac, the German crew walking alongside in their flight suits. The Spanish delegation bade them good luck. The aviatrix was already formulating plans to fly the Blutfahne back to Germany, to the Bavarian redoubt of Kehlsteinhaus at Berchtesgaden.

With the massive craft completely out of the hanger, the crew pulled themselves up and into the cockpit via the hatch just under the glazed nose. The pilots would sit up front, of course. Uhu entered the fuselage through the hatch near the tail. He occupied the seat in the waist of the fuselage, behind the empty bomb bay and the flight engineer and navigator. One by one the four powerful BMW engines sputtered into operation, the three-bladed props disappearing into a circular blur and blowing away their own exhaust smoke.

The sleek craft slowly rolled down the taxiway to the runway, navigation lights flashing, brakes squealing. The oversized tires looked strangely incongruent. Turning to line up with the runway, the pilot revved up the engines and it rolled forward and steadily gained speed until the massive undercarriage lifted off the concrete and disappeared into the wings. After a few moments, the twin tail and the blinking lights disappeared. Destination Amerika. After a few minutes, Uhu crawled onto an empty wooden shelf, stretched out, and fell asleep.

GWIN HEARS SOME GOSSIP
Mon., April 10, 1945, 2:00 am Central Wartime

On the north shore of a big bend in the Ohio River, klieg lights festoon cranes, rigs, and derricks, illuminating the ten building ways of the Missouri Valley Bridge & Iron Company, otherwise known as the cornfield shipyard. At night, the shipyard transforms into a black-and-white world of odd shapes, grids, and dark shadows, strung with wires of lights and broken by the crackling arc-lights of welders and the banging of steel against steel in a hundred different places, men yelling at each other, all echoing amongst the girders and plates. Eighteen thousand pipefitters and welders and manual laborers work around the clock in shifts to build the huge 328-foot-long ships that will land soldiers and Sherman tanks upon faraway Pacific shores. By the end of the war, the shipyard will have produced 167 such ships (LSTs-Landing Ship Tank) and taking only 60 days from keel laying to launching down the waterways into the river. One in six of the workers are women, drawn from the South and Midwest in pursuit of good-paying jobs. One of the best is Gwin Hamblen, a three-position welder—flat, horizontal, and vertical-overhead. She took the job because it pays $4 an hour. She lives in a barracks in the Diamond Villa project; she has a husband in Tennessee.

"Hey, Gwin, borrow me a smoke?" asked one lady welder to another atop the three-story scaffolding. They climb and perch on the tubular gridwork as naturally as primates in trees.

Gwin ignored her, finishing a weld on a plate marked S-67B in chalk. Randi slapped her mittened hand upon the shoulder of Gwin's overalls. Gwin twisted the torch's gas valve and lifted her mask high upon her head.

"Smoke?"

"Yeah," Gwin said with a sigh and glanced around. "Couple minutes won't hurt. Don't think Johnson's in this sector right now. He can't complain about the way we work."

"Fucking Aye."

Gwin pulled out two Chesterfields, lit one and gave it to Randi. The two women took a knee and then sat down. Gwin lit her own smoke with her stainless Zippo and flipped it shut. "I don't even know what day of the week."

"Monday, I think."

"Coming or going?"

"Coming."

The women dragged on their smokes and surveyed the scene set out before them. "Hard to believe. Look at this place!" Welding sparks lit up the scene like tiny explosions.

"Have a good time at the Trocadero last night? The boys from Camp Breckinridge there?"

"Oh yeah. Bunch of depraved degenerates," Randi said with a smirk and roll of the eyes.

"Did you hook up?" Gwin asked, referring to the depraved degenerates.

"Well, I actually found this GI that was kinda cute. But then I found out he was too drunk to do anything except pass out on me."

"True romance."

"Yeah, you said it. At least he didn't barf all over me. I did make a friend. I ran into this gal who talked about her sister in Knoxville getting lucky with some doctor."

Gwin sucked on her teeth. "Oh yeah. What else did she say?"

"She said her sister was Billie Jean. And the doctor was a guy named Marty. She said he was a married man."

Gwin tried to collect her racing thoughts. Was Randi playing stupid or was she trying to lay it out easy. "Not for long, if what you say is true," Gwin stated, inhaling deeply and blowing out a long stream of smoke. She twisted the cig on a vertical beam until the stub virtually disintegrated.

"Probably a coincidence. Lots of doctors in Knoxville named Marty."

"We'll find out this weekend when I go home," Gwin said. She had barely said it before she reckoned she'd go ahead and take a couple of days off mid-week. She was due. Marty's infidelity wasn't exactly a shock. He was a good looking guy, women were attracted to him, especially when they found out he was a doctor. They had been spending more and more time apart since the war started. Patriotism was a good excuse. Had she been chaste? Not exactly, but it didn't mean anything. Was it a fling in Marty's case or a love affair? Her anger grew from not knowing.

She flipped her mask down and closed it, lit the electrode, pulled on her mitten, and attacked the butt joint she was welding.

UHU LANDS IN AMERIKA
Mon., April 10, 1945, 3:00 am Eastern Wartime

The huge four-engine bomber droned on, flying unmolested at 15,000 feet over the North Atlantic with nary a hitch, already the longest flight of its type. Yes, there had been false overheating warning lights, but the glitch had been minor. The BMW radial engines were performing superbly. The Me264 Amerika bomber had been in the air now for more than ten hours as it entered US airspace and sought out the appropriate coordinates in the Appalachian foothills. It was nighttime with enough moonlight to recognize landmarks through the intermittent cloud cover. The first landmark was the beacon atop the Wright Brothers Memorial at Kill Devil Hills on the Outer Banks. Atop a hill 90 feet tall among the sand dunes on the narrow barrier island, the marine beacon, atop a 60-foot-high granite monument, was easy to see. The pilot noted to the co-pilot, "One side of the monument celebrates Deutsche aviation pioneer Otto Lilienthal, who experimented with gliders in the late 1800s."

The co-pilot thought to himself, "Hanswurst die historie."

Most of the Allied coastal-patrol planes would be flying grids at night over the water, searching for enemy vessels and submarines. They would not be on the alert for a hostile enemy bomber cruising at low altitude over the East Coast. In the event, the huge aircraft went undetected.

Continuing westward over the Piedmont, the Me264 flew dangerously low at two hundred feet over sparsely populated areas of North Carolina, avoiding the urban areas of Greensboro and Winston-Salem. One of the pilots quipped that they should land and pick up bushels of those good-tasting American cigarettes.

Then the behemoth encountered the foothills and the mountains. The aircraft easily surmounted the peaks of the highest mountains—Mount Guyot, Mount Le Conte, and Clingman's Dome, which are about 6,500 feet in elevation. Only then did they see the powerful beacon emanating from the roof of the lodge at the Top of the World. The beam of white light shot straight up into the night sky. The pilots and crew easily sighted the beam and opened the bomb bay doors. The aircraft carried no bombs, only its crew and special passenger. The pilot pulled back on the throttles as far as he could without stalling and made a wide circle around the beacon. They were low enough now to discern a smaller blinking light on the ground.

This stage was one of the most critical points in the plan, whether Uhu could safely drop out of a low-flying heavy bomber at night into a hilly and wooded "drop zone." He had about 400 feet to find out.

The Aryan paratrooper hung in the large opening, the treetops rushing below him, poised to fling himself into the darkness. The noise was deafening and the airflow strong. The co-pilot spoke in German, of course, and yelled "Bereit," then "Satz" and finally "Gehen!" The red light turned to green. The figure dove head-first out the bomb bay doors into the abyss, hit a brief moment of prop backwash, and immediately pulled the ripcord. He didn't have much time to drop at this altitude. Would his custom-built chute function properly? The chute jerked him in the harness and swung him around in a flat loop. Still falling rapidly, the trooper glided through a stand of pine trees, which snagged his chute and abruptly softened his descent. He ended up suspended about five feet off the ground, and when he unbuckled himself from the chute harness, he fell into a pile of pine straw. Pulling off his padded helmet and goggles, he could still hear the bomber as it swung around and headed south to the gulf coast.

He activated the small transmitter on his belt. Now he would have to wait for his accomplice to pick up the transmission, locate him, and drive him out of this place. He had no idea exactly where he was situated. Within moments he heard voices above the whisper of the pine trees. Not his accomplice but two men, with a mule. One was aged, the other much younger. The intruder moved quickly and quietly toward the point of their projected intersection. He wore the clip point knife in his right hand as if a claw, a part of him. The mule sensed trouble and brayed. Then it was over quickly.

IRIS ATTACKED
Mon., April 10, 1945, 3:00 am Eastern Wartime

It was a cloudy but moonlit night. Iris McCarthy sat on an overlook bench and petted Gunther, her German Shepherd. The dog panted and surveyed the surroundings, head on a swivel. He had not detected anything interesting yet but kept looking. Iris crossed her legs, pulled out a cigarette, stuck it in her lips, and lit it, and flicked the lighter shut. She turned both ways, even backwards, to make sure they was alone. She puffed on the cigarette as she gazed through the pines at the monument stretching out before them. Norris Dam rose 265 feet as one giant concrete monolith, backing up the Clinch River, and its crest was one-third of a mile in length. The spillway was stained dark greenish-black in contrast to the dry concrete beside it. The overlook was slightly higher than the crest of the dam, which also served as a roadway. The dam created an artificial lake covering 52 square miles. The dam sat 18 miles northeast of CEW.

Iris was one of a new breed of servicewoman. Most of the security guards at government facilities were single women under forty, former teachers and stenographers who were trained in combat techniques and even judo. They all carried .38-caliber revolvers and walkie-talkies. They were named the Women Officers of Public Safety or WOOPS for short. On her uniform was a patch stating "Electric Power Is A Weapon Of War."

She could hear the steady discharge of water as the turbines inside the Art Deco building generated kilowatts of power. The Tennessee Valley Authority operated seven hydroelectric dams and was busy building several more. TVA tripled its power production during the war to 12 billion kilowatt-hours. War industry used about three-fourths of that production. The aluminum plant near Alcoa (Aluminum Company of America), the largest of its kind in the world, required massive amounts of electricity to convert bauxite ore into sheets of lightweight metal used in all types of aircraft, from tiny observation planes to huge four-engine bombers. CEW also consumed nearly impossible amounts of electrical power, 24 hours a day, seven days a week. So much that the General ordered a supplemental power plant built next to the thermal diffusion plant at the far western end of the CEW reservation.

Security was tight at the dams and the electrical power lines and substations along the way. Even a slight outage of power—say a minute or two—could wreak havoc with the wartime industrial production. The aluminum works would literally seize up and possibly be ruined for any further use. Downtime at CEW might require days or weeks to gear up to normal workloads. A power interruption would be catastrophic to the United States wartime mission.

Iris's husband Arnold had worked for Public Safety Service before enlisting in the Marines and being shipped off to the Pacific. He hardly ever wrote, probably because he didn't have the time. That's what Iris told herself. Arnie was fighting the Japs, but he was still alive. He was tough. She couldn't explain how she knew he was alive, she just knew.

The war with Germany in Europe was all but over and the US was pounding the Japanese home islands. As the long days and short weeks flew by, it was becoming more certain that there wouldn't be any enemy sabotage or infiltration. Iris couldn't help but feel some complacency creeping in. These night patrols were actually quite peaceful.

Above the sound of the water falling and the swooshing of wind through the pines she detected a distant sound in the sky coming closer. The shadow in the night sky soared closer, blocked out the moon for moment, then droned out of view, dipping into a shallow turn. She knew of no reason for a heavy bomber to flying in this area at night. To the southeast she could barely see a beam of white light stabbing straight upward, like a searchlight, except that it didn't move. She could see the beam better when not looking directly at it. None of it made any sense.

Iris dropped the cigarette stub and carefully ground it under her boot. As she rose from the bench, Gunther growled and then barked. She knew what the sound of that bark meant. She whirled around and unbuckled the flap of her holster. The winged monster struck at her with nearly silent rage, sinking sharp claws into her shoulder. The massive shadow shuddered her, then lifted off. The assailant pulled at her clothing, trying to remove its claws from her uniform. Iris dropped her revolver, but then picked it up and squeezed off three rounds at the dark shape disappearing back into the gloom of the woods. Gunther was nearly crazed at the sudden, unprovoked episode, barking and pulling on his leash. Feathers whirled and fluttered. Her uniform was torn and her left shoulder was bleeding. After surveilling her surroundings, she holstered the weapon and summoned help on her walkie-talkie. She sat on the bench and thought about how to explain the incident. She had been attacked, but by what? All she could rightly recall was the terror of briefly confronting those two large orange eyes.

And she noticed that the white beam was now gone.

THE MOONSHINERS
Mon., April 10, 1945, 3:30 am Eastern Wartime

The Old Man, the young boy, and the middle-aged mule carefully navigated the switchbacks running along the steep wooded ridge. The moon was nearly full but sheathed intermittently by the overcast clouds. The youngster was tall and lean, lanky and awkward. The old man was still spry despite a discernable limp and a stiff back. The mule suffered silently with two full sacks slung over its back. The silence of the East Tennessee woods, foothills to the mountains millions of years old, was jolted by the cursing of the teenager.

"Dang it," he blurted as he tripped over an exposed tree root on the narrow trail and caught himself before falling.

"Keep your feet up, young'un," the Old Man instructed. "And be quiet now."

"Yessir," the young man whispered, concentrating on the trail and using tree trunks to steady himself. He bent his neck, thinking it would help him hear night sounds better. He thought he heard a soft humming sound in the sky that came and went, but he decided he had been wrong.

The Old Man was using his grandson as cheap labor and teaching him everything he could. For example, the way that revenuers can find a still by looking for black mold around the bottom of nearby tree trunks. Dead give-away.

A proficient moonshiner, the Old Man was famous in these parts for his annual batch of Jimmy Red Corn, using that unique corn grown only on the sea islands around Charleston. How he procured such exotic grain he never divulged. The water he used for distilling, low in iron, came straight from a limestone cave stream on the family property. He slung the double-barreled shotgun back around his shoulder, better to carry it. The thick cover precluded much of any wind yet in the distance came a faint thudding noise, like a steamboat in the forest. "I heer da thumper," the Old Man said with a grin. He yanked on the lanyard to the protests of the mule laden with supplies. "Don't be so stubborn, you ole coot," he said, oblivious of the irony.

Now they were descending into a narrow hollar where it was even darker and cooler. The clouds slid by the moon and illuminated their destination, a level clearing piled with tubs and tanks and copper coiling in addition to various other castoffs.

"We'll be here most the night. You up for it?"

"Yessir," replied the lanky young man, as if he had a choice.

The Old Man patted the chest pocket of his bib overalls. More than enough chaw to last the night, he thought. Just then, without warning, the mule released a stream of feces. The youngster jumped out of the way. "Damn!" he hissed. What's he feeding this beast, he wondered.

The Old Man hooted softly. "Be quiet now or I'll smack you in the hed. We gotta unload these supplies and start fillin' them jugs. First, we're gonna make a fire, a small fire. It's a mite chilly tonight."

The illicit production of white lightning, an occupation as old as the hills (or at least as old as the Scots-Irish settlement of such), was profitable during the war if a producer had access to the necessary supplies and a suitable distribution network. Most of the nation's distilleries were producing alcohol for military-industrial uses just as Detroit was producing Sherman tanks instead of Buicks.

The Old Man had started years ago with a modest set-up and corresponding yield, but he enhanced his skills over the years. One of his mentors was Popcorn Sutton himself. The Old Man was genuinely interested in making quality moonshine. The distillery and camp in the woods had grown to include a thumper and doubler and primitive bottling operation. Still backwoods, but a decent facility with a small shack in which to rest and guard the operation. No rusty radiators or rats in the mash tub, the Old Man vowed.

The old-timer crouched when he looked at his grandson. The young man froze, lifted an open hand, and scanned the surroundings without moving his head. The Old Man did the same. The mule stood unmoved.

"Whasisit?" he whispered.

"Thought I heardt somethin'."

"Whadid ya hear?"

"Don't know."

The two of them stood frozen, crouching downward with their ears wide open. They listened for several moments. Even the mule was quiet, his head down but his ears pricked. Nothing but steady muffled thumping. They eased a bit. The grandfather looked to his left, then to his right, and stood erect. Nothing.

"Reckon it was jest a raccoon or possum," he said. "I ever tell you the story of the great horned awl, the scourge of the Cherokee?"

"Yes, grandfather, many times. And I still hain't seen one yet."

"Not supposed to. He only comes out at night. He's very quiet. The great awl is an awesome predator. Sharp beak, round face, with claws like a bar. Rip a man to shreds in an instant."

"Yessir."

"They can see in the dark an' they can hear a mouse a hundert yards away. Swoop right down, real silent like, and carry 'em off before they knows what's happenin'." The Old Man was spooking his grandson and enjoying every moment of it.

The two moonshiners entered the small unoccupied camp and began unloading the mule. They never knew what hit them.

BILLIE JEAN AND THE PROFESSOR
Mon., April 10, 1945, 4:30 pm Eastern Wartime

Billie Jean Holloway liked her work at the university much more than monitoring calutrons eight hours a day at CEW. She was a librarian's assistant at the main building up on the hill, Ayres Hall, where the breeze was fresh and cool. It was much easier to see the doctor now and they could spend more time together, much of it close and intimate. She felt as if she knew him better; he was more willing to open up about his feelings although he still refused to speak of his wife, what she was like.

It was now late afternoon and the shadows were growing long on the great lawn as she made her way down the steps on the backside of the hill to the ornate Alumni Hall and down further still to the giant metal framework of the football stadium. Underneath the stands were small laboratories devoted to military research, a small barracks for researchers who kept long hours, storage facilities, and an old unused classroom with benches and a large blackboard at the front of the room. She took a seat in the back row of the classroom and waited. She wasn't waiting for the doctor, she was waiting for a man she referred to only as The Professor. He was a Russian émigré working on technical issues regarding mechanical devices used at CEW. How he gained access to CEW is known only to CIC. Perhaps his expertise and experience outweighed the doubts about his background.

This was not their first meeting. He never discussed his university work with her. His mission was much more consequential, at least that's what he had explained to Billie Jean, whom he found quite impressionable.

The Professor was an ungainly man built at odd angles and a face that seemed out of proportion. A faint mustache shadowed his lip, and a scar of indeterminate origin swept across his cheek from chin to left ear. He wore a hearing aid and walked with the help of a cane adorned with a crystal knob. Despite his undesirable looks, Billie Jean considered the Professor as her mentor. He had taught her a lot about the real world. The doctor did not know about their meetings, nobody did.

Billie Jean had been raised in the Baptist Church, learned the Scriptures, worshipped the Lord Jesus, and was taught to fear a vengeful God. Although a believer, she had doubts about the relevance of the Bible to modern times. Too many young men were dying for specious or unknown reasons; too many old men were enriching themselves building powerful and deadly war machines. Patriotism and devoutness didn't seem to make a whole lot of difference.

Perhaps the cruelest irony was that the Holloways, through no fault of their own, had been driven off their ancestral farmland because the US government needed the land to build war factories. And they didn't explain exactly what they wanted it for and why it was necessary. Billie Jean's family had two weeks to gather up their possessions and leave. Compensation was meager. Their farmhouse was demolished. No matter their love of country, it still didn't seem fair or necessary.

Like when the Northerners came to Knoxville eighty years before and confiscated whatever they needed, owned by loyal Unionist or not.

The Professor taught her that it was all part of the global conspiracy of rich capitalists to enslave the common man, to torture him at his own expense. The rich got richer while the commoners groveled for something to eat—the Great Depression had proven that well enough. It was so depressing that Billie Jean's father, Earl, suffered a nervous breakdown, developed heart problems, and drank himself to death.

Billie Jean had been exposed to a rural learning cooperative which promoted scholarship amongst young women, almost unheard of in this part of the South. In fact, the school was where she had been introduced to the Professor and his teachings.

"From each according to his abilities, to each according to his needs." The details would be hammered out by a cadre of highly trained and progressive intellectuals, i.e., high ranking party officials.

She got her first introduction to collectivism at the Ridge Runner Coalition School. She did not attend, of course, but learned a few things from hanging around the instructors, all of whom were so much smarter and brighter than her. Some of them even practiced free love—she blushed just thinking about such things. She relished the sense of freedom they projected, the potential possibilities of each individual if freed from toil and greed and closed-minded dogma. She couldn't spell it, but she knew what bourgeoisie meant. And proletariat. She knew that Karl Marx wrote the *Communist Manifesto* and wasn't related to Groucho.

The Professor had all the answers. He would say, only half-jokingly, that "those of you who think you know it all are very annoying to those of us who do."

There was a place in the world, far away, where there were no classes, where the common man ruled the means of production and all benefitted from a better life. Even the coloreds and other downtrodden ethnic peoples. Women were equal to men. That place was the Soviet Union, the Union of Soviet Socialist Republics. The Soviets were the ones battling Hitler and the Nazis to a standstill in the Great Patriotic War. After the war, which would be soon, the Soviet Union would ride the great tide of history, as detailed by Marx, and defeat the capitalists and the Jews and install a virtual Utopia on Earth. Socialism seemed so logical and ethical and doable, if only greedy and stupid people would behave as they should. It would be a beautiful world where everybody would love one another, live in peace, and not be diverted by notions of supernatural religion, nationalism, and superstition. Science and logic and reason would rule the day. This might take years to achieve, but the ends justified the means, and the mission was righteous.

Just look at TVA, the socialist government program that literally electrified the Mid-South. President Roosevelt needed innovative solutions if his New Deal was to lift the nation out of the depths of the Great Depression, and the TVA was one of his most innovative ideas. Roosevelt envisioned TVA as a totally different kind of agency. He asked Congress to create "a corporation clothed with the power of government but possessed of the flexibility and initiative of a private enterprise."

A BETTER WORLD FOR ALL
Mon., April 10, 1945, 4:30 pm Eastern Wartime

Of course, the Professor was careful not to preach Marxist philosophy or Soviet supremacy publicly at the university. He had been interviewed by the local FBI as to his beliefs and values. He was a naturalized US citizen and proud of it, at least superficially. He was not involved in any anti-war activity, or war production that would involve clearance or access to secret materials. He did not have a CEW badge. Nevertheless he was scrutinized and compelled to take a loyalty oath, which he readily did. Even he had to admit that he had no moral qualms. "By whatever means necessary" was one of his guiding lights. When the time came, sooner rather than later, those traditionalists or conservatives hostile to the progressive agenda would have to be re-educated or eliminated.

As Vladimir Ilich Lenin said, "The Capitalists will sell us the rope with which we will hang them."

But there would be no world peace if the United States was able to build the atomic bomb, the Professor instructed. Then the capitalists would rule the world and wars would become endless. The Professor informed Billie Jean that what CEW was really doing was enriching radioactive uranium so that it could fuel an atomic bomb. A bomb which would be dropped on Japan, killing hundreds of thousands, and then used against the Soviet Union. A weapon of blackmail. This must not be allowed to happen. Billie Jean had tried her best to sabotage the calutrons by fiddling with the dials and gauges and slowing down production. That wasn't working, the Professor insisted. Neither were efforts to unionize workers in the war industries and foment dissent. Instead they must intercept shipments of enriched uranium to New Mexico, where the bomb was being built.

As she pondered these secular wisdoms, footsteps echoed in the large classroom. She looked up and smiled. The Professor had arrived for their clandestine meeting, which would be brief, as always.

"Sasha," he beckoned warmly, for that was the code name he gave her.

"Hello. Nice to see you again."

"You were not followed, I trust," he said with his slight accent.

"Of course not," she replied.

He wasted no time with formalities. "Well, what do you have for me?"

"He's going to be out-of-town for several days, beginning Wednesday," she whispered, staring at him, knowing he would understand and approve.

"Good, good. I will set the wheels in motion," he said, pursing his lips. His facial expression indicated "you can go now."

She walked back the way she came, in the shadows of the exposed stadium girding. She really wished she knew what he was scheming, what the plan in detail would be. For they both knew that the good doctor Marty Hamblen only went out of town for several days on the train when the courier shipment was a real one and not a decoy. There would be green salt in the briefcase.

Billie Jean had no sooner disappeared down the stairway then a figure stealthily emerged from the shadows. It was Natasha, the Professor's assistant with the long, dark-brown hair and dark eyes.

"You'll be on the train Wednesday," he stated.

"Of course," she replied. "I'm going to intercept the package for the glory of Russia."

"For the glory of Russia," he pronounced proudly. "Be alert, for sometimes things are not what they seem." Natasha then fell back into the shadows and disappeared as quickly and silently as she had appeared.

The Professor had discovered, over time, that he actually enjoyed living in the US. The capitalists were greedy pigs, of course, but that did not preclude him from enjoying luxuries of his own and working to earn them. The principle of compound interest was fascinating. Invest your wealth and watch it grow, like magic. There's no harm in wanting the finer things in life, he mused, a notion also shared by Natasha. Capitalism can be catching. Fine wine, gourmet meals, men's fashions, jewelry, and so on. Of course, this was known by the CIC, which uncovered the Professor almost from the beginning. With some patience and applying ample inducements in the form of non-taxable cash, the CIC managed to turn the Professor. Turned him into a double-agent. They constantly threatened to deport him back to the people's paradise.

THE CIC TRAP
Mon., April 10, 1945, 6:00 pm Eastern Wartime

The Chief of Counter Intelligence Corps (CIC) was perusing the stack of daily reports on his desk when the second-in-command strode into his office at the Castle.

"Anything interesting?" the subordinate asked of his boss, nodding his head at the reports.

"Not really," the chief replied, picking up his cigarette and flicking the ashes into an ashtray fashioned from a brass shell casing.

"I've got a plan," the assistant said. "I need to get your opinion…and your approval." He sat in the chair in front of the chief's desk.

"All right," the chief said, wearily rubbing his face without removing his eyeglasses.

"As you know, we've been getting some alarming information from our Russian asset at the university. As I understand it, Soviet agents are going to hit the shipment on the *Southland* this Wednesday or Thursday. Two of them, highly trained. They will try to steal the package in the briefcase or perhaps try to destroy it."

"I want to divert the Soviets away from the couriers and their briefcase. Make them think the briefcase is just a decoy. The real tube-alloy will be contained in a crate in the cargo car at the front of the train. Accompanied by two military policemen."

"That's highly conspicuous, wouldn't you say?"

"Absolutely. That's the whole idea. At some point the Soviets are going to try to steal that crate, probably at the stop in Cincinnati or Indianapolis, or maybe at the station in Chicago."

"You have my permission."

"I'd like it in writing."

"You know better than that. Good luck. By the way, what's really in the briefcase?"

"Tube-alloy, as far as I know."

The chief considered what he had just approved and made a mental note to place several CIC men on the train. In civilian clothes, of course. This might be a special run, he feared.

THE FBI-KNOXVILLE
Mon., April 10, 1945, 2:00 pm Eastern Wartime

The Holston Building in Knoxville is one of the most desirable downtown locations to do business. The lobby is spacious, clean, and wrapped in glossy marble, granite, and tile. Much of the fixtures, fittings, and railings are shiny brass. The elevator has been modernized and retrofitted to hold a decent capacity and move briskly. The first two floors are dominated by Hamilton National Bank, with the vault on the ground floor. On the fourth floor, facing the street, sits the Knoxville field office of the Federal Bureau of Investigation. The Bureau maintains its own vault of sensitive information and wartime intelligence.

At precisely two o'clock the black teletype machine in the restricted alcove clattered into action, delivering the latest intelligence update from headquarters in Washington, D.C.

TOP SECRET
Date: 10 April 1945 14:00
FBI Headquarters, Washington DC
Forward: Knoxville Field Office
Attn: Special Agent in Charge
Intelligence from sources within Third Reich indicate Nazi military possesses technology which could threaten Eastern Seaboard with ballistic missile attack. Advanced U-boat design, known as Type XXI Electroboat, could travel underwater with reduced need for surfacing and detection. U-boat can tow tubular containers loaded with V-2 (Vergeltungswaffe 2), technical name Aggregat 4 (A-4) ballistic missile. Hundreds of miles to sea, container can be flooded into upright launch position and missile fired at US homeland. Probability of intercepting and/or shooting down such missile would be negligible (impact speed 2,200 mph).

Operatives in Norway report launching of flotilla of German U-boats, Group Seawolf (Gruppe Seewolf), from Bergen fjord Monday last, possibly eight in number and recent design technology allowing extended operation underwater undetected. Estimated destination US East Coast, specifically New York City and harbor. Unsubstantiated reports indicate possible "rocket" launch capability. US Naval Command stepping up frequency of aircraft and vessel patrols between Outer Banks and Cape Cod.

Myra ripped the sheet off the now-silent machine and stomped on her high heels into the office of the Special-Agent-in-Charge. "There you are, Roy. The latest reports." She stomped back to her office and began typing.

Roy "Slim" Gunderson eased back in his sturdy wooden chair and scanned the report. He wasn't quite sure what to make of it. The war in Europe was quickly coming to an end, and the Allies are winning. For years, attacks against the Eastern Seaboard had been a serious threat, although in recent years the US had become more proficient in sinking U-boats in the Atlantic. Nazi fanatics, perhaps SS men, could launch desperate attempts to thwart the Allied effort or at least inflict some serious damage. Some infantry in Germany were still fighting to the death. Even if the threats were real, an attack against the coast – 500 miles away – would have little effect here, he thought.

Gunderson pulled heavily on a Pall Mall and slowly released the smoke from his lungs.

Gunderson was somewhat of an oddity at the Bureau. For one, he was not married. The Bureau and the Director believed that agents should be family men. Another, he did not have a college degree or equivalent. But he was competent, efficient, and a long way from headquarters. He was working out well compared to his predecessor. What he was doing in Knoxville would not be tolerated at headquarters.

Gunderson put the report in the tray on his desk, got up, and darkened Myra's doorway. "Has Jimmy checked in yet?"

"Yes," she said with a sigh. "Nothing to report."

"I'm knocking off early today," he said, grabbing his fedora from the rack. "Up late last night. Care to join me at the movie show?"

She smirked and gently admonished him, "You know I can't."

"Would you if you could?"

She chuckled and shook her head. He didn't wait for a reply.

The field office was one of many workplaces located in the building dominated by the Hamilton National Bank at the corner of Gay Street and Clinch Avenue. His hard sole shoes echoed on the polished marble steps of the ornate staircases. Best to take the stairs. Keep in shape. The avenue was in shadows on this late afternoon. He ambled across the street and then to the opposite corner where the Tennessee Theater occupied a whole block. A huge vertical marquee adorned the streetfront of the theater. In the summers, he liked to sit in the huge air-conditioned auditorium, munch on popcorn, and think about things, not paying much attention to the movie. It was cool enough today that air-conditioning was not required. The late matinee drew a sparse crowd so he sat in the back near the aisle. The United News newsreel blared across the screen in black-and-white, martial trumpets in the background, with the narrator announcing:

"Leaving trails of steaming vapor in their wake, United States bombers head for Berlin to destroy armament industries in and around the Nazi war capital. In their 100th daylight mission over the heart of Hitler's fortress, American bombers, combined with British Air Forces, are pounding Germany with raids around the clock. One propeller out, a bomber limps home. In all, 68 American planes failed to return. But the next day and the next, American bombers returned in follow-up raids. Today, squadrons like these in ever-increasing numbers are taking the war home to Germany itself."

Gunderson pondered. "Sixty-eight planes down, that's nearly 700 men in one raid."

The narrator now shifts to the homeland:

"Nazi prisoners of war at a camp in northern United States. In full accord with the Geneva Convention, prisoners are well-housed, well-clothed, and well-fed. Although prisoners are not required to work, many volunteer as lumberjacks, for which they are paid 80 cents a day. A snow-shoveling detail. Prisoners keep their own camp in order. By doing work like this in the shoe shop, captives are able to buy cigarettes and other luxuries. War prisoners receive the same rations as American soldiers or an equivalent in their own type of food, if they prefer. These Signal Corps pictures show a fully-equipped recreation room provided for the captives, who even have their own band. America scrupulously observes the principles of humanity in her treatment of war prisoners."

Gunderson recalls complaints from local residents that the government "treats POWs better than they do their own citizens."

The matinee feature was a B-movie titled "My Boyfriend Was A Nazi Spy." Dramatic organ chords: "Saboteurs and fifth columnists in this country will stop at nothing. Poisoned water supply systems, poisoned milk for babies, blasts of huge magnitude in schools and department stores and other panic centres; bombs planted in the homes of high government officials, chemical poisons unleashed against men in army and naval training centres; wholesale murders of key war production workers—all that is definitely on the German sabotage timetable."

CATCHING NAZI SPIES
Mon., April 10, 1945, 3:17 pm Eastern Wartime

Gunderson sighed and rolled his head to stretch his neck. "On their timetable but haven't happened yet. These movies are something else," he thought to himself. "A Nazi spy under every bed. No wonder we get calls all the time from every Tom, Dick, and Harry. All of which have to be taken seriously, of course."

The Bureau was vigilant in its pursuit of Nazi spies in the US, and not hesitant to take credit for tracking down infiltrators, even when the Bureau really wasn't responsible. The Director was a master in promoting the Bureau and producing publicity that gained favor with the populace and members of Congress. The Bureau had earned its lofty stature by tracking down mobsters and gangsters during the Great Depression. The newspapers tended to sensationalize the cases when small-time hoodlums and miscreants robbed banks and pretended to be modern-day Robin Hoods. The Bureau preferred to go after Public Enemy No. 1, such as John Dillinger, and remove them from society, dead or alive.

During the 1930s Americans were in an isolationist mood, which some labeled as unAmerican. Charles Lindbergh's "America First" movement comprised 700 chapters with nearly one million members. Most of this kind of sentiment evaporated, however, with the attack on Pearl Harbor in December 1941.

During the early 1940s, before the US was formally at war, the Bureau identified 33 Nazi spies operating in the States and arrested them. All were convicted on espionage charges. A spy recruited by the German Secret Service had been turned by the Bureau and was directed to exchange hundreds of shortwave-radio messages with Nazi authorities overseas. He conducted dozens of personal meetings with Nazi spies and passed information to the Gestapo. The leader of the spy ring was Frederick Duquesne, a South African who became a naturalized US citizen. He provided information about US industrial production and methods to sabotage or bomb such facilities. Most of the Nazi spies in the US were native Germans who had traveled to the US during the 1930s and became naturalized citizens. They could not be tried for treason because the US was not yet at war with Germany.

In March 1942, the Bureau rounded up ten members of the "Joe K" spy ring, which had transmitted information on Allied shipping in New York

Harbor. They were convicted and sentenced to prison terms.

But the biggest bonanza came in June 1942 when eight German saboteurs were apprehended during a secret mission to attack American war production facilities, including the ALCOA aluminum plants near Knoxville. Two teams of trained agents were landed via German U-boats on beaches near Jacksonville, Florida, and Long Island, New York, within days of each other. Within ten days, all eight saboteurs had been arrested by the FBI before they could commit a single act of destruction. Led by the Director, the Bureau claimed responsibility for defeating Operation Pastorius and garnered much favorable press coverage. In reality, however, the leader of the saboteurs had grown despondent and turned against the mission. He called FBI headquarters and personally turned himself in to authorities, hoping to become a hero by disclosing information about the plot. The agents were tried by a military commission, found guilty, and all sentenced to death. Two of the agents received prison sentences instead for assisting the US authorities. The other six men, none of whom faintly resembled the public's notion of an evil Nazi provocateur, were immediately executed by hanging, one after the other, at the DC Jail. The bodies were buried secretly at a paupers' cemetery near the Blue Plains sewage disposal plant.

Relations between the FBI's Knoxville field office and the security and intelligence forces at CEW were strained at best. Most law enforcement agencies and intelligence bureaus are intrinsically hesitant to share their hard-earned information and tend to assume that any exchanges would be one-sided not in their favor. Adding to this tension was an incident in 1943 when a local agent of the FBI purposefully infiltrated the CEW reservation to test its level of security and ended up being exposed by flunking a polygraph test. The Director was not amused to put it mildly. Nor was the General. Any news or reports of this unfortunate incident was covered up, the agent was dismissed, and a new Special-Agent-in-Charge was moved in.

One investigation by the Knoxville field office really paid off, however. In the summer of 1944, a Nazi agent was tracked and arrested. He confessed but would not name any associates. Born in Germany he moved to the US in 1929 and became a US citizen. He became a leader in Friends of New Germany, later the Bund. He returned to Germany twice, and enrolled in an espionage training course. Back in the US, he worked as an electrician at Camp Pendleton near Norfolk, Virginia, and watched ships leave the harbor. He alerted the Germans, via drop box in Milan, Italy, about departures. He was placed on a watch list. He told the FBI he quit spying after Pearl Harbor when his acts would be treason. He moved to Knoxville and applied for work at CEW but was denied due to his German heritage. On his way to Federal prison in Atlanta to serve a 20-year sentence he told the FBI agent to check a steamer trunk at the YMCA, which contained a codebook used by Nazis. Among the entries recorded under Over-the-Rhine: Hammers, Uhu, Red Top Brew, Dayton Street. Contacts had been made at Coney Island.

Using the code book, which was easy to crack, the Bureau exposed letters referring to the Rhine, Bremen, Coney Island and numerous other references which made no sense. It made no sense because the wording referred to locations in Cincinnati, Ohio, which contained a large German population. The Rhine was the Miami & Ohio Canal which bounded the German-American neighborhood known as Over the Rhine. Bremen was not a city in Germany but a street name in Cincinnati before it was changed to Republic Street. And Coney Island was the huge segregated amusement park with the world's largest swimming pool, the Sunlite Pool, dating back to 1867 and located just upstream from Cincinnati on the Ohio River. The investigation remained open.

Besides CEW and ALCOA, another possible target was the Knoxville firm of Fulton Sylphon, which assembled a key component of the Norden bombsight, the thermodynamic device (metal bellows) invented in 1902 by Weston Fulton, a University of Tennessee meteorologist. He named the sylphon after the Norse goddess of weather.

When it came to Nazi sabotage in the US during the war, the Bureau had a clean record. Every suspect act traced to its source was the result of vandalism, resentment, a desire for relief from boredom, the curiosity of children "to see what would happen," or some other personal motive.

Now it is the spring of 1945 and the Germans are being squeezed by the Allies and the Soviets, and Wehrmacht soldiers are surrendering in an orderly manner by the hundreds of thousands. The threat of Nazi spies and infiltrators had come and gone, as far as the press was concerned. Now it was time, the Director announced, to check the advance of Soviet Communism, the atheist threat of worldwide totalitarianism. Back in the 1930s, Communism and Fascism had found favor with thousands of Americans who admired the concept while tending to ignore the harsh realities. Any agent who could identify and apprehend a nest of card-carrying Commies would stand in good stead with the Director, that was for certain.

Although the local FBI office receives dozens of calls each year, most turn out to be either pranks or misunderstandings. However, Gunderson was troubled by several anonymous calls he had received warning that special agents or infiltrators were planning to sabotage the aluminum plants at Alcoa, Tennessee. The Bureau had already rounded up the usual suspects to be held in custody and questioned or cleared of any suspicions. Headquarters and the aluminum plant security had been informed, but they did not seem all that concerned.

FBI INTERROGATES GERMAN POW
Tues., April 11, 1945, 2:35 pm Central Wartime

Another intelligence report rattled onto the scroll of paper in the FBI-Knoxville wire machine. The printed portion draped down the back of the machine against the wall. Gunderson ripped the paper off the machine after it had settled back into silence. The message involved the prisoner-of-war camp in Crossville on the Cumberland Plateau, 70 miles west of Knoxville. German and Italian infantrymen were detained there after being captured in North Africa or Italy and transported to America.

FBI Background Intelligence Reports
TOP SECRET
Date: 10 April 1945 14:35
FBI Headquarters, Washington DC
Forward: Knoxville, Nashville Field Offices
Attn: Special Agent in Charge
Claus von Kluge is a captured Wehrmacht soldier who participated in Operation Greif during the Ardennes Campaign. He speaks fluent English, being born of German parents in the US during the 1920s. He eluded execution by providing important information about German dispositions. He was then sent to the Crossville Internment Camp, where he again was interrogated by US military intelligence.

Von Kluge was slated to be transferred to a POW camp in North Dakota when he disappeared from Crossville. On 10 April 1945, his body was discovered near the camp in some dense woods wired to a tree and stabbed too many times to count. The birds hollowed out his eye sockets. Pinned to the body was the handwritten note "Verrater!"

This report for informational purposes only.

Gunderson pinched his nose between closed eyes and ruminated on this latest news. It was of particular interest to Gunderson because he had interviewed von Kluge in person at the camp in March. It is known that there are German hardliners at the POW camp who still follow Adolf Hitler and would not hesitate to injure or even kill inmates who cooperate with the US authorities. The G-man located the file folder on von Kluge and noted that the interview had occurred on March 23rd, more than two weeks ago. He sat down, lit a cigarette, and recalled the trip to the camp.

It was 65 miles of rough road between downtown Knoxville and the POW camp at Crossville. Kingston Pike turned into Highway 70, which winded past the southernmost perimeter of CEW to the town of Kingston, founded in 1792 as Fort Southwest Point, the boundary between the Cherokee and white settler territory. In nearby Monterey that boundary was marked by the Standing Stone, fifteen hundred years old. Harriman lays to the north along Walden Ridge, a company town based on industry and temperance. Neither concept proved sustainable. The first business into town now is a liquor store. Ozone is situated on the eastern slope of the Cumberland Plateau. At Crab Orchard, tunnels are drilled into the hillsides to extricate some of the finest granite and marble in the Western Hemisphere. Many buildings in the town of Crossville are built of Crab Orchard stone, which is a rare sandstone radiating various warm shades of color, like a Southwest painted desert. Crossville is a sundown town, where strangers are not welcome after dusk unless they are related to a local. Crossville developed at the intersection of a branch of the Great Stage Road, which connected Knoxville with Nashville, and the Kentucky Stock Road, a cattle drovers' path connecting Middle Tennessee with Kentucky. The POW camp is southwest of Crossville, a fenced compound of orderly barracks, guard towers, and numerous outbuildings. And lots of mud.

Gunderson drove to the camp in 90 minutes. He presented his credentials at the gate, accepted an escort, and was waved inside. He parked at the main building, where the commandant's car occupied its reserved spot. Gunderson got along with the commandant, Colonel James "Rocky" Briggs, a by-the-book officer with a sense of humor. The minimum-security camp allowed the trusted German and Italian inmates to work outside the compound, earning a wage as farmhands, bakers, tradesmen, and other jobs. Inside the camp, the inmates published their own newspaper, entertained as a chorus, played soccer (which was slowly being transformed into American football), and attended chapel. Movies were shown to the inmates, along with propaganda films promoting democracy and capitalism. Many of the inmates said they desired to relocate to America after the war. Some of the local black residents complained that the government treated the POWs better than it treated them.

One of the prisoners seeking special privileges was Claus von Kluge, a corporal born in Prussia who had been captured at Aachen. He spoke fluent English; in fact, he had resided in Cincinnati until he returned to the

Fatherland in the 1930s. At first enthralled with Adolph Hitler, National Socialism, and the fight against Bolshevism, he had become disillusioned as the war on the Eastern Front dragged on. He was a proud soldier and nationalist, but he disagreed with the politics of hatred, ethnic cleansing, and Hitler's micromanagement of his generals. As with many Germans, he had been enthralled with the Third Reich but fell into despair when it turned to war, especially since it was losing the war.

"Good to see you again, Roy," the commandant said, standing on the veranda and extending his hand. The veranda would be a great place to sit in a rocking chair and relax, but nobody does that here.

"Nice to see you, Rocky," the G-man replied, stepping resolutely up the stairs.

"Come, let's talk in my office." He pushed the simple, wooden door open and followed the agent inside. Von Kluge was seated near the commandant's desk, dressed in faded blue dungarees, boots, and cap in his lap. He looked rough but acted meek and mild. He stood as the commandant and FBI agent entered the room. He seemed eager and pleased to see them. In the corner sat the stenographer, a middle-aged woman in uniform behind her little shorthand machine, ready to chord and stroke.

"Let's have us some coffee," shouted Briggs to someone in the next room. The men sat and an aide brought in three mugs of black coffee.

Von Kluge nodded his head in appreciation and took a tentative sip. Then a longer one, and he placed the mug on the desk, not to disturb it again.

Briggs did the introductions and added an aside to the stenographer. Gunderson settled down on the table with his notebook and pen, and lit a cigarette.

NAZI SYMPATHIZERS IN AMERICA
Tues., April 11, 1945, 4:15 pm Central Wartime

Von Kluge began his soliloquy (some wording has been revised for clarification):

I remember the great celebration known as German Day hosted by the German-American Bund (Amerikadeutscher Volksbund), previously known as the Friends of Hitler Movement or Friends of New Germany. This was in July 1938. Participants from all the 19 Midwestern groups came to Coney Island, just upriver from Cincinnati, to celebrate. German heritage was honored by thousands of marchers wearing Nazi armbands and carrying both the Nazi flag and the American flag. We sang the "Horst Wessel" (the official Nazi song) and displayed a replica of the sacred Blutfahne, the Munich banner bearing the bloodstains of the fallen Nazi patriots. I remember the Sunlite Pool, the largest swimming pool in the world. Appropriately it was off-limits to Negroes and other miscreants. Ludwig Thon, the editor of the *Cincinnati Freie Presse*, spoke at the festival, and in his speech, he attacked the press, claiming that reports about the persecution of minorities in Hitler's Germany were overblown and hypocritical.

We believed that American values and the values of the Third Reich were compatible. After all, the founding fathers were apprehensive about democracy and mobs, and formed a republic, which like National Socialism, is the enemy of worldwide Communism. The food at the festival was German and plentiful, lots of warm beer and bratwurst, bread and cheese, and lots of German folk music.

The featured speaker was Gerhard Kunze, the German-American Bund's public relations officer, who was touring the country on a recruitment drive. As you know, in January 1938 the US Attorney General announced the conclusions of an FBI investigation and cleared the Bund of any federal wrongdoing. The emboldened Bund launched membership drives that included Kunze's trip through the Midwest.

Kunze the orator tried in vain to imitate der Fuhrer in his delivery. He stated that "the Bund was against any and all atheism, against all subversive internationalism and against the indiscriminate mixture of Aryan and Asiatic or African races. We want to preserve the culture in which America has been built and keep people of our own kind controlling the public mind."

Some elements of the crowd, no doubt fueled by alcohol, became aggressive and threatening. There were fights with anti-fascist protestors and amongst themselves, and a few arrests. The Bund crowd was so large, however, that protestors dared not challenge them forthright. Thus ended von Kluge's speech.

After smudging out his cigarette, Gunderson pulled a black-and-white photograph out of its envelope and showed it to von Kluge. "Do you recognize this man?"

Von Kluge took the photo and stared at it. He thought he knew who it was but he wanted to make sure. "It has been awhile, but that resembles Heine Hammerschmidt. I remember him from the old neighborhood, Over-the-Rhine in Cincinnati. It's called that because the German neighborhood was on the other side of the Miami & Erie Canal. His uncle Heinrich was born in Germany turn of the century. He emigrated to America and ended up in Cincinnati. He married a local girl, Heidi, whose father owned the brewery where Heinrich worked. The ceremony was at Philippus Kirche. Their son born in America was Hans Hammerschmidt; he would've been born in or around 1924. Earning a decent living turned out tough for the family and there was some anti-German hostility, even in that neighborhood. Down with the Hun, you know. So the family moved back to the Fatherland in 1935. By that time Heidi Hammerschmidt's parents had died. I don't know much about them after they went back to Germany."

"So who is Heine Hammerschmidt?" Gunderson wanted to know.

"He is the son of Heinrich's brother, Lothar. What's interesting is that Heine Hammerschmidt emigrated to the U.S. the same year the Hammerschmidts moved back to Germany."

"You've been very helpful," Gunderson said to von Kluge, terminating the interview.

The commandant smiled and told von Kluge that he should go back to his barracks. He advised the FBI agent, "You should come back when you have time for a hunt." Gunderson grunted his approval and thanked Briggs.

Gunderson considered von Kluge's testimony driving all the way back to town. Mainly because the photo he had shown von Kluge was that of Daniel Ross, aka Big Dan the Hardware Man. The FBI agent was deep in thought and he did not recall the drive back to town. When he got to his office he headed straight to the file cabinet and withdrew a dated bulletin.

Date: 6 July 1938

FBI Headquarters, Washington DC
Forward: Knoxville Field Office
Attn: Special Agent in Charge
Hundreds of members of the Northwest Georgia Communist Party are sickened with ptomaine poisoning at an outdoor festival in Atlanta suburbs. The poison is believed to have come from rancid potato salad. A Bund operative known as Andy Anderson of Cumberland County, Tenn. is a prime suspect, but his whereabouts are unknown. Attached is composite sketch of possible suspect.

Gunderson pondered the sketch, which somewhat resembled the photo of Heine Hammerschmidt.

Gunderson recalled an anecdote that Myra, his secretary, had shared with him. Myra was a friend of the mayor's wife.

Myra told Gunderson a story she had heard from the mayor's wife about a visit the mayor had made to Big Dan Ross's lodge in the foothills. Up at the lake in the sky. Such outings are restricted to men only and consisted of fishing, drinking, relaxing, swimming, boating, and other male bonding. The mayor's wife didn't know about the party girls, but she had heard rumors. Knoxville is a small town. Anyway, the mayor told the story about a black bear crashing one of their outdoor celebrations and giving the guys a hard time. They put out a pot of beer (the high-octane good stuff) and the bear drank a lot of it. He rolled around and danced and then stumbled off into the woods. The guys all had a great time unwinding and getting snockered. You know, that's how Big Dan gets a lot of his inside information. Alcohol loosens the tongue. Apparently that also applies to Big Dan, who tried to teach a drinking song to his guests. A favorite in Munich during Oktoberfest goes like this:

Die Kruge hoch! (Raise your steins!)
Ein Prosit (A toast)
Der Gemütlichkeit (To the coziness of it all)
Oans, Zwoa, Drei, g'suffa! (One, Two, Three, Drink)
Zicke Zacke Zicke Zacke
Hoi! Hoi! Hoi!

Of course, none of the guests, including the mayor, could remember the words the next day, but Gunderson looked it up. The song is "Ein Prosit."

Big Dan's from Cincinnati, of German heritage. Hundreds of thousands of Americans have a German heritage. But one might have thought that drinking song came straight from München. Big Dan sounded natural affecting a Deutsches accent.

G-MAN DETECTS INFILTRATION
Tues., April 11, 1945, 2:30 pm Eastern Wartime

The call came in from one of his informants who knew what was going on in the sheriff's office, sometimes before even the sheriff knew. Two bodies—an older man and his grandson—had been found up in the hills, the victims brutally murdered. They were known moonshiners, found not too far from their still, about fifteen miles southeast of Knoxville between Maryville and the Foothills Parkway. At first, investigators worked on the supposition that the killings were a backwoods feud, perhaps even rival shiners, although that sort of violence was uncommon in those parts. Both of the victims had been stabbed to death, actually slashed, the old man first. The boy had defensive wounds on his hands. The cuts were made with precision with a razor-sharp, curved blade. Two quick slashes to the neck. The first slash targets the vagus nerve, which immobilizes the victim, then a down stroke that cuts the bleeders. Minimal arterial spray; the victim bleeds out in thirty seconds. No noise. Obviously the work of a professional. Cold-blooded killings.

Gunderson asked the informant, "Where's the sheriff right now?"

"Well, after looking at the bodies and handing them over, he headed to the family home in hopes of preventing further bloodshed. You know, retribution."

"Where is this home?"

"It's up Bucksnort Mountain and down the holler alongside Turkey Creek. Hell, I'll take you there myself. Meet you down at the street."

The informant, known as Buzz, was a flinty man with beard stubble who wore a beaten-down fedora on his bald head. His suit hung off his frame as if he had lost a lot of weight lately. He drove a pre-war Ford that swayed alarmingly—new springs and other parts were difficult to procure these days. He had virtually made a living of hanging around the county courthouse and doing odd jobs for the sheriff's office. Some said Buzz was a retard; others claimed he was a savant. A full-grown adult, he sometimes acted childish, deriving great pleasure from such behavior. The first time you meet Buzz he'll ask for your name and Social Security number. If you bump into him five years later he'll tell you your name and Social Security number.

Buzz took the Henley Street bridge over the river and headed down Highway 33 to Rockford and then through the small town of Maryville.

Montvale Road led to Sixmile and Butterfly Gap Road. Soon they were rambling down improvised roads under a canopy of oaks, elms, and hackberries. The dirt road hugged the course of the creek, which was flowing rapidly from the spring rains.

"I hope you know where you're going."

"Oh yeah," he replied with a grin. As he drove he snapped the chewing gum in his mouth.

As expected the log house was ramshackle with a long porch up front and wooden shingles. An agitated man in his twenties wearing bib overalls waved them off with a double-barrel shotgun. He eased off when he recognized the driver.

"Sheriff here?"

"Yeah, he's inside." The gunman eyed the passenger of the sedan wearily. "Who's he?"

"A friend of the sheriff's," Buzz said, which was true. Buzz knew better than to identify him as an Federal agent. The sheriff liked Gunderson a whole lot better than his predecessor.

The sheriff met them on the porch, followed by a gruff old man sucking on his stained teeth, what was left of them. He spat some tobacco juice onto the floorboards. At least he turned his head to do so.

The sheriff greeted them by name. "Buzz, you been behavin' yourself?" he asked rhetorically.

Gunderson said, "Hello, sheriff. Understand there's been some trouble."

"You could say that." The sheriff needed a new uniform or at least a laundered one. Folks tended to lean informal around these parts.

The FBI man gestured him off the porch. Buzz and the old man stayed put.

"Can you show me the site?

"Sure. I'll take you in the cruiser." Buzz said he'd like to tag along, and the sheriff did not object.

The moonshine distillery wasn't difficult to find. A dirt trail led from the outhouse out back. The still was fairly elaborate as far as these backwoods rigs go. The sheriff pointed to two disturbed spots on the ground. He explained how the bodies had been found by a relative of the family. They had been moved before law enforcement got there. There wasn't much of a crime scene to examine. The law shut down the moonshine operation; the mule still stood there, a mute witness.

"Like somebody or something just swooped down on them." The sheriff swooped his arm to demonstrate.

The FBI agent said he'd like to look around for a while.

"Sure. Help yourself. I'll be right here," said the sheriff, lighting up his pipe.

Gunderson indicated that he would head off to the left and work his way around; he told Buzz to do the same on the right side.

He tried to walk lifting up his feet. He stumbled a couple times on exposed tree roots but managed to stay upright. Here and there he spotted various items of debris. Broken glass jars, rusted pieces of metal, even an old wheelbarrow with a sapling growing up through the tub. He noticed a licklog, its notches void of salt. A sinkhole of some size was being used as a backcountry dump but nothing seemed to have been disturbed recently. He found some sort of buckle on the ground. It was shiny and looked new.

Over to his right something hanging from a tree limb fluttered in the breeze. It was a patch of fabric about the size of a small kitchen towel. He wadded it up and held it in the crook of his arm. He craned his neck and examined the trees until he found what he was looking for. It was up high, far out of reach. Soon he met up with Buzz and they both headed back to the killing site in a direct line of travel.

"Find anything?" Gunderson asked.

"Nope. What you got there?"

The agent held up the piece of fabric. "Might be evidence."

"Looks like a parachute to me," said Buzz.

Let's just keep this between you and me, okay?" He tucked the material into his waistband beneath his coat jacket and went to see the sheriff.

Buzz motioned that he was zippering his mouth. He participated in courthouse gossip as much as anyone, but he could keep a secret.

GUNDERSON AND THE LIBRARIAN
Tues., April 11, 1945, 5:45 pm Eastern Wartime

The University of Tennessee graduate library shared stacks with the Law Library. Gunderson found the stone building with English Tudor-style windows nestled in a small stand of tulip poplars off the winding street up The Hill. The library closed at six; he arrived about 15 minutes beforehand. The dim hallway echoed his shoe falls, but otherwise was quiet. The place seemed deserted; the students were away at war. The female librarian emerged from the shadows so stealthily that he was startled. In spite of her middle-aged, formal demeanor she couldn't help but giggle.

"You startled me."

"I noticed. Can I help you?" she said, sizing him up. She wore her reading glasses on a chain around her neck and her reddish-brown hair pulled back into a tight bun.

He had this notion that female librarians harbored repressed sexual tendencies, suppressing their feminine qualities. Probably just a typical male fantasy.

"I need to find some translations, German to American, uh, I mean English."

She met his glance perhaps a little too long. "All right. Walk this way." She turned and swished her legs inside an impossibly tight skirt. He watched with fascination and lust, thinking that he couldn't walk that way if his life depended on it. She was not unattractive.

She turned left, sashayed past three or four stacks, and stopped midway down the aisle. She browsed for a moment and pulled a large volume from the row.

"Wow. That's a big one," he said.

"Yes, yes it is," she said. "Heavy too."

Gunderson offered and took the book from her. She indicated a nearby table. He placed the book on the table and sat, following her lead.

She scooted her chair closer to his. "I have studied several foreign languages, which might be useful."

They were the only ones in the room, perhaps the entire library. She smelled of spring blossoms, not too different than Myra's scent.

"Okay," she said.

He pulled a scrap of paper from his jacket and positioned it next to the book.

"Grün salz," she said. "That's relatively easy. It translates as green salt."

She poked at the scrap with the long nail of her index finger.

"Fallscgirmsprung. Fairly sure that means parachute." She looked it up in the book. "Yep."

"Next is Geheimnis, which means secret. Leuchtfeuer means beacon," she said after looking it up.

"Uhu means eagle owl," she stated. "It's pronounced as ooh-who."

"I need to look that up in a bird book."

"Okay," she said, pushing away from the table. "Follow me."

He needed to learn about Uhu, but he had forgotten where he'd heard that word.

Further back in the stacks, she found a section with books on biology, and fauna and birds. She pulled one out and put it on another nearby table. Under raptors, she found the entry titled Eurasian Eagle-Owls. He sat down to read. Now she loomed over him. He smelled faintly of smoke and aftershave alcohol, a manly scent for sure.

She watched intently, silently, as he read the description:

"Eurasian Eagle-owls combine fast and powerful flights with shallow wing beats and long, fast glides. They also soar on updrafts, displaying a type of flight similar to that of soaring hawks like the Red-tailed Hawk. Eurasian Eagle-owls are among the world's largest owls. Their pumpkin orange eyes and feathery ear tufts make them one of the most striking owls in the world.

"Eurasian Eagle-owls are found throughout much of Europe and Asia and in parts of northern Africa. They live in a variety of wooded habitats.

"With their bright orange eyes, mottled feathers, and ear tufts, Eurasian Eagle-owls are visually striking animals. Their large, powerful feet and strong flight make them effective hunters. Like many raptors, these owls are top predators – they hunt other animals for food but no animals hunt them on a regular basis. For most top predators, their only threat is human.

"Eurasian Eagle-owls are mostly nocturnal, or active at night. They spend their days roosting, or resting, in a safe perch. If they spend too much time on the ground, even these top predators may fall prey to opportunistic ground predators like foxes.

"Each hoot consists of two notes slurred together, the first higher and louder than the second."

Gunderson slammed the book shut, creating a slight cloud of dust.

"This is all very interesting," she said in a sly manner. "If I may ask, what do you do? Are you a German bird-watcher?"

He chuckled and told her a cover story which wasn't very convincing. She didn't seem to care. She moved closer and peered into his face with lovely, captivating eyes.

"You know, it gets lonely in here. As a matter of fact, we're the only ones left in the building."

"You don't say."

She made her move, and he had no intention of stopping her. She let her hair down, shook her tresses out, and pushed herself against him. She was soft yet assertive. An aggressive librarian, what a grand idea.

"Ooh-who," he exclaimed more than once. His outbursts echoed throughout the hallways and lonely stacks.

"This isn't my first rodeo, cowboy," she explained.

BIG DAN FLIES AWAY
Wed., April 12, 1945, 2:45 pm Eastern Wartime

The FBI SAC, Slim Gunderson, spent most of Wednesday morning putting the pieces together, connecting the dots, as they say, and piling up cigarette butts in his desktop ashtray. His desk was littered with report files, wire dispatches, photos, and other paraphernalia. He tried to forget about yesterday's tryst with the red-haired librarian, but flashbacks kept intruding onto his mental gameboard of clues. He made a note to call her as soon as he could. He knew he would need to see her again, perhaps this time at his place (home not office). After he firmly rooted that scenario in his mind, he could proceed with more urgent matters. It was well into the afternoon when he decided to set things in motion.

He dispatched his subordinate, Jimmy Rucker, to track down Big Dan Ross and field-interview him. Gunderson told Rucker, "I'm going to get on the *Southland Express* headed to Chicago today. I do believe there's going to be some mischief. I'll probably check back when I reach Cincinnati."

He warned Rucker, "Be careful with Ross, he's a big man around town and I don't want to spook him. Don't let him know that he's the subject of an investigation."

"Gotcha, Chief," Rucker replied. Big Dan might be able to figure that out on his own, he reckoned. "I'll check his shop, his home, and his weekend getaway, if I need to."

Gunderson left the office for the train depot. After a few minutes on the phone, Rucker learned that Big Dan was most likely alone at his lodge at Top of the World, 45 minutes away. Rucker drove the big sedan over the swirling Tennessee River headed towards Chilhowee Mountain and the Smokies. He skirted the town of Maryville and hooked onto Butterfly Gap Road, which zigzagged up the steep ridge with several sharp switchbacks. The trees were beginning to leaf-out and the sheer roadside rock walls were wet with spring seepage.

Rucker drove under the Foothills Parkway and up onto Flats Road. The lodge was located on Big Bass Lane on the southwest shore of the small lake. A dirt road circled the small reservoir shaped like a boomerang or a banana. Rucker found Big Dan's place, by far the largest and most opulent of the community. He could hear the banging of a hammer wielded by a homeowner making springtime repairs. Big Dan's place was on a small hillside, an A-frame with stone foundation, flanked by one-story wings with huge windows onto the lake. He pulled into the steep driveway flanked by stone pillars and parked next to Big Dan's utility truck. Leaves were rustling and songbirds chirping. The air here was cooler and invigorating. In the near distance, windchimes jangled gently. Nice place up here.

Rucker sauntered up the paved walkway and yelled "Hello!" He crested the top of a gentle slope where he could now see the shoreline. Suddenly a gunshot rang out and echoed against the trees along the shoreline. Rucker heard the round zing over his head and he hit the ground. He quickly pulled out his service revolver and scanned the back of the lodge for the shooter. Down the incline to the lake he heard the heavy pounding of shoes on wooden deck planks. In the small cove, Big Dan had built a covered dock equipped with an avgas tank for his floatplane and was hastily climbing aboard. Apparently Rucker had interrupted preparations for his departure. Wearing some sort of flight suit, Big Dan pushed the aircraft away from the dock while boarding and within moments the engine had started up with blown bluish smoke and the whirling of the twin-bladed propeller. Rucker could not tell whether the small, two-man airplane carried a passenger or not. He knelt and fired off a round, both hands on the piece. The bullet missed the aircraft, glanced off the surface of the water and whizzed away into the far woods. The Stinson L-5 floatplane, painted bright yellow and radiant against the dark blue of the water, was moving away quickly. The surface of the water was smooth and peaceful. Rucker could have shot again but he figured the odds of hitting a small, moving target was slim. He stood up and ran down to the dock. By the time he reached the dock the airplane had hoisted up on its floats and was lifting off the water with a final burst of spray. The plane climbed quickly out of sight leaving only the echoes of the engine behind. Only a highly skilled pilot could take off or land on such a small lake.

"That worked out well," Rucker grumbled. The FBI agent strode up the hill to the patio and entered the large lodge, the door left unlocked. There was nobody inside, but he found evidence of a second person staying there. He looked for clues and found nothing other than a marked-up flight map that might prove useful. He used the phone in the cabin to call the field office and report his findings. Myra said Gunderson had left for the train depot.

Initially, he had to assume there were no witnesses to the shooting.

BUSHWHACKERS IN POSITION
Wed., April 12th, 1945, 2:15 pm Eastern Wartime

The day had come for Operation Brilliant. The four-man crew met at Pinky's for one last review of the plan and the hoisting of whiskey shot glasses for good luck. In two cars, Bum and Big Donnie drove them all to the scene of the upcoming crime on Solway Road. They were lost in their thoughts. All of them had big plans for themselves after the heist:

- Large Donnie planned to buy a yacht with his share of the diamonds and stock it with booze, big cigars, and a scantily clad female crew.

- Bum was going to travel around the world on a luxury ocean liner, dress like ole Scarface, and meet all kinds of exotic women.

- Pecker was going to buy or build his own saloon, a classy place with fine liquors and showgirls that would put Pinky's to shame.

- Hacksaw wanted a huge estate on the lake, a house with 40 rooms, horses, and a 1935 Duesenberg SSJ, just like the one Gary Cooper drove.

Meanwhile, LT and Sarge, the couriers, were leaving Building 9733-1 at CEW. They passed the huge billboard with a hatless Uncle Sam rolling up his sleeves and warning "Loose Talk Helps Our Enemy. So Let's Keep Our Trap Shut."

LT kept the briefcase on the bench seat between himself and Sarge in the back of the beige 1939 Chevrolet sedan. The unmarked car bore Tennessee plates registered under the name "Special." Before the routine inspection by the MPs at the Solway Bridge gate, the unremarkable sedan was hosed down to lessen the overwhelming amount of mud splatter. The sedan was driven by an armed guard, also dressed in a civilian suit. Sarge brought a suitcase that contained clean underwear, a towel, a baton flashlight, and other gear. His lucky coin was in his pocket. The Chevy trailed another sedan, this one a Ford V-8 of the same vintage. Two heavily armed MPs occupied the Ford vehicle, also in civilian clothing. They had a pump shotgun right underneath the front seat. They headed out of the reservation toward Robinson's Crossing. There were three routes that they could travel into downtown Knoxville to the train depot—the Knoxville Highway, Middlebrook Pike, or Kingston Pike. On each 17-mile trip, they took a different route. Today, they were headed to Middlebrook Pike.

Nearly two-and-a-half miles from the Solway gate they would cross Beaver Creek, about fifty feet wide, on a simple concrete culvert with no railings.

This particular afternoon a motley crew awaited at the Beaver Creek bridge with a special welcome. They had it all planned out, like clockwork. Large Donnie was on the north side of the bridge with binoculars, ready to signal when the caravan was approaching. He wore denim bib overalls with red t-shirt and an odd-shaped felt fedora. His vehicle was an old Chrysler 1934 Airflow, an innovative vehicle for its day. For the past decade, however, the faded blue beast had been used to transport hootch into Knoxville. Much of the booze was loaded onto trains to Chicago, where certain bosses ran illegal bars called speak-easies.

Large Donnie would give the signal—the waving of a handkerchief —and then get behind the wheel, drive onto the pavement, and block the pike after the CEW procession passed by.

Bum was stationed on the other side of the bridge, the south side, where he would park his car on the pike, lift the hood, and wave for help. Once the heist was effected, Bum would drive them all away from Knoxville headed west on the Hardin Valley Road. His vehicle, a roomy Lincoln Zephyr sedan, was well maintained in contrast to Large Donnie's Chrysler. The beast was nearly 17 feet long, weighed a ton-and-a-half and sported a Ford V-12 powerplant. That's more than one hundred horsepower.

Once the CEW cars were blocked on or near the bridge, Pecker and Hacksaw would emerge from the south tree line and attack the vehicles. Pecker was armed with the Thompson submachine gun and Hacksaw wielded the bazooka, which was already loaded. With any luck, the crew would not be noticed by any motorists passing by. The pike was not too busy this time of day, rush hour having come and gone.

Bum anxiously tapped his fingers on the enormous steering wheel of the Lincoln Zephyr, which sported a suicide knob in the form of an eight-ball. He nudged the gas pedal to keep the engine running in neutral. He could just barely see Large Donnie on the other side of the bridge, standing and peering through his binoculars. Bum had rolled the window down, and the bugs were busy pestering him at this location near the creek tree line. He could not see Pecker or Hacksaw on the other side of the slightly elevated road. Bum kept nipping at the flask of whiskey he had brought with him. It was getting emptied fast.

Pecker was crouched near the intersection of the concrete bridge and the pike, down and out of sight. He grasped the submachine gun with the pistol grip and laid it across the top of his thigh. The damn thing was heavy, weighing well over ten pounds. The day before, he took 45 minutes to handload the fifty rounds of .45 ACP into the relatively delicate drum magazine, which rattled noisily even when fully loaded. It was getting hot and humid this time of the day, his handkerchief already wet from wiping perspiration from his brow. He glanced back at Hacksaw, who was crouched behind him.

"Watch where you're pointing that thing," he hissed at Hacksaw, indicating the bazooka.

"You ready?"

"Ready as I'll ever be."

After their toast at Pinky's, Hacksaw had taken the opportunity to swig a mouthful or two of liquid courage in the form of Southern Comfort. Now his head felt as if a hot ball of fizz was knocking around inside. He needed to prop the rear end of the bazooka into the ground behind him to keep his balance.

"C'mon, c'mon," he nervously muttered.

The two heavily armed hooligans would need to run up an incline of grass still wet with dew. At least there were no mud patches on that gradient. Pecker could barely see Large Donnie across the creek and through the tree line; Hacksaw could not see him at all.

Large Donnie was on the southwest shoulder of the pike, concentrating on observing the CEW vehicles as soon as he could, the slight bend in the roadway notwithstanding. His Chrysler was down a slight incline, perpendicular to the roadway, engine idling and driver's door open. He had a .44 Magnum revolver laying on the front bench seat, ready for use if needed. He had to signal the others, then get into his car and drive it up onto the roadway just north of the bridge, blocking the government vehicles from retreating. Then he would have to make his way across the bridge and get into Bum's vehicle for the getaway.

The ambush had been precisely planned and explained to all the participants. The real problem was that they all had several days to mull it over and experience growing doubts. None of them had slept well the night before. It's difficult to deliberately not think about the day to come.

"Fuck it," Pecker had told them. "We're doing this. This is big time."

Bum muttered to himself, "I hope I don't fuck this up."

How did the motley crew know when the government vehicles would approach the bridge? They had lookouts, secret operatives, and informants just as military intelligence did. They had kept a close eye on the couriers' routes even before hatching the ambush scheme. This was the logical place to hit the CEW caravan. Had to be someplace between the Solway gate and Robinson's Crossing.

Large Donnie took one last drag on his Old Gold before flicking it down onto the pavement. Now the time of reckoning had come. The CEW vehicles rolled down the Solway Pike toward the small bridge, the structure barely noticeable even when you're driving right over it. The vehicles kept close, about 15 yards apart. Traffic was light. Beautiful spring day. Looked like another milk run.

AMBUSH GOES AWRY
Wed., April 12th, 1945, 2:15 pm Eastern Wartime

Large Donnie caught a glimpse of the lead car's huge chrome grill coming around the bend of Solway Pike. He waved the white rag over his head excitedly. He bounded down the shoulder, buckled under his notorious "trick knee," slipped on the wet grass, and lost grip on the binoculars. Cursing profusely, he then noticed that the Chrysler's engine had stalled. Wet and stained, he grabbed the open door to pull himself onto the front seat, and cranked the ignition as he slammed the door behind him.

There was no traffic in front of the government vehicles so Bum, on the south side of the bridge, sprang into action. Bum hit the gas and immediately spun the rear wheels, gaining no traction. "Shit, damn, fuck," he cursed, throttling the steering wheel in anger. He was feeling a little groggy, his perceptions a quarter-second behind his actions. He knew he needed to keep his cool. Moving the shift lever furiously, he managed to rock the big beast and move forward. Nursing the engine, he stalled it but recovered remarkably well for a knucklehead in his condition. He nudged the Lincoln up onto the pavement and pointed it toward Knoxville. He then rushed out of the car, feet skittering about, fumbled with the hood latch, and finally raised it as a (phony) distress signal. He then stood at the left front fender and waved down the caravan.

The MPs in the lead car looked at each other, and one exclaimed, "What the hell?"

"This does not look right," stated the driver.

"Do not stop," ordered his partner, who reached for the pump shotgun. Once in hand, he briskly pumped a shell into the chamber. The shell contained a lead slug, more lethal and accurate than buckshot.

The couriers and driver in the second car did not know what was happening, but they saw Large Donnie moving his Chrysler up onto the road behind them. Sarge pulled his .45 semi-automatic from the holster and held it with the muzzle pointed upward.

Once clear of the concrete bridge, the lead driver veered left of Bum's car and drove down the embankment, headed at an oblique for Pecker and Hacksaw. Bum brandished his handgun, a cheap Saturday night special with a history in Chicago, and began shooting wildly, endangering his buddies more than the MPs.

Pecker was pedaling on the wet grass like a hamster on a treadmill, but he managed to stay half-upright and steady himself. He brought up the tommy gun with both hands and squeezed the trigger. The submachine gun sprayed the scene with a burst of loud gunfire, hitting nothing because Pecker had lost control of it as it recoiled and ratcheted upward from the blasts. Pecker lost his footing but hung onto the weapon. When he tried to fire again, nothing happened. He had hit the ground with the drum magazine and now the gun was jammed, and no amount of working the bolt would fix it. He threw the tommy gun down and pulled his sidearm from his hip holster. By the time he had crouched into a firing position to draw down, his feet slid out from under him and he slithered down the incline, desperately trying to gain a handhold. His outburst was laced with the most vulgar obscenities.

Meanwhile, Hacksaw wiggled over to avoid Pecker, abandoned the notion of moving any closer, crouched down on one knee, and aimed the loaded bazooka slightly upward at the profile of the government vehicles. The backblast of the rocket launcher knocked him over and deafened him. He had forgotten to put in his earplugs. His head was ringing and his vision blurred. He was facing the ground.

The MPs yelled, "Incoming!" and hit the ground.

Unfortunately, Hacksaw had aimed too high to begin with. The projectile zoomed over the sedans with a horrid hiss and trail of smoke. Turns out, the projectile hit the roof of a barn ("See Rock City") owned by farmer Jerald Caswell and scared the hell out of a mule, the livestock, and family members inside the farmhouse.

Hacksaw had no more rockets to fire. They had figured that one shot would do the trick. Even if he had more he probably wouldn't have bothered trying again.   .

"Get us the hell out of here!" the MP in the lead car yelled at the driver.

The MP wheeled the sedan around Bum's Lincoln and managed to land a glancing blow to the sodden gunman. Bum hit the pavement like a sack of potatoes and didn't get up. By this time, Large Donnie had arrived at the scene, only to confront Sarge standing outside his sedan, aiming a large handgun at him. Large Donnie wheeled around on one stiff leg, steadying himself with one hand on the blacktop, stood up, and ran to his vehicle. He swung the Chrysler around and headed northward away from the bridge.

"Get in," LT told Sarge.

"Why didn't I shoot the motherfucker?" Sarge cussed.

The couriers pulled around the Lincoln and caught up to the lead sedan. The two cars stopped on the shoulder a hundred yards from the ambush site. LT got out and instructed the MPs, "Let's keep moving. Let's get to the depot. We're supposed to take Middlebrook Pike but let's take Kingston Pike instead. Okay?"

Once back inside and moving, LT listened to Sarge as he glanced back through the rear window. "How do you like that? Those were a bunch of rank amateurs."

"Well-armed amateurs. That was an M1A1 recoilless anti-tank rocket launcher they had."

"Thank God they don't know how to shoot."

"They must've been trying to steal the briefcase. No other reason to do what they did. They don't know what's in the briefcase, only that it must be valuable."

"Well, what now?"

"We need to stay alert, for sure, but I don't think we're looking at any more trouble. Let's notify CIC when we get to the depot, and get on the train and in our cabin as soon as possible. The MPs can hang around longer than they usually do. We might need all the help we can get."

Meanwhile, the guards at the Solway gate, having heard the blast of the rocket launcher, went to investigate and ran into Large Donnie fleeing the scene. They took him into custody without incident. When they reached the scene, Bum was still prone on the pavement being attended to by a passing motorist.

"We'll take over," the guards told the motorist.

"What happened? I don't think he's dead."

"Multiple car accident. Nothing to be worried about."

"I heard an explosion."

"Must've been a car backfiring."

"Whatever you say," said the civilian. "Hope he's okay."

Meanwhile, Pecker and Hacksaw were making their way along the creek bank, heading back toward town. They eventually caught a ride in the truckbed of a farmer heading toward town. Left behind, the Thompson submachine gun and the rocket launcher were discovered and confiscated.

"We may have some explaining to do," said the CEW guard. "Let's clear it with HQ. Probably list it as a multiple-car accident. I don't think there were any eye-witnesses."

"I'll be interested to find out the real story when we question that mutt we collared."

BILLIE JEAN'S SURPRISE
Wed., April 12, 1945, 6:00 am Eastern Wartime

Doc Hamblen got up before sunrise that morning, careful not to disturb Billie Jean lying next to him. They had tried something new that night, and the experience had been exhilarating, and exhausting, in a good way. He worked it so hard his sweat dripped onto her back. She was young; she still had the energy later to roll him over and straddle on top. Nature had awarded him great stamina and he lasted a long time. Once she got going and hit the right spot, she couldn't stop until she literally bounded off him, shreiking and screaming. Then when they cuddled, she would coo. They both slept well; both trying to avoid the wet spot. Upon awakening and seeing the time, he needed to shower and dress quickly to get to the depot. He dressed comfortably in civilian clothes, a sportscoat without a tie. He packed a small bag with toiletries he could sling over his shoulder. His radiological equipment, including a portable Geiger counter, was contained in a leather grip. A crate full of other equipment and gear would be placed in the cargo car for his use, if necessary. He needed to get to the depot early and into his cabin so that the couriers, who arrived later, wouldn't see or recognize him.

Billie Jean was stirring now, rolling over to grab for him and finding only a pillow.

Doc Hamblen let Billie Jean sleep some more. She practically lived there now, setting up a household, preparing for her perceived future as Mrs. Marty Hamblen. The doctor was certain to leave his wife, who basically lived her own life, traveling with her boyfriend, who happened to be married himself. That much the doctor had told her. The damned war was playing hell on traditional marriages.

The good doctor had been extremely selfish when he reported to supervisors that Billie Jean was pregnant and couldn't work the calutrons anymore. He wanted her all for himself, even to the point where she assisted him with minor duties at the university medical offices underneath the football stadium. At first, she was furious at his ploy, but eventually she came to believe that he had done that for her own good. He never lied to her about her being pregnant.

Now that she actually was pregnant she couldn't wait to tell him, but she also was terrified at his possible negative reaction. Surely this would be the impetus that would prompt him to get a divorce and marry her. On a whim, she couldn't help herself, she got ready and dressed to go to the depot herself that morning. She would buy a ticket to Chicago and she would surprise him with the good news on the train. They could celebrate in the big city. Champagne and all. It would be gay.

Although she slept later than the doctor, she was the first out the door, heading to the lab underneath the stadium.

The CEW car came for Doc Hamblen around 8:00 am, parking outside his bungalow in the Fort Sanders neighborhood. The driver was a Medical Corps corporal who was busy chomping on a wad of gum.

"Yo ho," the driver greeted him informally.

"Same to you, fella," Doc replied.

The route took them past the obelisk monument at the corner of Clinch and 16th. It noted that the 79th New York Highlanders had successfully defended Fort Sanders approximately eighty years ago. Apparently the soldiers assaulted the fort while screaming the rebel yell until they realized nobody remembered to bring the scaling ladders. The Yankees lost 13 men while the Confederate casualties totaled 813. One of the most lopsided battles, albeit a small one, of the entire war.

Doc Hamblen arrived at the L&N depot ahead of the couriers and everybody else. He took his usual assignment in the the first cabin car.

PASSENGERS CONVERGE ON DEPOT
Wed., April 12, 1945, 7:00 am Eastern Wartime

The Louisville & Nashville Railroad depot in Knoxville is an ornate red-brick Victorian structure sitting along the tracks just north of downtown. It straddles the east bank of Second Creek, and was designed to incorporate the creekbank's downward slope. The building is L-shaped, with wings projecting west and south of the northeast corner tower. The northeast corner tower, which rises three stories, is topped by a pitched, clay-tiled roof with decorated dormers. The heavy entrance doors gleam with brass, frosted glass, and glazed transoms. The waiting rooms are in the west wing, a dining room in the tower, and a kitchen, lunch counter, and baggage areas in the south wing. The waiting rooms include a general waiting room, a ladies' waiting room (with a private entrance and an entrance from the general waiting room) on the northwest corner, and a "colored" waiting room on the southwest corner with a separate entrance.

In the morning, like the city itself, the station slowly awakes to the rhythm and intensity of the day.

The depot is busy that morning with servicemen arriving and departing, civilian travelers of all sorts, and the normal crew of clerks, engineers, porters, and baggage men. The large waiting room reverberates with the sounds of squealing children, the opening and closing of doors, background chatter and radio dialogue, the scuffling of shoes on stonework, and the occasional intercom announcement. The intensity and endurance of the echoes reflect the volume and configuration of their source.

The passage of time. It's all about time here—conducting commerce, meeting deadlines, completing schedules, and the consummation of logistics, as well-oiled as the locomotives humming outside on the tracks. Overlooking all is the big, round clockface ticking away the seconds and minutes. Arrivals and departures are listed on the giant grid-like L&N schedule. It's not all action and movement—as the Army says "Hurry up and wait."

Servicemen in uniform carrying duffel bags saunter through the main lobby. Some sit and light up cigarettes with black crackle-finish Zippo lighters. A few Navy men in white cluster and separate themselves from the khaki-colored Army GIs. A younger lady in a scarf and light coat guides her newborn in a carriage. Men in coat and tie sit and read the latest newspapers from the newsstand while a couple of businessmen sit at the shine stand with their scuffed shoes up and on display. Waiting for their trains, passengers sit in long wooden pews, back-to-back. A few patrons perch on stools at the luncheonette and sip coffee from heavy ceramic mugs. The interior stonework is accented by polished brass handrails and decorative cherubs and other mimetic nick-nacks. A dissociated other-worldly voice, like the god of locomotion, announces arrivals and departures over the public address system.

As passengers make their way down the wide stairs to the platforms, sleek, streamlined locomotives pull their trains of colorfully painted passenger cars held together with orderly rows of round-headed rivets. The locomotives throb with the vibrations of their diesel engines and sound off with horns. Waning but still operative are the antiquated coal-fired steam engines with their whistles, their sooty residue bound to linger for decades.

At the end of the platforms, baggage handlers use all sorts of conveyances to load and unload crates, boxes, and barrels, and steamer trunks festooned with travel decals.

CIC agents planted here at the depot look for workers with loose lips and any other suspicious behavior. Several uniformed MPs loiter about, observing the crowd, on the lookout for known AWOLs, and fiddling with their nightsticks.

Now in its so-called berth, the *Southland Express* boasts a gleaming, streamlined diesel locomotive in the Art Deco style painted burnt-orange and dark-blue, now somewhat faded. Even at rest, engines humming, it exudes the look of speed. The lead locomotive is paired with another behind, followed by a freight or cargo car. There are three Pullman sleeper cars with ten seats/bunks each. Mostly servicemen and rural folks occupy these sparse quarters banked by windows. Then come three luxury cars, each with six private cabins. These cabins feature comfortable bench seating, luggage racks, pull-down bunks, private lavatories, and a large window allowing passengers to enjoy the scenery along the route. Next come the bar and dining car with maximum seating of 16 diners. Then the kitchen and crew car, followed by the baggage car, and finally the caboose.

Wed., April 12, 1945, 10:00 am Eastern Wartime

Tommy "Toothpick" Tarantino always stays at the swank Andrew Johnson Hotel in downtown Knoxville when he accompanies a shipment of contraband from Chicago. Upon arrival, he supervises the unloading of crates of counterfeit coupon books printed in East Chicago and destined for distributors in East Tennessee. He enjoys getting out of town, and why shouldn't he? The rooms at the hotel are plush, and he can always summon female companionship. He also likes to eat although he remains thin in stature. In particular, Toothpick loves the fried catfish dinners served in the Cumberland Room with all the fixings—hush puppies, cole slaw, potato pancakes, and a tangy house sauce.

That morning he got to the railroad depot just in time to supervise the loading of the crates intended for Chicago. Each crate held a dozen jugs of prime red-corn hootch packed snugly in excelsior. Each crate is stenciled with the symbol of an ear of corn. The crates ride in the freight car directly behind the locomotives. Conversely, the baggage belonging to the passengers rides in the baggage car directly in front of the caboose. Many riders keep their smaller bags with them. After paying off the foreman handsomely, Tommy retires to his private cabin, lays down, pulls his hat over his face, and goes to sleep, toothpick still in his mouth. The rhythm of the wheels on the rails are hypnotic.

Wed., April 12, 1945, 11:00 am Eastern Wartime

Law enforcement ran in the blood of the Crunkleton family. James was the sheriff of Macon County, Texas, experienced in dealing with modern-day cattle rustling. His brother Rowdy served as a Texas Ranger and participated in closing down the State Line Gang in Beaumont. Crusty Crunkleton, son of James, went to the police academy in Fort Worth and ended up serving as a Military Policeman in the US Army, assigned to special projects, such as guarding shipments of CEW materials crucial to the war effort. His partner on the reservation was Lincoln "Lenny" Brewster from Rockford, Illinois. Brewster had emerged from the police ranks in that gritty city known as Little Chicago. He along with others kept the peace on the notorious west side of town.

Together, Crusty and Lenny found themselves driving a crate of material in an escorted caravan from CEW to the train depot in Knoxville. They were assigned to guard the simple wooden crate in the freight car of the *Southland Express* headed to Cincinnati and then to Chicago. They had orders to hand off the crate to couriers on the *Santa Fe Chief* heading out west. They were not told the contents of the crate, only its importance.

The CEW couriers were ordered to ride the overnight route in the freight car, allowing for restroom breaks one at a time. During the trip, a waiter from the dining car was instructed to deliver their dinner and breakfast, just like room service. The couriers were uniformed with MP armbands and armed with handguns. Heavier weaponry was available in another crate, along with tactical gear they might require in a confrontation. Although it was frowned upon, both of the couriers lit up cigarettes en route. They were careful to thoroughly extinguish their butts. It wouldn't due to ignite the cargo car on fire. Although warned beforehand by CIC, Crunkleton and Brewster did not expect any trouble. Their biggest problem was not falling asleep when it was their turn to stand guard. Crusty arranged some crates and boxes so as to form a decent platform to sleep upon. The rhythm of the wheels on the rails is hypnotic and soothing. Lenny found a chair to sit in while he kept a watchful eye. He began to feel a bit claustrophobic stashed away in this railroad car with no windows. There was a skylight in the roof but that did no good at nighttime. Two railroad lanterns hanging and swinging from the ceiling provided just enough light to illuminate the car. Time dragged on and the only way to defeat the boredom was to sleep.

Wed., April 12, 1945, 1:35 pm Eastern Wartime

The man, codename Boris, was tall and lanky, and the same could be said for his occupational spouse, Codename Natasha. They both wore long, dark-colored coats under which one could conceal nearly anything. Boris sported tousled sandy brown hair and Natasha had long, dark-brown hair parted down the middle. He wore boots and she low-heel shoes. Lord knows, she complained, nylons could not be found these days at any price. She had been in the States so long she was beginning to think like an American. She spoke fluent "American" and well. Boris was a man of few words. He ordered two tickets to Chicago in the Pullman sleeper, as no private cabins were available. They were posing as man and wife, a married couple. The arrangement was close to the truth except for the actual wedding vows. And the honeymoon. They had no idea when they'd be able to return to the Motherland. They hunkered down to get comfortable in their seating. The conductor came down the aisle punching tickets. He wore a vest and a gold-plated pocket watch on a chain.

The Soviet mission was to intercept the crate in the freight car delivered from CEW. They did not know what was in the crate but their superiors, their handlers, certainly did. The crate was guarded by two US Army policemen. They would wait until arriving in Chicago to make their move, sooner if the occasion arose.

Previously, the Soviets had tried unsuccessfully to kidnap the one person who knew as much about the Manhattan Project as the General himself and that was his secretary, known as Major or by her initials JOL. The General kept her informed about all the details in case he himself was incapacitated or killed. The Soviets planned to capture her on a train trip out of Washington, DC, but JOL changed travel plans at the last moment. After learning about the couriers transporting enriched uranium via train to Chicago, the Soviet handler decided it would be more advantageous to steal the package. The agents used the resources offered by gullible Americans and "useful idiots" who were members of CPUSA (Communist Party of the USA).

Wed., April 12, 1945, 1:45 pm Eastern Wartime

The driver of the sedan dropped off his passenger several blocks from the train depot. The serviceman could walk the rest of the way. The sedan pulled away as the serviceman in uniform strolled to the L&N depot. He was a corporal in the U.S. Army and he had the insignia and papers to prove it. He was stationed at Fort Campbell and on leave to see his folks in Cincinnati. His stature cut a sharp figure in the crisp khakis. He carried a small suitcase. The heavy stuff, the tactical gear, had already been stowed in the prearranged spot in the baggage car.

Making his way into the waiting room, the serviceman bought a ticket and sat in the pew for the long wait. A man in a coat and tie sidled up to the pew and flipped open a credential with a badge. An Army intelligence man, rank of major.

"Can I see your papers, please?"

"Sure," the corporal said, fumbling with his blouse pocket. "Looking for some AWOL?"

"Something like that." The agent examined the papers and glanced back at the GI. "Where you headed?"

"Cincinnati."

"Where you from?"

"Stationed at Fort Campbell."

"Roundabout way to get to Cincinnati."

"Yessir. I looked up a buddy here in Knoxville."

He handed back the papers. "Have a good time, soldier."

The CIC agent talked to a few more passengers in the waiting room and then joined another man, obviously his partner, near the newsstand.

"See the fella at the end of the pew over there?"

"Yeah, what about it."

"Keep an eye on him. Something suspicious. His ID card was spelled correctly. The real cards misspell the word 'identification.' His card isn't misspelled."

"Interesting. Yeah, let's keep an eye on him."

Wed., April 12, 1945, 2:55 pm Eastern Wartime

The two sedans, one with a bullet hole in the fender, arrived at the depot just before 3:00 pm. Normally the MPs in the lead car would head back to the reservation, but today they reconnoitered the parking lot and main waiting room before giving the couriers the all-clear signal. They hung around the waiting room just in case there were follow-up attacks. LT and Sarge did not need to buy tickets; their accommodations had already been arranged, as usual. Sarge sat on a bench and lit up a cigarette. He was anxious, not afraid but high on adrenaline. He quickly took several puffs before settling down. Funny how you needed a cigarette first thing in the morning to wake up, then relax by smoking them during the day. LT thought that the key to destroying America would be to confiscate all the coffee and cigarettes.

They needed to remember not to call each other by their "military" names—Sarge and LT. Their civilian names were Bert and Ernie. They sold fasteners of all sorts to government contractors.

"Okay, let's go and get in our cabin," said LT.

"Sure thing." Sarge ground the cigarette into the sand of the receptacle, got up, and walked away. Each man carried a case, LT's briefcase strapped to his arm. Just then, a GI in uniform barged into Sarge, grabbing his arm for a moment.

"What the hell?" Sarge said in anger. "Soldier, are you drunk?"

"Oh no, sir. Sorry about that. My fault. Sorry."

Sarge glared at the serviceman, who quickly turned away and went to a bench to sit. The CIC agents took notice.

Sarge felt for his wallet, his holster and handgun. They were still all there.

The two couriers walked briskly through the waiting room to the terrace and onto the car with their private cabin. The same one they always used.

Something about that grunt didn't sit right. Sarge didn't believe their collision had been an accident. But then what? Too many strange things happening this morning. Sarge was glad to settle into his seat in the cabin and relax a little.

Wed., April 12, 1945, 2:55 pm Eastern Wartime

FBI SAC Slim Gunderson took a taxi to the train depot. He purchased a ticket to Chicago. The PA announced that Gunderson had a call waiting. At the ticket counter, he took the call from Agent Rucker, who relayed what he had found in Big Dan's lodge, that Ross had shot at him, then taken off in his plane with the floats. Gunderson had a hunch some kind of larceny was going to happen. He didn't exactly know what he was looking for. Mostly suspicious characters. He knew the CEW couriers were on the train in their special cabin with their special briefcase. He knew the Germans wanted that briefcase as did the Soviets. He suspected that German and Soviet agents would be on the train. He carried an ONI in a shoulder holster under his coat jacket. A Smith & Wesson Model 19 combat magnum with four-inch barrel and round butt. These guns had been acquired from the US Navy, Office of Naval Investigations. The handgun was relatively small, easy to conceal, and packed a punch (.357 Magnum cartridge). The Bureau wanted him to give it up for a standard piece, but Gunderson managed to stand fast and hang onto his model. The cabins on the train were all occupied so he took a seat in one of the Pullman sleepers.

SARGE FEELS SICK
Wed., April 12, 1945, 3:15 pm Eastern Wartime

With all aboard, the porters jumped onto the stairwells and the
Southland Express glided out of the L&N station in Knoxville, final
destination Dearborn Station in Chicago, roughly 500 miles to the north.
Slowly, smoothly, the train gained momentum until it was out of the city
and cruising at speed. The *Southland Express* rolled through the Tennessee
countryside on its journey into Kentucky en route to Cincinnati and points
thereafter. As the train advanced in a northerly direction the sun sparkled
off the paint on the port side of the cars. From a bird's eye view, the
Southland might appear to be a colorful slithering snake following a shiny
ribbon through the woodlands.

Sitting in their private cabin, the two couriers began to settle in, but
Sarge began to feel weird. His ears felt hot and he heard a whooshing
sound like a sea shell held up to the ear. His vision clouded over like a veil
had been thrown on his face, and he felt groggy as if he had imbibed one
too many shots of whiskey. He looked at LT, who casually returned his
gaze and then leaned forward, looking concerned.

"You okay?" LT asked.

"Feeling kind of woozy, and I think it's getting worse."

"Something you ate? Or drank?"

"No. It was that grunt in the waiting room. I wasn't sure, but now I
think I am. He pricked me with something, I just know it. In the thigh."

Sarge was turning pale; sweat formed on his brow. He took off his
jacket, exposing his holster rig. "Damn, I feel hot. Giddy, woozy, nervous.
I feel like I'm falling off a cliff."

LT moved over to the opposite bench seat and sat next to Sarge. He felt
his forehead with his free hand and it was indeed hot. He loosened the
briefcase from his wrist. He pulled out a handkerchief, managed to wet it in
the closet sink, and applied it to his buddy's forehead. Could Sarge be
experiencing some sort of flashback or combat-related episode? A nervous
breakdown?

"Stay with me. Keep your eyes open," he ordered. He pulled the cord
to summon the porter.

After a few moments the porter, a thin black man in uniform and cap,
knocked at their door.

"Got a sick man here," LT said. "Need some ice...and a doctor."

The porter came back promptly with a small bucket of ice. He was followed by Dr. Hamblen.

"What's the matter with this man?" the doctor asked LT.

"I don't know. He just all of sudden started feeling sick."

Sarge managed to mutter, "I think I've been poisoned. The guy in the depot. The corporal."

"Poisoned?" the doctor reacted.

Now that Sarge was being tended to, LT asked, "Aren't you from the reservation?"

"Yes, I am. And you two are the couriers. How do you feel?"

"I feel fine," replied LT. "Concerned but fine."

Hamblen opened the top of his briefcase, pulled out a small tubular sensor on a twisted cord and finagled a few dials on the machine inside. He then waved the sensor all around Sarge and listened intently. No feedback from the machine. He then waved the sensor at LT with similar results.

LT looked at the device and then at the doctor. "What, radiation? Is that what you think?"

The good doctor waved his metallic wand over LT's briefcase and sighed a little with relief. "I thought it was possible but not likely now. No readings. Could be simple food poisoning. He's not having a heart attack, I'm fairly sure. He's not in shock."

LT gently slapped Sarge's face, but he was losing him. Sarge passed out and went limp.

"Lay him out on the seat here and elevate his feet. Loosen his clothing. Give him some water and see if he keeps it down."

LT tended to his associate as the cars kept rolling. He moved his briefcase to the opposite bench seat, next to Sarge's suitcase. He removed Sarge's shoulder holster and placed it next to the briefcase. The doctor's briefcase/device sat on the floor.

A knock came on the door. Must be the porter, LT thought. He opened the door.

GWIN MEETS BILLIE JEAN
Wed., April 12, 1945, 2:00 pm Eastern Wartime

"Hell hath no fury..." the saying goes, and Gwin was furious with her husband. She required payback. She was part Cherokee and part Scots-Irish. She had high cheekbones, dark eyes, and straight raven hair, cut short due to her job requirements. She didn't know for sure that her husband was guilty, but she desperately wanted to believe it. She wasn't in love with him anymore but the thought that he was cheating on her had festered in her mind the entire time. She had to do something.

She took the morning bus from Evansville to Nashville, then hopped on the Tennessee Central train to Knoxville, a journey that took about eight hours. She stayed the night at a friend's house and borrowed the friend's sedan and some gasoline ration stamps. She brought along her Ruger five-shot pocket pistol with .38-Special rounds in the cylinder. The lightweight snub-nosed gun could fit easily in a purse or pants pocket. It didn't really pack a punch like some other handguns on the market, but it was enough to get the job done.

She parked the sedan across the street from her bungalow in the Fort Sanders neighborhood, just north of the university campus. She saw Billie Jean leave. She was cute, Gwin had to admit, with blond hair tucked underneath a head scarf. She wore sunglasses. Not long after she drove off, the car and driver came for Doc Hamblen. They backed out the driveway and down 15th Avenue to the Hill. Down the incline on Cumberland, left on Hensley, and then pulled into the L&N railroad depot lot. She made sure he didn't notice her following him. She parked several spaces behind his vehicle. After he entered the lobby, she walked over nonchalantly, stood in front of his left rear tire and poked a hole in the sidewall with her Case Pigsticker. She had thought about sticking her beloved husband with it, but she decided that stabbing would be too messy and take too long. And she didn't want to go to prison.

She went to the ticket counter and bought a round-trip ticket to Chicago. He would be long gone before they arrived in the Windy City, she vowed to herself.

Gwin sat in the second Pullman sleeper car, taking an aisle seat. She knew that Doc Hamblen would be in a private cabin, but she didn't know which one. Scanning the passengers getting onto the train, she noticed with a grin that Billie Jean was onboard. She wasn't wearing the scarf or shades now. Her eyes were a cornflower blue, the favorite color of the Dutch painter Vermeer. Gwin got up and sat next to Billie Jean and made a scene of getting comfortable. She wore plain pleated pants and a blouse, with a sharp military-style jacket void of any insignia.

"Hi, how you doing?" Gwin said in a neutral tone.

"Fine, fine. And you?" replied Billie Jean.

"Fine and dandy. Where you headed?"

"Chicago. Going to meet someone. Hope to do some celebrating."

"That sounds nice. Boyfriend? Not to be nosy but I didn't notice a wedding ring."

"Oh, yeah. He's a nice guy, a doctor. I'm Billie Jean."

"Gwin," she stated. "Just got here from Evansville. Kind of funny, but my husband's a doctor."

"That's nice." Billie Jean flushed and dropped her chin to her chest as if to hide. Her heart was in her throat. Could it be possible?

"Yep. My husband's name is Martin, Marty for short." She stared at Billie Jean, showing no outward emotion.

Billie Jean couldn't speak; she didn't know what to say or how to handle such a shocking situation. The only thought in her mind was that she was glad she hadn't mentioned she was pregnant.

"I know who you are," said Gwin, breaking the awkward silence. "How long have you and my husband been seeing each other?"

"Not long," she managed to utter. "You must be Gwin. What are you going to do?"

"As far as you're concerned, honey, nothing. You seem like a nice kid, albeit confused. I haven't been around town here much lately. I can see how most any guy would be tempted. That's not going to get him off the hook."

"Please don't do anything…" she couldn't supply the correct word to finish her sentence. She thought to herself, don't do anything violent to the father of my unborn child.

"Well, a divorce is preeminent, that's for sure. But not before I extract my ounce of revenge." Gwin wasn't certain about actually shooting her husband, but she sure as hell wanted him to think she would. It's the least she could do.

The conductor walked up the center aisle, asking if any of the passengers were a doctor. "I have a sick man who needs attention."

Gwin pulled gently on the conductor's jacket. "There's a doctor named

Hamblen in the private cabins. I don't know which one, but he's a doctor."

"Thank you, ma'am." He strode off toward the cabins at the rear of the train.

THE PACKAGE
Wed., April 12, 1945, 4:12 pm Eastern Wartime

The flimsy door to the cabin burst open. A young man dressed as a U.S. Army corporal moved into the compact compartment and knocked out the doctor with a blow to the temple. The doctor fell to the floor like a sack of cement. Next, the intruder disabled LT with an open hand to the side of his head before he could reach for his firearm. The intruder grabbed the briefcase as Sarge awoke and lunged at him, flailing at shadows. Using the briefcase as a shield, Uhu chopped at his opponent. His strength having been sapped, Sarge fell to the floor clumsily. Immediately Uhu vacated the cabin with his prize, shutting the door behind him. He made his way toward the back of the train, dashing through the dining car and pushing a waiter over into the diners and spilling his tray. Once through the kitchen car with some banging of pots and pans, he entered the baggage car slowly and confidently. Quickly he moved to a large trunk and unlatched it. He withdrew a sizeable backpack from the trunk and hunched it onto his back, securing the arm straps. Using a special prying tool, he cracked open the briefcase and lifted out the heavy package. He placed the package into a custom-made tote bag and strapped it across his chest. Finally, after donning a pair of goggles and fingerless gloves, he pulled the final pieces of gear out of the trunk. Some sort of lightweight tubular metal brace and an oblong rigid loop covered in canvas.

Uhu moved to the back of the baggage car and through the exit. He entered the open-air gap just in front of the caboose. The trees on either side of the track whooshed by in a blur. The rhythmic noise of the wheels on track was quite loud. Clickety-clack over and over. The setting sun stabbed through the pine trees to the west like a strobe light.

Uhu climbed the ladder at the rear of the car and onto the flat roof and into the windstream. There he fastened the tubular brace to the metal seam of the roofline. He climbed in front of the brace, facing backwards so that his weight secured his lower body against it, as the car bucked side to side. He retrieved the large canvas loop from the brace and held it in front of him. Everything had been timed so meticulously, every second counted. He could see but not hear the bright yellow floatplane approaching from the south; he could not see the trestle ahead. Once on the trestle and free from any overhanging trees, each second would count in his attempt to hook up with the aircraft.

REVENGE ON THE TRAIN
Wed., April 12, 1945, 4:15 pm Eastern Wartime

"Please don't do anything crazy," Billie Jean begged of Gwin. She grabbed Gwin's jacket and her arm. Gwin squirmed and broke the handhold. She strode deliberately toward the back of the train, having to make her way through two Pullman sleepers and two cars with private cabins and all their occupants standing in her way and Billie Jean tugging at her from behind. She came to the final cabin car and ran into the conductor just as a groggy Doc Hamblen was leaving the cabin in pursuit of LT and Sarge.

"Please take care of this lady," Gwin told the conductor, indicating Billie Jean.

Billie Jean managed to bypass the conductor and caught up to Gwin in the dining car.

The diners were still talking amongst themselves and reacting to the three guys who had just lumbered and clamored through the car. Boris and Natasha were enjoying a roast beef dinner after several vodka martinis. Most of the other diners looked at each other and muttered, "Wonder what that's all about," and then went back to eating.

Next was the kitchen service car, full of stainless-steel counters, pots and pans, tables and sinks. The car smelled like steaming vegetables, horseradish, and cleanser. The chef observed the commotion with a cleaver in his hand and remarked with an accent, "What the hell was that all about?"

Hamblen ran toward the rear of the car, holding his hands up and declaring, "That's my wife. She's going to kill me. Stop her." Nobody took him up on that.

The women walked briskly through the baggage car only to run into two men firing handguns up into the air between the baggage car and the caboose. They were shuffling about in that cramped space, craning their necks, trying to get a bead on their target. The brakeman high in his lofted seat in the caboose had a front-row view of the action. He wasn't sure what to do.

The gap outdoors between the cars seemed like an acceleration of time into a different dimension of flashing colors, pounding noise, the sensation of speed, and the fresh air.

Having seen his wife still moving toward him with Billie Jean in tow,

Doc Hamblen made his way into the caboose with the two women right behind. They bypassed the gunmen and the man on top of the railcar; their focus was on the doctor.

"Marty!" Billie Jean blurted. "Careful, Marty. I think she wants to hurt you."

"What are you doing here, darling?" the doctor said firmly and calmly.

"Don't darling me, you cheatin' bastard."

Gwin rushed him; Billie Jean lost her grip and her ability to impede; Hamblen fled the scene toward the end of the train.

Gwin then strode into the caboose and slammed the door behind her, shutting Billie Jean out. At that moment, the train left the trestle behind and entered the woods again.

"Think about what you're doing," the doctor yelled frantically at his wife.

"Oh, I am," she replied, pulling the pistol from her pocket. A great big smile erupted on her face. Was she mad?

The brakeman sat high and unmoved in his perch in the cupola. "Hey, you're not supposed to be in here." He looked up and noticed that the man standing on top of the train was now gone.

Hamblen opened the final door on the train and stepped out upon the platform. No more train, just lots of scenery flying by him and converging in the distance.

When Gwin pulled the door open from his grasp, Hamblen went to and down the sidesteps. "You don't want to do this," he pleaded. "Think about what you're doing, for Christ's sake."

"Oh, I'm not going to kill you," Gwin had decided, pointing the gun at him. "I'm just going to neuter you."

She pulled the trigger, aiming between his legs. The shot rang out, but at that precise moment Hamblen had closed his eyes and jumped backward off the train. The pistol jumped in her hands despite her best efforts to dampen the recoil. By the time Gwin realized what had happened, Hamblen had rolled down the embankment out of sight.

Gwin was momentarily stunned, not knowing for sure whether she had shot him or not. Time stood still but the train kept on rolling, oblivious to their drama. For a fleeting moment she thought about jumping after him. She wiped the pistol on her pants leg and threw it as far from the train as she could, in the opposite direction from Hamblen's jump.

RENDEZVOUS ATOP THE TRESTLE
Wed., April 12, 1945, 6:15 pm Eastern Wartime

Big Dan had planned and trained for so many months for this moment. He was piloting the floatplane in a north by northwest direction from Tennessee into Kentucky airspace, droning along slightly higher than the treetops. He knew the terrain well, having practiced several times during the train's actual trips. About two miles south of the Grand Gulf Trestle over Laurel Hill Lake he caught up with the northbound train, descending and trying to match the train's speed exactly. Then he saw Uhu, his cousin, climbing on top of the baggage car near the end of the train. The route of the tracks curved through the woods and the steep limestone cuts. There was really only one place along the route that the rendezvous could be made and that was on top of the tall trestle. The top of the spindly trestle consisted only of track bed with no superstructure overhead. But only for 1,125 feet, about four football fields long. Facing the rear of the train, Uhu was secured against the brace by the inertial force of the train. All the time the train kept up its diesel-propelled pace. Big Dan closed in on the train, aiming for the crew car just in front of the baggage car, trying not to overcompensate with the controls. The train was now approaching the trestle. Off to his left was the rapidly setting sun, at an angle where it did not blind his view.

Coming closer now, the bright yellow Stinson L-5 hovered over the baggage car, matching the speed of the train. Uhu was holding the loop upright now to catch the hook which hung down between the twin floats of the plane. He pushed the loop forward but just missed contact. It took all of his strength to turn the loop upright again. There were two men between the baggage car and the caboose shooting at him with handguns. He heard the bullets whiz by his head. Some ricocheted off the backside of the railcar. The plane bobbed slightly from an updraft but settled down for one more attempt. The opposite bank with its gauntlet of tall pine trees was rapidly approaching. The side window pushed open, Big Dan yelled wildly at the man on top of the train, caught up in the excitement of the moment.

This whole desperate process seemed to incorporate all the basic tenets of physics, ballistics, and gravitational space-time with some elements of relativity thrown in. Uhu pushed the loop forward again and missed the hook again. He could not see the end of the trestle; he was facing toward the back of the train, watching time disappear. But he could sense it. In a split-second of disappointment he realized there was no time left for another try. His training kicked into high gear. Now for Plan B. Instinctively he tossed the loop to the side and pushed against the brace as he leapt off the moving train to his left. Big Dan hit the throttle and pulled the yoke back to clear the trees rushing into his view. Instead of converging, Uhu and Big Dan were accelerating away from each other.

Almost immediately Big Dan saw the red-and-white parachute blow open but not fully, having been caught in twisted shroud lines. With any luck, the drag of the chute would soften his cousin's fall enough for him to survive. Uhu hit the water awkwardly at speed and quickly began to sink due to the weight of the package still strapped to his chest. Immediately, underwater, he unfastened the parachute harness and pulled the vest cord. Compressed carbon dioxide from the metal cylinder on his backpack quickly inflated the Mae West life jacket and lifted him slowly toward the surface. He fumbled with the small emergency oxygen bottle and dropped it when he tried to fit it to his mouth. It sank to the bottom of the reservoir. He was gasping for breathe. Everything literally was all tangled up. He had to rely on Big Dan getting to him on time.

The planners had wanted a large inflatable bladder to bring him to the surface in case he had to jump into the lake, but the rig was too large and heavy and they couldn't figure out how to get his head above water as he would be holding onto the bottom of the large bladder. So they opted for the life jacket, which proved to be unable to keep his head above water.

Big Dan cursed out loud when Uhu missed the hook with the loop and immediately swung the floatplane into a wide curving arc over the reservoir east of the trestle. Landing would be similar to dropping down onto the lake at the lodge. He had no time to spare. As he glided onto his approach and then his final leg, he spotted the orange life jacket bobbing on the surface under the trestle. The water upstream was quite still. The plane came in toward the trestle and gently let down on the surface of the water, plowing toward Uhu. As the plane slowly lost speed and moved toward Uhu, the prop stopped spinning. Big Dan got out onto the left float and grappled the body with a metal hook. He pulled the body toward the plane, actually pulling the plane to the body. Close enough and still secure, he pulled Uhu's lifeless body to the side of the float. Only the difference in their weights made it possible to pull and drag the body onto the float. He punctured the life jacket and pulled if off the body. He cut the strap securing the package and placed it behind the airplane's front seat. Uhu was gone, drowned.

"Verdammt! Scheiße!" Big Dan cursed in German at the death of his cousin. He had not seen him in many years and now he is seeing him in death, dressed in the uniform of a US army serviceman. Alive just a few minutes ago. What a waste!

Big Dan sat with his cousin hoisted up upon the spar of the float and scanned the countryside, searching for witnesses, looking for answers. He knew he must deliver the package, and soon. Otherwise, all is for naught. The U-boat waiting off the Outer Banks could not wait long without being detected. Time was of the essence. Although deeply saddened at the death of his cousin, he had to finish the mission. There was nothing else to do except to flee the scene and carry out the remainder of the mission. There was no way Big Dan could lift the body into the aircraft. He would have to leave the body there. He pulled off the backpack, placed it in the plane, and gently pushed the body away. Before he climbed back into the cockpit, Big Dan gave the salute and shouted "Heil Hitler!"

A fisherman was upon the lake, but he was too busy yanking a huge snapping turtle from underneath the northern bank of the reservoir to witness the floatplane scenario.

Big Dan turned the aircraft around and took off the opposite direction that he had landed. He held the yoke full back to force the aircraft's nose up; the engine manhandles the floats onto their rear step. He then lowers the nose to just above level attitude so that the drag of the water is minimized and the airplane can accelerate to takeoff speed. Soon the trestle disappeared among the trees in the rear window as he flew away from the sunset and toward the Outer Banks, roughly 470 miles away.

Dusk was approaching fast. From his calculations, he knew he did not have enough fuel to make it all the way to the East Coast. The tank held only 50 gallons. The plane could accommodate an extra fuel bladder for additional range, but the added weight of the fuel would have made maneuvering highly difficult if not impossible. The whole plan, even Plan B, depended on securing more fuel.

G-MAN STARTS PURSUIT
Wed., April 12, 1945, 6:30 pm Eastern Wartime

Sarge and LT gained consciousness about the same moment, laying helter skelter on the cabin floor. Their porter was at the door. "He went that way," he said, pointing toward the rear of the train.

LT glanced at his arm and scanned the cabin for the briefcase even though he knew it was gone.

"How you feeling?"

"Like I got hit with a bag of nickels," Sarge moaned. "But I'll be alright. You know, once I actually did get hit by a bag of nickels. In Vegas."

"We gotta get that briefcase," LT said. "What's the next stop?"

"Lexington," said the porter.

"Is there a two-way radio on this train?" LT asked.

"No, sir. We just got one, but it don't work right yet."

"Damn! Let's go."

The two groggy couriers got up and more or less stumbled toward the back of the train, through the dining car and service car. Everyone got out of their way, at this point out of habit. They found the German agent had climbed on top of the railway car. They withdrew their handguns and began aiming and firing at him, and then at the small aircraft. Each man had to grab a handrail to steady himself against the rolling, bucking train; shooting with only one hand was wildly inaccurate. Before they had expended all their ammo, the agent jumped off the train. And then the train had sped off the trestle. They holstered their weapons and made their way back to their cabin. They had no idea where Doc Hamblen had disappeared to.

"We'll get off at Lexington," LT announced. "If I can clear my head we can figure this out."

"Go ahead, I'm listening."

Before LT could speak, Slim Gunderson the G-man darkened the doorway. The couriers knew him, but they were incredulous that he was on the train. He had to have gotten aboard in Knoxville. The couriers knew the G-man, mostly by reputation, and liked him because he was so much better than his predecessor.

"Gentlemen, let me propose a plan," he said, staggering into the cabin and taking a seat.

"The asshole got away with our briefcase," complained Sarge.

"Yes, I know. I've been investigating this guy for a while. I've got a fairly good idea where he's headed. His code name is Uhu." He pronounced it correctly as ooh-who. "He parachuted into Tennessee a few days ago. His real name is Hans Hammerschmidt and he's a well-trained German operative. He's already killed two men and shot at my subordinate. I know it's hard to believe, but Big Dan Ross, Big Dan the Hardware Man, is actually Heine Hammerschmidt, his cousin."

At this point, they would have believed anything.

Sarge stated, "He got on top of the train. As far as we know, the aircraft picked him up. I don't think we hit him or the plane."

Gunderson began to explain. "They're headed to the East Coast to rendezvous with a German U-boat offshore. Most likely around Nags Head or Kill Devil Hills. There's a monument with a signal at Kill Devil Hills. A guiding light. They'll probably meet inland. That floatplane can't land on the open sea. They'll meet with some of the crew and paddle a raft out to the submarine. There's something in that briefcase that they want real bad. I believe it's explosive or radioactive or both."

"The only hitch in their plan," said Gunderson, "is that the pilot will have to refuel at some point along the route. That plane, with two passengers, will run out of fuel short of the coast. He has to land on water, and the only logical place for him to land and stop along the route is in the vicinity of Clarksville, Virginia. There's a large man-made reservoir there. I'd be willing to bet there's an accomplice waiting there with some aviation gasoline."

"We need to get off at Lexington but then what? We can't drive fast enough on these country roads to catch them."

"I have yet another plan. I need to call somebody as soon as we get to Lexington. Their Stinson L-5 lacks speed and range. Its engine can cruise at only 100 mph with a range of 375 miles and endurance of 3.5 hours. The fuel tank holds 50 gallons."

FOUR MEN ON AN AEROPLANE
Wed., April 12, 1945, 8:00 pm Eastern Wartime

The three men—Sarge, LT, and Gunderson—rushed off the *Southland Express* even before it had settled into its berth at the massive train shed in Lexington. Gunderson made several quick phone calls from a wood-and-brass booth lining the wall of Union Station's central dome.

"The car should be here in a few minutes," he announced.

Meanwhile, LT was on the phone to call CEW, but the switchboard was down and he couldn't get through to Capt. Zimmer. He wasn't anxious to announce they had lost the briefcase. Perhaps through some miracle they could retrieve it before the whole world (at least the world of military intelligence) knew about it. He shuddered to think how the General might react.

The G-man lit up a Pall Mall, clicking his lighter shut. The couriers joined him, LT with a Lucky Strike, Sarge with a Camel. Gunderson led them through the terminal to the horseshoe-shaped drive up front. The street lights were on. They waited on a bench, minutes turning into epochs in their anxious state. LT got up and began to pace back and forth.

"I know this town fairly well. I was stationed here for awhile," said Gunderson between drags.

A large pre-war limousine, a black Packard, pulled up to the curb at a distance calculated not to smudge its massive white-walled tires. There was plenty of room for the four of them in the back, bench seats facing each other.

"I feel like Douglas Fairbanks Jr."

"Or Al Capone."

Gunderson got into the passenger side up front. Driving was a dark-complected man in his fifties dressed in a sharply creased suit over his pajamas. "What, no chauffeur?" Gunderson cracked wise.

"Welcome aboard," the driver greeted them with an Italian accent. "You'll excuse me while I enjoy my coffee. Normally this is my bedtime," he said, intimating that he did not normally drive at this hour.

He pulled out a leather-wrapped flask and tipped a dram into his mug.

"In case you're wondering, it's bourbon, of course. Old Grand-Dad."

"Let's get there today," Gunderson remarked. "The Bureau frowns on drinking and driving."

"So let them frown. This guy, always in a hurry. All righty then," the driver said, manhandling the large steering wheel of the land cruiser. "Please do the introductions."

"Of course, you know me," said Gunderson with a grin and a chuckle. "We call the husky guy here Sarge, that's his rank. Combat veteran. And the distinguished looking lieutenant, we call him LT."

"As you well know, Mr. G-man, I love the boys in uniform and I'm honored to do anything to help the war effort."

"Like bootleg whiskey, black market goods, and counterfeit ration stamps?"

"Well, not that I am admitting to anything, but one must do what one must do," he replied, tipping up the flask, putting his right shoulder upon the backrest and turning to greet the guys in the backseat. The big sedan slid across the centerline, producing some wailing car horns.

"Whoa, fella. Just keep your eyes on the road, hands upon the wheel."

Gunderson shook his head and turned to the backseat. "This, gentlemen, is Earl "Bunny" Briscoe, man about town, dealer in underworld matters, and king of the numbers racket in this part of the world."

"Don't forget the horses. I love the horses, my whiskey, and..."

"Fast women?"

"Ah-huh! Yes, you are correct, but I was about to say fast aeroplanes. I'm a certified fly-boy, you know. How many grand pooh-bahs do you know that can fly an aeroplane? First-class, of course."

"That's where we're headed," said Gunderson. "Old airstrip south of town. The ground crew should have the plane ready to go when we get there."

"*Darling Darla*, that's her name," Bunny said proudly.

"Bunny here owes me and the Bureau a favor and he's going to help us out."

The limo rolled down long lanes bordered by dark bluegrass meadows lined with white fencing. Miles and miles of straight-board fencing. Occasionally they caught sight of a few thoroughbreds out to stud along with some haggard mules. They passed a distillery set back from the road, a conglomeration of buildings pumping plumes of steam into the air. "Those are the rickhouses over there," Bunny pointed out. "Mostly empty these days. Government, military, gets most of the alcohol these days. Torpedoes run on alcohol, I've been told. Unaged, of course."

The limo pulled off the road near a gate in the fence, now chain-link. "There she is, boys," Bunny said. Sitting on the strip, engines running, was a Boeing 247D twin-engine tail-dragger, a small airliner adorned in bold blue stripes. On the nose was a semi-nude pin-up girl with *Darla* underneath in a fancy typeface. "I learned to fly from barnstormers and walked the wings a few times. My first plane was a Ford Tri-Motor, a Tin Goose, and then I stepped up. I considered a Lockheed Electra but settled for the Boeing. Only seventy-five of these beauties ever made."

"He's going to fly that thing?" LT asked Gunderson. "With us aboard?"

"He's better at flying than driving."

"That's not saying much. Why is he doing this?" LT asked with emphasis.

"Let's just say he owes me and the Bureau a favor and wants to stay in our good graces. Hopefully he's afraid of me. The Director for sure."

"Wouldn't miss it for the world," Bunny said in his best W.C. Fields impression.

Two crewmen stood by the parked aircraft, its rear fuselage hatch open with stairway down.

The aircraft boasted sleek lines, two robust radial engines with three-bladed props, and five passenger windows per side. Oddly, the framed windshield was sloped forward instead of backward. Boeing must know what it's doing, for gosh sakes, they designed and built the Superfortress.

The warm backdraft from the engines blew open the men's jackets and mussed their hair. Boarding up the slim ladder steps required some coordination. Once inside the upholstered interior, however, the noise and commotion abated. The felt seats were comfortable and spacious. Gunderson sat in the co-pilot's seat (the righthand one) although he didn't know a thing about flying. Bunny buckled up in the lefthand pilot's seat and tested the radio mike. Fussing over some engine gauges he yelled back at the passengers in the cabin, "Once we're up, help yourselves to a cocktail back there. This luxury liner carries a fully stocked bar."

It was a moonlit night with good visibility. The airstrip did not have runway lights but the stripe down the center of the runway was fairly new and visible. The men inside buckled up and kept their thoughts to themselves as the craft gained groundspeed. The tail lifted up first, then they were off the ground, the retraction of the landing gear quite noisy. Gunderson had a flight map on his lap as they tried to figure out the required compass heading.

They were flying at about five thousand feet and searching for landmarks on the ground. They could discern the city lights of Blacksburg and Roanoke. The latter city even had a lit-up airport with the city's name painted on top of the small terminal. The towns were lit up much more than usual for some reason. Gunderson consulted the flight map and told Bunny the appropriate compass headings. The ride was smooth, there was little if any turbulence.

Bunny proved to be a decent pilot and a loquacious raconteur. He told them about Chicago mob boss Tony "Big Tuna" Bombazi, who would stay at his hotel in Lexington, reserving the entire top eighth floor, en route to deep-sea fishing in Florida. Bunny said that the boss preferred a batch of handmade bourbon that only Bunny could procure.

An authority on horse flesh, Bunny owned several thoroughbreds that had finished well at Keeneland and Churchill Downs and sired many champions when put out to stud, including *Sword Dancer*. He personally knew Jimmy Stout. He had played poker with the Cincinnati Kid and billiards with Minnesota Fats (he fell short of bragging that he had beaten them).

He personally feted Bette Davis, Hedy Lamarr, and Betty Grable, during bond drive visits to his city. He met Charles Lindbergh and took a ride in his plane (not the *Spirit of St. Louis*). He advised Howard Hughes on aviation projects and played golf with Bobby Jones, who told Bunny he had a natural swing. Elliott Ness targeted him for prosecution, but Bunny beat the rap.

And on and on it went, Bunny barely stopping to take a breath. If he were telling the truth about ten percent of his tall tales it would make for a fantastic life.

Of course, Bunny knew of Big Dan the Hardware Man but hadn't met him. He was surprised to learn that Dan was piloting the airplane they were chasing.

Meanwhile, as they passed over Danville, Virginia, the passengers couldn't help but notice the town lit up and lights along the north-south railroad line. Hundreds of people lined the tracks. As Darla droned on past, heading east, they noticed the locomotive's headlight and the cars of the train, some of which were lit up.

"Who died?" Sarge asked nobody in particular.

Another surprise came during the night flight when a light homed in on them from eight o'clock high. As the other airplane bounced them from on high, Bunny and Gunderson got a good look at the unidentified flying object. Painted all black, the Northrup P-61B "Black Widow" featured twin engines and a twin tail, looking like nothing they had ever seen. Luck would have it that the P-61B pilots recognized that *Darling Darla* was not the aircraft they were searching for. The night fighter boasted amazing firepower—four .50-cal. machine guns and four 20mm cannons. The dark craft swept past them as if they were standing still and soared eastward toward the full moon with a ring around it, a halo.

U-BOAT ARRIVES AT OUTER BANKS
Wed., April 12, 1945, 11:00 pm Eastern Wartime

It takes a certain kind of man to be an Unterseebooteneer in the Kreigsmarine. All of the crew are volunteers who have undergone extensive training in classrooms, on sea trials, and in coordination with other members of their boat. Every crewman has a specific duty and may be trained to perform several other duties. Those suffering from claustrophobia and/or unstable emotions (Blechkoller or tin fright) are obviously unsuitable. They must be able to live and work harmoniously with other crew members and steadfastly obey commands from their superiors, all in a cramped environment and at sea for months at a time. Military deportment is relaxed due to the circumstances, but the fate of the vessel and all souls aboard depend upon teamwork and performance of duties. Crews sleep in shifts and share bunks in close quarters. Despite efforts at ventilation, the dank interior recks of oil and grease, diesel fumes, flatulence, and other body odors.

By this late in the war, more than 600 U-boats have been sunk either by patrol aircraft or surface destroyers. And their destination—the Outer Banks—is known as the Graveyard of the Atlantic for a reason. Over several centuries, three thousand vessels have met their doom on these islands, usually by running aground. In fact, exactly three years ago, U-85, commanded by Oblt. Eberhard Greger, sank off Cape Hatteras struck by gunfire from the destroyer USS *Roper*.

Only two hundred yards off Kill Devil Hills, an American tanker sank in 1927, and two years later a Swedish freighter ran ashore, struck the tanker and cut it into two pieces.

Fregattenkapitan Karl-Friedrich Scholtz had these wrecks on his mind, along with their main mission, Feldzug Ultimativ Vergeltung (Operation Ultimate Vengeance), as he approached the East Coast of the United States, undetected. Also tormenting him was an infected tooth, which ached despite the application of benzocaine. The medical officer threatened to pull the tooth if Scholtz complained any more of the pain. He knew he'd have to have it pulled soon.

The U-3008 had not crossed the Atlantic without incident, however. Halfway across, in grid 42A, the Type XXI U-boat had been at shallow depth using its Schnorchel for running its diesel engines and charging its massive load of batteries when screws were detected and the boat was forced into an emergency dive to 800 feet, close to the maximum depth, aka crush depth. The Type XXI was advanced in design and was built by assembling pre-built sections. However, the quality of construction lagged during the last year of the war and the crush depth was less than previous types for that reason. Long story short, Scholtz could not be sure how deep to dive to avoid the newly designed Allied depth charges and still avoid the crush depth. Of course, he did not share his doubts with the crew or even his executive officers.

For hours the U-boat lay suspended underwater, its crew waiting for the sounds of wabos (depth charges). Several times the sound of screws were detected approaching and then leaving overhead. There were no explosions. The U-3008 finally slipped away after launching a motorized Sieglinde (sonar decoy) behind them.

Scholtz considered himself lucky. They were operating in radio silence and knew nothing of the outside world for most of the past week. The high command had assumed that the Allies had broken the Ultra code used by their Enigma machines. But they had lost time avoiding the destroyers in mid-Atlantic and now needed to proceed underwater with all due haste. The waters are turbulent at the Outer Banks, where the Gulf Stream and the Labrador Currents collide and head eastward toward Europe. The strong currents, ebb and flow of the tides, and shifting sandy coastline combine to make the Outer Banks a mariner's nightmare.

The Nazi plan calls for the U-3008 to surface at night near Kill Devil Hills, where the width of the barrier island is the narrowest. A party will be put ashore to cross the barrier island on foot to Albemarle Sound and meet with the agent delivering the package. The U-boat will remain on the surface for five hours before leaving the area, hopefully with the package and undetected during that time period. Scholtz knew that was an awful long time, considering the frequency of air and naval patrols by the Americans. Another worrisome variable. In addition to carrying no torpedoes, the U-3008 did not even boast an anti-aircraft deck gun. But their luck had held so far.

Just off the coast, at the appropriate gridlines, Scholtz ordered the boat up to periscope level. In the darkness he could see no vessels or other silhouetted objects on the horizon. To the northwest, he did sight the Wright Brothers beacon so he knew he was in the proper location. He knew the boat was in shoal waters, but that was one drawback that they would just have to deal with. The landing party was at the conning tower preparing to leave the U-boat. The captain was so busy calculating their odds and making sure everything proceeded according to plan, his tooth stopped aching. Hah!

Then there was a sudden boatwide lurch that nearly knocked the submariners off their feet. The control room pitched over and stuck. Scholtz knew immediately what had happened, but he couldn't believe it. Their luck had run out. The U-3008 had run aground on a sand bar, the length of the boat parallel to the shore and listing. The captain ordered the engine room full speed ahead and then full speed astern. Then once again. And again. It was no use. They were stuck on the bar, completely at the mercy of any aircraft or shore patrol that might sight them, until the tide rolled in and floated them off. With any luck.

BUNNY IMPROVISES
Wed., April 12, 1945, Midnight Eastern Wartime

The mini-airliner raced along at almost 200 mph at five thousand feet elevation and skirted the lights of Roanoke, Virginia, to the south. Bunny adhered to a compass bearing of 150 degrees. He worked the foot pedals, which controlled the rudders, to keep on a constant bearing (yaw). Turning the yoke kept the aircraft level, as indicated by the artificial horizon gauge (roll). He kept constant altitude by watching the altimeter and pushing and pulling the yoke correspondingly (pitch). He left the throttles alone while monitoring the engine gauges. He was cruising along at a speed calculated to give the craft the most range.

Giving in to their full day of activity and the droning not only of the twin engines but also of the pilot, LT and Sarge slept fitfully in their secured seats. LT snored as was his habit. Gunderson would nod off only to startle himself awake again.

The moon was full with a ring around it, a halo, and the skies were relatively clear. After sighting the lights of the small town of South Boston, Virginia, Bunny bore more to the east. When he noticed the large body of water ahead, the shoreline of which he recognized as the Buggs Island Lake, he flew southeast down its length, dropping altitude. Up ahead he saw the fluorescent green runway lights at Clarksville, more than half a mile long. As he descended over the small town below he realized that the parallel set of lights was actually the fishing lights of the concrete highway bridge over the lake. Just past the narrower iron railroad bridge.

Bunny waggled the wingtips to rouse the passengers.

"Well, gents, we are here," announced Bunny. "Nothing suspicious," he added, referring to the apparent absence of the yellow Stinson floatplane.

"Does this place have an airport? Airstrip?" Gunderson wanted to know.

"Hell if I know," replied the pilot. "Look at the map."

"Don't see one. And the terrain around here does not look flat."

"What about that?" Bunny pondered, pointing out the highway bridge.

"What about it?"

Bunny thought about it some more, then figured, why not? The paved bridge was not humped in the middle all that much, it was reasonably level. It was straight and long enough, but was it wide enough? No vehicles on it this time of night. The wingspan of the Boeing 247D was 74 feet, wider than the bridge, which would be about 60 feet. But if the bridge's railings were no more than three feet high it wouldn't make any difference. All he had to do was keep the nose of the aircraft pegged to that center stripe.

"You're kidding, right?"

"What else can we do?" chimed in Sarge.

"We could circle around and wait for Big Dan."

"We'd use up a lot of fuel and maybe scare him off. If we get on the ground, alive, we can call in reinforcements and report back in."

Bunny was determined to land on the bridge, more as a challenge to his piloting skills as anything else. "Going to give it a good look-see before I do anything," Bunny said, circling around that section of the narrow lake. "However, I am going to require a bracer, a stiff belt of Old Fitzgerald, if you please."

Although normally hesitant to help a pilot behind the controls become intoxicated, under the circumstances LT figured what the hell, it might actually help. Crouched and bracing himself, he made his way aft in the plane, opened the cover to the wet bar and spotted the requested bottle. He brought the bottle and glass forward and carefully poured some whiskey into the glass, not too much. He handed it to Gunderson, who held it out to Bunny. The mobster took the glass and downed the whiskey in one swift gulp.

"Oh yeah," he said, smacking his lips, and handing the glass back to Gunderson.

Bunny circled the bridge, keeping the wingtip low, observing it carefully and came around to his approach. The passengers craned to look out the windows for any traffic approaching the bridge. Nothing. Bunny lowered the landing gear and dialed in the flaps. He gently pulled back on the throttles. The roar of the twin engines now settled into a low hum and wind noise became noticeable. The landing gear dropped and locked into place with a jolt. The wings tilted and drooped like a teeter-totter as the airplane gently rolled back and forth.

"This might be a little bumpy," warned Bunny. "Hard to gauge how far to the ground."

"Here we go," said Gunderson, buckling up tight.

LT closed his eyes and braced for a hard landing. Bunny set *Darla* down in a perfect three-point landing, but then the plane bounced from front gear to rear wheel like a bucking horse. Then the wheels set down nicely and all was going well until the right wingtip hit the thin vertical pole on the bridge marking the channel below. The plane scooted 90 degrees clockwise and the port landing gear collapsed, breaking the left wingtip and contorting the three-bladed propeller on the port engine. By that time the plane slid to a stop with a raucous round of metallic screeching, the threesome aboard high-tailed it out the door. Due to the tilt of the fuselage, they literally spilled out of the craft onto the pavement.

"We made it, thank God. That was some damn fine flying, Bunny."

"I owe it all to some fine Kentucky corn squeezings," he said, channeling W.C. Fields again. "Speaking of which, I forgot something," Bunny crawled back into the aircraft and emerged with a bottle of booze which he carried like a trophy.

The government men moved briskly from one side of the bridge to the other, trying to spot Big Dan's floatplane down on the water. Just when they had given up and lit cigarettes, a quiet drone emanated from the west heading towards them with the breeze. It was quiet enough at night to hear the plane touch down on the water and the engine noise drop off. They could plainly see the yellow aircraft now and identified it as Big Dan's. Who else could it be? They drew out their firearms, aimed earnestly, and fired at the aircraft. "Try to hit the engine, that's the biggest thing to aim at anyway," shouted Gunderson. Handguns are notoriously inaccurate beyond twenty yards.

Before they could home in on their target, the aircraft revved up and took off, veering to their left. And then it was gone. They had made enough noise to wake up the whole town, but apparently Clarksvillians slept heartily. Maybe they were used to gunshots in the night.

Gunderson shook his head wearily, knowing they needed to resume the chase and meet the yellow floatplane at Nags Head. First, they needed to get in touch with their superiors and report the briefcase stolen. Gunderson could have sworn he has seen only one person, the pilot, in the floatplane at Clarksville.

BIG DAN AT CLARKSVILLE
Thurs., April 13, 1945, 12:15 am Eastern Wartime

Heine Hammerschmidt, aka Big Dan Ross, was keeping the floatplane as close to the ground as possible. It wasn't easy following the contours of the foothills of eastern Kentucky and the Blue Ridge Mountains of Virginia. He followed his compass heading until he could discern the town of Roanoke (elevation 1,000 feet above sea level), which meant he was halfway to the refueling point at Clarksville, Virginia. He was heading almost directly away from the sun setting behind his back. Sunset would be at 7:29 pm Eastern Wartime and the visibility would be wonderful under the moonlit sky. The confrontation at the trestle and the shock of finding his long-lost cousin dead from the ordeal had clouded his mind and left him exhausted and fighting the urge to close his eyes and rest. The droning of the small engine didn't help either. He had had doubts about continuing the mission after leaving the body in the lake, but he quickly concluded that finishing the mission was the only logical decision for him to make. Hans certainly would have wanted him to continue. After all, he did have the package in his possession, and the U-boat was waiting off the Outer Banks for him to arrive. He couldn't fly there directly; he didn't have enough fuel to make it. The floatplane could have accommodated an extra fuel bladder, but the extra weight would have make the small, under-powered aircraft too ungainly to take-off and land. The midway point in his flight and the only decent place to land a floatplane worked out to be Buggs Island Lake at Clarksville. A dedicated member of the local Bund would be waiting there with a hundred gallons of aviation fuel to add to the plane's tank and get him to the Outer Banks. The man on the ground would signal the aviator with a lantern fitted with a red lens.

About 8:45 pm, much later than planned, Big Dan found the large black mass of the reservoir spreading out beneath him and he recognized the shapes of the shoreline. Up ahead he could see the green fishing lights on the bridge at Clarksville. He would aim at the center of the span and put down to the starboard side where the small sleepy town was situated and look for the flashing red light of his accomplice, whom he had not met before. His name was given as Phillip, which sounds like fill 'er up, he mused. Just a coincidence? Who cares and what does it matter.

The surface of the manmade lake was undisturbed until the twin pontoons of the Stinson cut through the water. He let off the throttle and then cut the engine entirely and glided, looking to the shoreline on his right for the red light. Other than the bridge lights and a few streetlights up in the town there were no signals. Then he noticed the people up on the highway bridge, pointing at him. Who the hell were they? Fishermen? Not way up on the bridge; too high to fish from. Whomever they were, they were not likely to be friendly. At least, that was not the plan.

Desperately he scoured the docks, rocks, and piers at the waterline and saw nothing. Some object zinged over his plane like a meteor; then there were tiny sprouts in the water in front of him. The strangers on the bridge were shooting at him! Either they were deranged miscreants getting some twisted kicks or they knew what he was doing there. None were in uniform. They knew his mission probably. As much as he hated to do it, he had no other choice than to start up the engine, push the throttle steadily forward, pull back on the yoke at just the right time, and lift off the water. As soon as he did, he made a steep climbing turn to the right and flew over the town, leaving the shooters on the bridge behind as fast as he could. He found the main channel of the reservoir again and set his course bearings for the Outer Banks, more specifically the night beacon at the Wright Brothers Memorial, Kill Devil Hills. From now on there would be few landmarks to guide him. On the other hand, the terrain fell into the level plains of the Piedmont and the swamps and tidal flats surrounding Albemarle Bay. The U-boat would be laying off the coast just north of the beacon. At that point, the barrier island is barely 1,000 yards wide. A landing party from the U-boat would make their way across the sandy beach and would be waiting for him on the other side, which is where he would approach them from the west. At that point, the water would be only about five feet deep. He would deliver the package and follow the crew back to the submarine in their inflatable rubber landing raft. He would then be dependent on the fate of the U-boat. The floatplane would be left behind. That is, if he had enough fuel to reach Albemarle Sound, the inland waterway. He was not confident.

NAZI AGENTS AT CLARKSVILLE
Thurs., April 13, 1945, 12:15 am Central Wartime

In Clarksville, Phillip had brought an accomplice with him in the pickup truck, a fellow mechanic by the name of Ron. He wasn't real bright and probably would never figure out exactly what was going on. For all he knew, he was helping a buddy deliver some fuel to a boat out on the river. The pair drove to the railroad bridge over the river and rolled down the steep bank to the landing, which was used only for fishing during the war years. If there were folks down there, what would they care? The locals kept to themselves and tried to keep out of unwanted trouble with the authorities. As it turned out, the only persons there had wandered far downstream in search of better fishing.

Phillip maneuvered the truck in the lot so that its bed faced the river. He had four metal canisters of aviation fuel that he had bought on the black market for a handsome amount of cash. Each held twenty gallons, 120 pounds. A hand pump and hose would deliver the fuel to the aircraft. This was the last chore, Phillip figured, before he lost himself in the crowd and disappeared from the scene. There wouldn't be much use in the US for Bund hardliners such as himself when the Reich fell, which was imminent. He had done his duty; now he wanted to get "lost" and make some money. The small yellow plane was scheduled to land on the river about 8:00 pm Central Wartime, so he might have some waiting to do. He hoped that the pilot, whose name he did not know, knew how to land the floatplane in difficult situations because the Cumberland River made a big bend here in Clarksville, Tennessee, and the swirling currents are tricky. In the event, he smoked half a dozen handrolled Bull Durham cigarettes before giving up his wait. The floatplane never showed up. The current was so swift that Ron's slashed and bloated body wasn't found until May. It had floated downstream nearly to Dover, Tennessee.

A DEATH IN THE FAMILY
Thurs., April 13, 1945, 12:30 am Eastern Wartime

Leaving Bunny behind with his beloved *Darla* still on the bridge, the FBI man and the two military policemen jogged down the highway towards town. A rusty sign proclaimed "Clarksville—The Oldest Continuous Tobacco Market in the World." They needed to find a telephone. The only building with lights on and cars parked outside was a late-hours riverside tavern catering to the local blue-collar workers and men seeking relief from their wives. The storefront bore a small Schlitz Beer sign that announced Tiny's Tavern, a rough wood facade, and a large glass window that had been painted dark.

Sarge peered into the narrow gap between the buildings, stepped inside, and relieved himself. After Sarge reappeared, LT shrugged, said what the hell, and followed suit. Gunderson swung open the glass door of the bar and they entered the dimly lit room. The clientele were propped on stools at the bar nursing mugs of beer and hand-rolled cigarettes producing coils of white smoke. The clacking of billiard balls could be heard in the back corner. The jukebox softly played "Too Late to Worry, Too Blue to Cry" by Al Dexter and His Troopers. The joint wasn't exactly a bucket of blood, but it wasn't an upscale, classy pub either.

The hefty bartender sauntered over, wiping down the bar as he went, raised his double chin and enjoined, "What can I get you fellas? You ain't from around here, are you?"

Gunderson took the lead, ordered three longneck bottles of beer, and asked to use a phone. He was directed to a coin machine on the wall near the pool table.

Gunderson nodded and moved to the phone, dropped in some coins, and dialed the number. The others heard some loud conversation but couldn't make out the words. The G-man came back to the bar and stated, "They'll be here asap."

LT proceeded to the phone and called CEW, finally getting through, an orderly waking Capt. Zimmer from his nightly slumber. An animated conversation followed, and LT finally hung up the receiver with a grim expression on his face. He returned to his cohorts.

The bartender stood behind the bar in his stained apron, wipe towel in hand. "You guys heard the news? Roosevelt died."

LT and Sarge did a double take, expressions of doubt on their faces.

They had no reason not to believe the bartender, but they found it difficult to accept the news. "No shit. What happened?"

"Just heard it on the radio. He died in Warm Springs, Georgia, of a cerebral stroke. He was 63." The bartender had a difficult time pronouncing the word cerebral.

"Damn, hard to believe. Well, so now who's President?"

"The vice-president, Truman."

"I've heard of the guy. I guess he'll do alright. He's from Missouri, I think."

The bartender turned away and adjusted the big radio sitting on the bar between the cash register and the big jar of pickled pig's feet. Truman was talking in a bland, unpretentious Midwestern accent. "The world may be sure that we will prosecute this war on both fronts, east and west, with all the vigor we possess, to a successful conclusion."

"Funny story on the radio," the bartender said. "Truman was having drinks at the Capitol with his buddies and they called him over to the White House. They told him Roosevelt had died and Truman asked Eleanor if there was anything he could do for her. She asked if there was anything they could do for him. He was the one in trouble now."

"Can't remember who was President before Roosevelt."

The customers at the bar considered the question, coming up with Coolidge? Hoover? They could not have known it but back in Washington, D.C.—

Within 15 minutes of the press office's death notification, all major American radio networks had issued bulletins, and they stopped their regular programming. News reports were mixed with solemn music and interviews with shocked citizens. At 7 p.m., Truman convened his first Cabinet meeting, which was a short session. But after the meeting, War Secretary Henry Stimson pulled President Truman aside to tell him about a secret project to produce a "new explosive of almost unbelievable destructive power." Two weeks later, Truman would be fully briefed by the General on the Manhattan Project and the United States atomic program.

The bartender wagged a finger at the three strangers. "I think I know who you guys are. We ain't in any trouble, are we? Just a smalltown bar trying to serve our customers and make a living." He must have noticed their firearms under their coats.

Gunderson shook his head, "Nah." He turned to the drinkers at the bar. "Who owns the '41 Buick Roadmaster out in the lot?"

The bartender pointed at a customer at the bar. "He does." The bar patron wore a coat and tie with the knot loosened and the top of his shirt unbuttoned. He was middle-aged, balding, and heavyset. He had been at the bar for a while. He was damp with sweat. He acted peeved but let it pass.

"Yep, I do," he said, looking sullen.

Gunderson moved toward him and discretely showed his FBI credentials. "Look, we need some transportation fast. The Bureau needs to commandeer your vehicle. This is a national security matter. Some agents will be arriving in due course and will compensate you. Do we have your permission?"

The drunk gazed at the somber faces around the bar as if to get their approval.

One of the boozers challenged him. "Is that really real?"

"Yes it is. I am the Special Agent in Charge at the Knoxville field office."

Murmurs traveled up and down the bar. The pool game stopped. "The hell you say. What are you doing here?"

"We got here by landing an airplane on the bridge over the river," he said matter-of-factly as if it were a daily occurrence. "We need to catch a suspect headed to the coast."

"That's a long ways, mister."

"He's a Nazi spy and I'm not joking."

The owner of the car stood up against his stool and said, "Yeah, sure, go ahead. What the hell. My wife, er, ex-wife, that bitch, will probably get it anyway. This guy's story is so whacked, it's got to be the truth. Wouldn't want to get on the wrong side of the F-B-I." He raised his beer glass and took another gulp. He separated the big car key from his ring of keys and handed it to Gunderson. "Matter of fact, just got a full tank of gas, don't ask me how. Pulls to the right."

"Thank you very much," Gunderson said, holding up the key as the three of them headed to the door. Several boozers slowly followed them, most likely to see if an airplane actually had landed on the bridge. The local constable was now on the bridge, scratching his head and working his camera in order to get a photo of the bizarre scene. He burned flash bulbs until he deleted his supply.

Bunny had a lot of explaining to do. With the assistance of the Bureau, the incident was recorded thusly: when Bunny went flying at night for relaxation, he ran out of fuel over Clarksville, 350 miles away. The wings were detached and stowed alongside the fuselage, and the aircraft hauled on a lowboy truck back to Lexington. Bunny would have tagged along, but he was having too much fun holding court at Tiny's as the toast of the town late into the morning.

CIC MAKES THE CALL
Thurs., April 13, 1945, 1:16 am Eastern Wartime

Gunderson had called the special station at headquarters in Washington and spoke to the station's chief deputy. He told him where he was located and where he was headed. He reported that a briefcase holding enriched uranium had been stolen off the train in Kentucky by Nazi infiltrators, that a small floatplane with pilot and passenger was heading due east to meet with a German U-boat near Nags Head on the Outer Banks. Two teams of two agents were dispatched from Norfolk, one headed to Clarksville, the other to Nags Head, one hundred miles and two hours away. After hanging up, Gunderson quickly brought LT up to date.

Capt. Zimmer took the news from LT with some astonishment but surprising composure. He noted that the odds would be unlikely of stopping or intercepting the floatplane before it reached the coast. He would notify the closest Army airbase, which could dispatch an assault plane to the Nags Head area, along with alerting all shore patrols and any aircraft or ships in the vicinity to be on the alert. In addition, he would arrange for an assault team, with radiation monitoring equipment, to be dispatched to the area from Fort Bragg (home of the 82nd Airborne Division), North Carolina, two hundred miles away.

Capt. Zimmer had been updated on the amateur ambush on Solway Pike early that afternoon and concluded that the attack was unrelated to national security. Now the briefcase with the package had been stolen by foreign experts and the chase was on. He decided to allow events to take their course. He contacted the Chief Engineer, who just about blew a gasket but acknowledged that nothing much else could be done. He agreed that neither CIC nor the General needed to be informed at that time.

He had heard no news regarding the Soviet agents and the crate in the freight car of the *Southland Express*.

DESPERATE ROAD TRIP
Thurs., April 13, 1945, 1:45 am Eastern Wartime

The 1941 Buick Roadmaster was a behemoth, one of the last models produced before the carmakers switched to war production. The Fireball-8 engine cranked out 165 horsepower and featured compound carburetion, which increased the fuel induction the faster the engine revved. The land yacht was cream-colored with red leather upholstery and whitewall tires. The body was streamlined heavy-gauge steel and featured a large chrome grill and motorized ragtop. After starting the inline engine, which rumbled ominously, Gunderson was happy to find a four-speed shifter on the steering wheel stalk instead of the usual three. The transmission probably was custom-made for speed. With the top down, the passenger vehicle seemed even larger.

The responding FBI agents would be arriving at the tavern soon, but Gunderson couldn't know when, and there was no time to waste. He stomped on the gas pedal and sprayed gravel all over the lot. He had to manhandle the large steering wheel. He realized it would take a little time to acclimate to the vehicle's handling characteristics.

Big Dan was piloting an aircraft that could only fly a little more than 100 knots per hour. As far as they knew, Big Dan had not been able to refuel. He would get to the Outer Banks before they could drive there if he didn't run out of fuel. The highways they needed to use were four-lane divided highways with at-grade intersections. At least most of the way at first. There would be light traffic during the night. And animal crossings. Gunderson had to drive as fast as he could while still maintaining some level of safety.

The Roadmaster had seat belts, usually only found on race cars like at the Indy 500. The passengers buckled up as the land cruiser swayed and jerked to and fro. The trees swished by their doors as the Roadmaster roared down the highway with a noisy gusto. Gunderson was really pushing the beast, hoping to avoid hitting any deer or other nocturnal animal. If they hit a squirrel, they'd probably never even know. A grown deer could really put a serious hitch in their pursuit however. The headlights illuminated the pavement in front of him for a respectful range, allowing him to avoid most potholes, jerking the large steering wheel back and forth, making the heavy vehicle sway like a boat in rough waters. The potholes he did hit he could feel in the wheel, but the suspension absorbed most of the impact. By the time they were 40 miles from the tavern all four of the chrome hubcaps had flown off into the ditch or shoulder.

The task of driving as fast as possible while maintaining control and concentrating on the roadway ahead lit by the headlights was daunting and highly exhausting. Plus the noisy airflow around and down into the passenger compartment kept the others from snoozing. In the event, the three of them took turns driving, each for about one hour.

At one point, sitting in the back seat, LT caught a bug in his mouth, quite the foul sensation. He tried to cough it out, failed numerous times, and then finally swallowed it, glad he didn't know exactly what it was. Sarge conjured up a small bottle of rye belonging to the previous owner and tucked between the seat cushions. LT took a big swig to wash down the insect. At one point, they thought they saw a huge flock of bats flying across the halo moon.

They followed Route 58 north out of Clarksville to South Hill and then on to Lawrenceville. Virginia was full of small towns, virtually villages all closed up for the night. Unless they ran into a nighttime sheriff's patrol, they wouldn't have to worry about being pulled over. Emporia came and went, then flying by Franklin until veering off onto Highway 32 to Highway 158. Several stores along the way had spread out black bunting in honor of the fallen President. They were in North Carolina now, across the invisible state line. They really were making good time even though it felt as if the roadway stretched in front of them infinitely as the nighttime stretched on. Insects of various sizes and wetness smashed on the windshield with regularity. At times, a heavily loaded eighteen-wheeler would blow by at an excess speed that shook the heavy vehicle. They ran into, figuratively speaking, only one old-timer in a pick-up truck wavering down the road, all over both lanes. Probably a drunk making his way home ever so slowly. Gunderson timed it masterfully and passed him as the truck skittered along the right shoulder. The snockered driver probably never even noticed.

The communities of Camden and Barco came and went as they headed southward toward Point Harbor and the bridge across Albemarle Sound to the Outer Banks. As they sped across the bridge, Gunderson turned off the headlights. The darkness closed over them from all sides. Past the bridge, he could see the road well enough, so he left the lights off. Just as he had driven the first stint, Gunderson was at the wheel during the last.

It crossed his mind that if they wandered off the road in these lowlands they probably never would be found, the car swallowed up by the swamp, and all the creepie creatures feasting on their corpses until the car carried only skeletons. Back to reality, he forced himself.

They had driven through flatlands and into swamp territory, full of sloughs and brackish backwaters, then onto the strip of barrier island bordering the sea.

The barrier island was quite narrow and the road swept close to the dunes and the beach. Waves crashing to their left, the trilling of swamp insects to their right. The road was rugged and irregular so they could not cruise at high speed. He stopped, cut the engine, and they got out and listened. They staggered for a few brief moments as they gained their solid-ground balance again. They heard the surf crashing and rolling to the east, and in the opposite direction a vibrating blanket of sound produced by tree frogs, bull alligators, and many species of tidal insects. They had driven about 200 miles in just over three hours on rural roads. Gunderson was dead tired, drained of adrenalin. He was so punch drunk he was actually giggling. He suddenly realized the other two were staring at him and he quieted down. He took the moment to light a cigarette, took several drags and then extinguished it. Shouldn't give their location away, he had realized. Where were the FBI agents from Norfolk? They should be here by now, he figured.

Talking amongst themselves, leaning on the car, they thought outloud that Big Dan was headed toward the Outer Banks where the German U-boat would be waiting. Big Dan couldn't risk trying to land the plane on the ocean so he would logically land in Albemarle Sound. And they were situated now at the narrowest part of the barrier island. They got back into the car, drove a couple hundred yards further and stopped again. Gunderson could swear that he had grown so accustomed to the darkness and sound that he could hear and see beyond the blackness and background noise. "You hear that?" he asked Sarge and LT, gesturing for them to be quiet. "Hear it?" he whispered this time.

Damn if they didn't hear it, a low rumbling sound coming from the sea along with spurts of an engine whining and grinding in low register.

"You smell it?" Gunderson said, smiling. "That's diesel exhaust. That's a U-boat out there stuck on a sand bar or something. Trying to work itself free."

Sarge pictured a whale floundering out of water on a spit of sand. They peered out into the surf, but they could see only the whitecaps of the breaking waves.

"I think we are where we're supposed to be," said the FBI agent. He checked his handgun and reloaded it. The others did the same. "I'll bet there is a landing crew of German sailors right over there," he said, pointing to the west. There was no place to hide the car so they left it where it sat. The terrain was sandy, of course, with a light cover of scrubby underbrush.

"Hope the water moccasins are asleep," Sarge commented.

They headed west towards the theoretical meeting place, about a thousand yards away, the length of ten football fields. As they moved forward in a crouch, the sound of the surf passed away behind them in exchange for the sounds of the swamp. The dunes were far behind now and the ground felt damp and cushy. The breeze off the ocean was replaced by the odor of decaying vegetation and pine. Up ahead the sand disappeared; they were looking out over the dark quiet water of the sound. The inland shoreline was covered with cattails, saltgrass, and reeds. Soon they heard voices sounding as if arguing with each other. They were close enough they could hear what the strangers, surely the U-boat shore crew, were saying. But they did not understand because they were speaking in German. The faint smell of burning tobacco could be detected.

CLACKING CLAUSTROPHOBIA
Thurs., April 13, 1945, 2:55 am Central Wartime

Besides trips to the cramped public men's room, the two of them had been cooped up in the musky cargo car of the *Southland Express* for nearly fifteen hours now and they'd be in here for another three of four, they reckoned. They were hardened military law enforcement, but they were still human after all and there was no fighting to be had, except amongst themselves. The prohibition against smoking had been broken hours ago and they were bored to death. Naps only lasted a handful of minutes, fitful under the circumstances. The porter had brought dinner, as promised, which was fairly decent. They arranged some boxes so they could sit at a "table" and enjoy the plates of corned beef hash topped with a fried egg, and the pound cake for dessert. Crusty Crunkleton and Lenny Brewster had doffed their helmets and loosened their ties in that swaying, darkened room crammed with freight. They tried playing craps but the jerking of the car on the rolling of the dice produced only squabbles. The Texan and the Midwesterner argued about the relative merits of the Fighting Illini and the Hook'em Longhorns, despite the fact the two teams had never played each other and each team barely had a .500 season in 1944.

GUNFIGHT AT KILL DEVIL HILLS
Thurs., April 13, 1945, 4:45 am Eastern Wartime

Big Dan could now see the beginning of Albemarle Sound, a large body of flat, smooth water reflected in the moonlight. The Roanoke River angled into the sound and from there on east in a straight line for 50 miles lay the waters of the sound. At points, the water was up to ten miles wide. He had to get as close as he could to the coast; he was amazed that he hadn't already run out of fuel. He could barely make out the beacon at Kill Devil Hill atop the 60-foot-high granite monument. He reckoned he had flown over the sound near the convergence of Perquimans River and needed to aim the plane at Powells' Point, where Route 158 turned east and across the Currituck Sound, just north of Kill Devil Hills and Avalon Beach.

He needed to put down at the furthest eastward reach of the sound, miles away. He cursed his luck when the aircraft engine began to cut out and sputter, and soon the prop came to an abrupt stop as the fuel ran out. He had no choice but to glide the plane down upon the waters of the sound near the swampy northern shore. He could get out and paddle the plane the rest of the way but that would take all night, even if his strength didn't give out. Instead, he landed the plane near the shore and reached for the inflatable raft in the back of the fuselage. He made sure he had enough clearance away from the craft before switching on the compressed-air tank that brought the form of the raft into reality. The raft settled on the water with more than enough room for him, the package, a life-jacket, and a paddle. Making sure he still had his sidearm, he slipped down into the raft carefully, holding the package tight to his side. He placed the package in the front, carefully slipped into the raft, and paddled away from the floatplane. It had carried him here from the foothills of Chilhowee Mountain. He thought about his wife and children back in Knoxville. They were Americans, of course, and he cared for them deeply. Perhaps when the war was over he could come back for them. How would he explain his disappearance, assuming that he escaped safe and sound and was not connected to the mission? These were matters that would have to be answered in the future. For now, he had a lot of paddling to do. He signaled with his flashlight and the U-boat crew signaled back. He was perhaps two miles away. Would they paddle out to him? Would an alligator get to him first? He was terrified of those creatures.

Gunderson knew that they had to wait at least until Big Dan and Uhu arrived at the inland shore with the package. Then they had to attack the Germans and recapture the package. No telling when, if ever, the trailing FBI vehicle would arrive. It was about midnight now and they were out in the middle of nowhere. There were three of them, each armed, against a German crew of three sailors, plus Big Dan and Uhu. It was likely that all of them were armed; perhaps one or two of them weren't. They weren't expecting visitors or trouble, but Big Dan would certainly alert them to the threat. Big Dan didn't know for certain that the three of them were already here. The Germans would guard the package at all costs. Their goal was to deliver the package to the U-boat, get onboard, and escape beneath the waves.

Gunderson figured they would have to surprise them, shoot and kill them all, or possibly take some prisoners. Would the U-boat send another landing party ashore? Most likely. They would need to capture the package and drive away from there.

The four-man Scout Team Zebra, in full camo and heavily armed, watched the two groups of soldiers carefully from their position 150 yards to the south. They had arrived from Fort Bragg in a Sikorsky R-4B helicopter equipped with pontoon landing gear. The rotary aircraft were experimental in all but name, difficult to fly, and pilots found that the control stick shakes like a jackhammer. The helicopter could carry a pilot and two passengers. Scout Team Z worked their way north until they heard voices speaking in German. They were ordered to surveil and monitor movements of the groups, especially the Germans, and take no action unless absolutely necessary. They were there to ensure the package made it to the U-boat, without revealing their existence. Strange, but orders were orders.

The Germans welcomed Hammerschmidt ashore and took possession of the package. They consisted of Able, the commander, and Baker and Charlie, the sailors. They moved quickly across the barrier island toward the seashore where the U-boat awaited. Guns brandished, Gunderson, LT, and Sarge emerged from the scrub cover on either side of the Germans and demanded that they halt. Startled, the Germans reached for their firearms without thinking and began shooting blindly into the darkness. Sarge took a bead with his .45 and dropped Charlie in his tracks. The Germans quickened their pace toward the shore, leaving Big Dan to keep up the pace, but he couldn't. LT braced his pistol with both hands, aimed at body mass, and shot Hammerschmidt in the back. He fell forward with a loud thud and a final bellow. Able and Baker disappeared into the darkness with the package as the three men took count of themselves and assessed the damage. To beat all hell, Sarge took a bullet to his right foot but could manage to limp along. He'd had lots of practice with foot wounds. LT and Gunderson glared at each other, trying to think of something to say. The gunfight had stupefied them. They then realized that they still needed to chase the bad guys. Big Dan or Heine Hammerschmidt or whomever he was, was dead as a doornail, for what that's worth. Uhu was nowhere to be seen. Charlie would never make it back to the Unterseebooten.

By the time the three of them got to the seashore, the Germans were paddling for all their worth toward the stricken U-boat still floundering on the sand bar. Fortunately for the Germans, the high tide was rolling in and lifting the submarine off the bar. LT and Gunderson had reloaded once again and were drawing a bead on the life raft. They'd have better luck trying to shoot at the moon. Sarge pulled off his shoes and socks and pants and limped down the swash flat and into the surf, diving into an oncoming wave.

"What the hell?" LT shouted. "Get back here!" Instinctively he knew it was no use trying to call back Sarge. The lunkhead was thrashing in the surf, actually making headway towards the raft and the U-boat. LT and Gunderson stopped shooting and watched the drama unfold as the waves pushed and then pulled against their ankles. They stood hands on their hips. The full moon created shadows stretching back up the beach.

The bobbing raft made it to the U-boat just as the behemoth finally rolled up in the advancing tide and floated free from the sandbar. After a brief moment of celebration, the deck crew lifted the German sailors up out of the water and secured the package. The empty raft floated away as Sarge, foot wound and all, reached the vessel. The U-boat was drifting away from the shore into deeper waters as Able and Baker climbed to the conning tower and lowered themselves down the hatch on the ladder. They secured the hatch just as the U-boat reached the deeper shelf and began to dive below the surface. Sarge climbed up the hull on a discarded line and clambered onto the deck and then up onto the aft empty gun platform as the bow disappeared below the waves. He was holding onto the railing like a rodeo rider might wrangle a bucking bronco as he and the submarine disappeared below the surface. He twirled his free arm in circles. The surf drowned out his hoots and hollers. In moments, all that remained was a swirling of disturbed water and an empty raft.

They waited, examining the surf for signs of Sarge but saw nothing. LT had the feeling that Sarge was going to ride that U-boat down into the depths as far and as long as he could.

"For shit's sake," grumbled Gunderson.

LT ran out into the surf to look for Sarge. Gunderson jogged out until the water reached halfway between knee and waist; he wanted to make sure that LT didn't drown trying to save Sarge. In ten minutes, LT came back towards shore with the rubber raft but nothing else.

LT shook his head as if to clear it. He couldn't believe that Sarge was gone. Perhaps he would survive the ocean, but LT knew that he was gone. And the package too. After all of the chase, the prize slipped out of their fingers. What would he tell the officials back at CEW? He was convinced that he and Sarge had done their best. Sarge had made the supreme sacrifice. LT knew that none of their exploits would see the light of day. Maybe as evidence at a secret court-martial?

LT grabbed Sarge's clothes on their way back to the Buick. On a hunch, he reached into the pants pocket and found what he was looking for—a 1923 Peace silver dollar.

At the Buick, Gunderson and LT waited for the other vehicle to arrive. They toweled off as best they could and put their pants back on. Gunderson was certain that eventually they would be found, hopefully before daybreak. He wanted the other agents to see the "crime scene" and collect the bodies. He had been the only one to connect the dots and foresee what was about to happen. Scant reward considering what actually transpired. He had no idea where Uhu might be. He was too involved in the past day's activities to see the bigger picture clearly. He wondered what Bunny was doing right now. He laid back and instantly fell asleep.

LT shook his head and pinched his nose, between his eyes. He was dog-tired and still trying to digest the repercussions of their actions, or lack of action.

They still had no idea where Uhu was or what had happened to him.

With any hope or luck, the U-boat would be destroyed before inflicting any damage. It was out of his hands. The PBYs and Liberators, along with the destroyer fleet, were already on high alert for a U-boat that may or may not be able to launch a missile at the homeland. Fighter planes were in the air to protect the New York-New Jersey-Connecticut area. Nothing further could be done.

A much smaller possibility was that the U-boat would carry the enriched uranium back to Germany for use during a hold-out in the Bavarian Alps or the Great Third Reich Redoubt.

Gunderson had a great story to tell, that is until the word came down from the Director that no mention of the thief on the train, the subsequent pursuit, and the gunfight at Kill Devil Hills would be made, publicly or privately. The nation was too busy mourning the death of their beloved President to notice much else going on. Gunderson was likely to keep his job. After all, he was much better than his predecessor.

SOUTHLAND ARRIVES IN CHICAGO
Thurs., April 13, 1945, 6:00 am Central Wartime

The ruckus on the *Southland Express* on Wed., April 12th was explained to the passengers, if they asked, as a domestic disturbance gotten out of hand. Apologies were profuse. The only eyewitness to the entire fracas—the gunmen shooting at a man on the roof, the floatplane hovering over the train, the man jumping off the train—was the brakeman in the caboose. Through no fault of his own, he was transferred later to the godforsaken line running out of Saskatoon, Saskatchewan. But who would believe him anyway? As for the infuriated Gwin and pregnant Billie Jean, they were caught up in their own little interpersonal crisis. In reality, however, most Americans were consumed by the alarming news of the day.

The train's passengers and crew heard the news at the Cincinnati stop in the middle of the night. President Franklin Delano Roosevelt was dead. Died of a cerebral stroke earlier that day in Warm Springs, Georgia. Vice-President Harry Truman had been quickly sworn in as the new President. The news was shocking, especially since the country was still at war. Roosevelt had occupied the Oval Office for the past 12 years. An incredibly wealthy man, he won the hearts of even the most modest citizens. He had guided America through the Depression and the Second World War. He had spoken to the people through the radio as if they were neighbors and friends. Many couldn't remember the country having any other President.

The mood aboard the train changed from anxious to sober. The sound of quiet sobbing permeated the cars on the train. Tears ran down the porter's face. Several riders in the dining car raised glasses of bubbly in honor of FDR.

With the sun rising over the raggedy grasslands of flat Indiana and the profusion of railroad tracks and sidings sliding into view, the *Southland Express* passed the gigantic Union stockyards of holding pens, slaughterhouses, and processing plants, and Comiskey Park, home of the White Sox, and pulled into Dearborn Station in Chicago right on time, as indicated on the depot's tall red-brick clock tower. Black bunting festooned the station's exterior. Flags were flown at half-mast.

As one might expect, the two uniformed MPs in the freight car were anxious to transfer the wooden crate with the rope handles to the new team of couriers waiting at the station. Although unaware of the routine, the couriers would accompany the crate on a new train to the lab in New Mexico.

At the cargo docks at Dearborn Station, the side door of the cargo car rolled open and stopped with a thud, revealing the adjacent cargo platform. Stevedores were already up and into the car, loading various boxes, crates, and trunks onto conveyances and over to waiting trucks. The MPs grabbed the handles to the box and prepared to exit the freight car. Several large imposing men in overcoats and fedoras assumed position in the door and blocked their way. Their stylish wardrobes contrasted with their ruddy, scarred faces and crooked noses. They looked like they meant business and usually got their way.

Toothpick Tarantino, onboard all the way from Knoxville, stood amongst them, looking small and inconsequential. He was responsible for delivering the goods to Chicago, but once there he could not issue orders to this crew. "We're here for our merchandise," one hardnose announced. Two of the men swept Thompson submachine guns out from under their coats and brandished them menacingly. The guns had dual pistol grips and clip-type magazines. The MPs instinctively grabbed their holsters, ready to unsnap and draw their sidearms. They were obviously outgunned. Just then two suspicious-looking characters strode into the freight car and demanded the box guarded by the MPs. They were dressed in black; one was female.

"I don't give a shit what you assholes want," the largest of the mobsters sneered with relish. "We're here to pick up our delivery; nobody goes nowhere until we do."

The sinister thin man in black declared, "We want the wooden box with the rope handles." He seemed to be a true believer in the invincibility of the new Soviet man. He slowly pulled his hand out from his jacket and displayed what was in it—a fragmentation grenade. He used his thumb to pull out the pin, which ended on the floor. His companion behind him pulled out a Russian PPSh-41 with 35-round magazine, a nasty automatic weapon.

Immediately, with one smooth move, the first thug blasted a series of slugs from his tommy gun, literally ripping the grenade holder in half, from crotch to wicked grin. The noise inside the car was deafening and shocking. The grenade lever popped open and the explosive pomegranate dropped to the floor. The PPSh-41 fired into the floor as the second sinister Soviet caught several slugs of lead from the mobsters and collapsed on top of the grenade. The gunshots rendered the close quarters with deafening noise, the smell of cordite, and the pinging of spent shells on the flooring. All of this commotion seemed to occur in slow motion.

Meanwhile, the MPs dropped to the wooden floor still grabbing the box. The grenade went off, lifting the two Soviet agents slightly off the floor and demolishing the end of the freight car. It would have been much worse if not for the Soviet bodies muffling and muting the explosion.

The mobsters recovered quickly, apparently inured to this kind of work. The lead mobster strode over to the rear of the car and motioned his pals over to grab several boxes marked with the symbol for an ear of corn. He grinned at the MPs and told them, "All we want is our hootch. We come back without it, our boss does a number on us." The men grabbed a handcart and loaded it quickly with half a dozen wooden crates. Just to be sure, one mobster counted the cases out loud and referred to the manifest in his hand. The boxes were loaded onto a truck and the tailgate slammed shut. The number-one mobster shouted, "We're good to go. Let's get outta here."

By this time onlookers were crowding onto the freight platform, risking their lives to see what was the commotion. The MPs with the wooden crate waltzed out of the freight car before the local authorities arrived. They hurried to Room A-20 and waited. Eventually two couriers showed up with the proper credentials and took possession of the crate. They hauled it off to another platform. The MPs went off in search of a men's room and then drained several mugs of strong, black coffee.

The war in Europe was not over yet, and the death of the President who had guided the nation through warfare on two fronts since the end of 1941 hit Americans hard. The train terminal had already been festooned with black crepe and patriotic banners in the wake of the President's death. Flags were flown at half-mast. Some citizens were still sobbing or crying at the news. Many dabbed the moisture from their eyes. Some whispered prayers and attended Mass. Many were worried about the fate of the nation.

Gwin took Billie Jean under her wing and found her a place to stay in Evansville. Eventually the both of them shared an apartment and got along well. Gwin went back to work welding. Billie Jean found work as a clerk at the shipyards. She was due at the end of the year; she hadn't decided yet if she would keep the baby or not.

U-BOAT THREATENS TO LAUNCH DIRTY BOMB
Thurs., April 13, 1945 3:18 pm Eastern Wartime

Fregattenkapitan Karl-Friedrich Scholtz, commander of the U-3008, was well satisfied with the performance of the Type XXI Electroboat. The submarine could remain submerged for much longer intervals than the older boats, which had to surface frequently to run their diesel engines. They've had two close calls. First, eluding British destroyers in mid-Atlantic and then getting unstuck from a sand bar at the Outer Banks. A crew member on shore duty had been shot and killed, and both Nazi infiltrators had been terminated, but the package of highly enriched uranium-235 had been stolen and secured.

Onboard, the forward torpedo room had been dedicated to housing the chemical-operated steam generator or Dampferzeuger, which would propel the buzz bomb or cruise missile along the launch ramp on the forward deck of the U-boat. This room was also where the package of green salt was "unwrapped" and inserted into the V-1 warhead.

The Schleichfahrt (silent running) took them approximately 12 hours to reach their destination undetected. Once they had moved past the appropriate grid, it was time to settle just underneath the surface and raise the periscope and Schnorkel tubes. Squinting into the eyepiece the captain rotated slowly until he sighted the stubby Romer Shoal Light and its signal (flashing white twice every 15 seconds). There were no patrol ships in sight. He checked with Petersen and Roach to make sure they and their crews were ready. Then he gave the command to surface and position watchmen on the top deck of the conning tower.

Once surfaced, Petersen's highly trained crew elevated the launch ramp on the front deck of the U-boat and made ready. Meanwhile, Roach and his men opened the waterproof chamber and dragged out the buzz bomb. The warhead and the two stubby plywood wings were then attached to the fuselage of the missile. The fuse was set to 13.5 miles. Normally when the fuse ran out, the jet-pulse engine stopped and the buzz bomb dropped and exploded on the ground. This time, however, the fuse was set to detonate the explosive warhead at 2,000-foot elevation and spew radioactive U-235 throughout lower Manhattan, rendering it unfit for human habitation for hundreds, if not thousands, of years.

The 27-foot-long buzz bomb was aligned with the ramp and the steam-driven launch piston. Written prominently in chalk on the forward fuselage was the tribute to der Fuhrer—*Alle Gute zum Geburtstag.*

More and more, Scholtz had considered this a suicide mission. It was highly unlikely they could successfully perform their duties, escape detection, and make their way back home. Being captain he would go down with his ship, never see his family back in Hamburg again. Perhaps the crew could be rescued by patrol vessels. Thoughts racing through his mind. He had thought about the possibility of surrendering his boat following the launch. He also pondered whether the high command would order him to scuttle the boat after finishing the mission. He considered his crew a fine group of highly trained men who had served him well. Perhaps they would catch a mariner's blessing. If they were lucky enough to ignite a dirty bomb over Manhattan, making it inhabitable for decades, his crew would probably not be treated kindly by their captors.

The watch crew scanned the horizon and blue skies for sight or sound of a patrol boat or plane, such as a Consolidated PBY. If such a flying boat caught sight of the U-3008, they would be sitting ducks. The aircraft would strafe the deck and drop aerial torpedoes that would rip the hull in half. And there would be no time to submerge. Scholtz preferred not to think about it.

The ramp catapult was powered by the Dampferzeuger, which mixed hydrogen peroxide with sodium permanganate to produce steam. The pulse-jet engine on top of the buzz bomb was started by the Anlassgerät, which provided compressed air for the engine intake, and electrical connection to the engine spark plug and autopilot. The missile was launched with a full head of steam past its stall speed of 200 mph; the pulse engine surged up to full speed in seven seconds.

Standing on the deck next to the missile, Roach consulted his foreman and then signaled affirmatively to the captain standing up in the conning tower. Scholtz smiled and pointed toward the city. Roach moved back to the side of the conning tower and gave the order to fire. There was a momentary delay when nothing happened (was this weapon a dud?), then with a huge hiss and mighty roar the missile shot down the ramp and headed toward Manhattan, its pulse-jet creating a unique throbbing noise and the launch piston splashing down into the sea.

The launch was caught on film for posterity by a Third Reich cameraman on the conning tower. The target was Wall Street, a largely symbolic gesture since the missile lacked the guidance system to hit specific targets. Manhattan was big enough.

No sooner had the missile left the U-boat then one of the spotters yelled "Feind Flugzeug!" and pointed to an approaching aircraft. Immediately the captain gave the emergency dive order.

The crew on the deck raced for the conning tower as the behemoth ran its engines forward and filled its ballast tanks with water. Four sailors did not make it to the hatch in time. The blue and white Catalina flying boat with the US Navy insignia soared overhead and dropped aerial mines, looking like oil drums, from underneath its wings. The U-boat was not yet fully submerged. Didn't matter anyway. The explosions, almost as one, cracked the exterior hull and left the U-boat helplessly sinking to the bottom of the channel. Soon all that remained was a swirling cauldron of water, oil, and scattered debris.

In the event, only two of the U-3008 crew were rescued alive. Due to the launching of a flying bomb against a large East Coast population center, the captured sailors were interrogated vigorously. Under intense pressure, they did not reveal any other missile-launching U-boats; later it was confirmed that there weren't any others. Most of the U-boats in Gruppe Seewolf had either been sunk or captured; none were equipped with V-1 launch capabilities.

BUZZ BOMB OVER NEW YORK CITY
Thurs., April 13, 1945 3:28 pm Eastern Wartime

Calvin Jefferson, Jonny's boy, was an anomaly in the U.S. Army Air Forces during the war. Although one of the Tuskegee Airmen trained under Alfred "Chief" Anderson at Moton Field in Alabama, he was not assigned to the Red Tails unit in Europe. Those airmen flew P-51 Mustangs with tails painted red and escorted bombing missions, usually composed of hundreds of B-17 Flying Fortresses. The airmen fought off Me109s, Focke-Wulf 190s, and the new-fangled Me262 twin-engine jet fighter. The legend which claimed that the Tuskegee Airmen never lost a bomber under their escort had already taken hold although far from the truth. The reality, however, is that the Tuskegee Airmen were highly skilled, highly effective, and highly sought after by the bomber crews.

Calvin was culled from the ranks of the Negro flyboys by a certain colonel at Mitchel Air Force Base on the Hempstead Plains of Long Island, New York. This officer caught hell in 1943 when a P-47 under his command crashed on take-off and struck Hofstra University's Barnard Hall. The pilot was the only fatality. After that embarrassment, the colonel choose his aircrew carefully. It didn't matter that Jefferson was black, he was an exceptional pilot with an exceptional training record. Calvin came to Mitchel Field's 301st Fighter Wing with another Tuskegee airman to help alleviate any harassment the black flyers might encounter from other pilots. The two Tuskegee men bunked together, got along fine, and there were few incidents of any consequence.

That is how Calvin Jefferson from rural Kentucky came to be flying a P-47 Thunderbolt patrolling the skies over the tri-state region. Calvin harbored mixed feelings about his assignment. He enjoyed his duties, which allowed him generous flying time in his machine *Glorious Gladys,* named after his mother, now deceased. He worked well with his maintenance crew, no problems. And he enjoyed being stationed on Long Island. Off-duty trips into Harlem offered entertainment, jazz nightclubs, great soul food, and last but not least, the women. At times, it seemed as if there was no war going on at all. On the other hand, he was missing all the action and glory of fighting in Europe. He had to wonder what he would tell his grandchildren about his war duty. At least he had the distinction of being a US Army Air Forces pilot protecting the homeland.

When you start the radial engine of a Republic P-47D Thunderbolt fighter plane, the noise of the eighteen pistons coming to life sounds like God coughing, followed by a belching of white oily smoke from the giant exhaust stacks and the whirling of the gigantic four-bladed prop. What begins as a clattering racket becomes a steady, whirling powerhouse. The whole airframe shakes from the vibration of the engine, which can produce up to 2800 horsepower. This beast is known as the Jug for its large shape. The bulky airframe was designed to accommodate the radial engine and an extensive system of ductwork feeding a supercharger. The pilot enjoys great visibility due to the new "bubble" canopy. This late model was built in Evansville, Indiana. If the P-51 was a stallion, the P-47 was a bull.

Roaring through the sky at up to 420 miles per hour, the pilot, snugly strapped into the cockpit, becomes part of the machine, combining exceptional vision with hand and foot coordination on the joystick and foot pedals. Calvin has flown this mammoth warrior so many times he doesn't have to think anymore, it is pure instinct and muscle memory gained from hundreds of hour in the air. He can perform aerobatics and dogfighting maneuvers gracefully and without effort, the only real limitation being a relatively slow rate of climb. Once at altitude, however, say 24,000 feet, the Thunderbolt can dive upon any target at ferocious speed with the "bounce and zoom" maneuver.

In Europe the P-47 is a workhorse ground-pounder. Using its guns and rockets it can swoop down on enemy vehicles and trains and destroy them with one well-placed volley. And it can take a licking from ground fire and anti-aircraft shells and get its pilot back home in one piece. In one incident, a Thunderbolt took an eight-inch flak hit on a propeller blade and continued on its mission without a hitch.

Today, however, the Thunderbolt is armed with eight .50-cal. machine guns and a belly tank of extra fuel. Its mission is interception of enemy missiles or projectiles and assisting in coastal patrols seeking out surfaced German U-boats. Under-wing rockets would not be suitable for the mission. The machine guns are powerful enough against any aircraft—one five-second burst produces 500 rounds of ball, armor-piercing incendiary, and tracer projectiles into a three-by-three-foot target 366 yards away. That's 50 pounds of bullets fired at 2,900 feet per second.

Well, the war against Germany was almost over. Calvin was aware that German U-boats conducted Operation Drumbeat, also known as the Second Happy Time (Zweite glückliche Zeit), back in 1942 when the submarines enjoyed sinking hundreds of thousands of shipping tonnage off the East Coast. Since then the Battle of the Atlantic had been won through the use of aerial patrols and the breaking of the German signal codes. Much of the time, Calvin was busy fighting complacency, which he knew full well could get a pilot killed.

In 1945, however, there had been much talk and press coverage of rumors that German U-boats had been dispatched, reportedly from bases in Norway, to strike the East Coast with V-1 buzz bombs and even V-2 ballistic missiles. The missiles would be towed in separate containers across the Atlantic and then positioned upright to fire the rocket. Speculation ran rampant as to whether such technology was feasible. The most likely scenario is that a state-of-the-art U-boat could surface and fire a V-1 buzz bomb at an inland target. This is the same weapon that Hitler had turned upon England in great numbers. Almost 2,500 buzz bombs reached England, causing 24,000 casualties (6,184 deaths). However, the buzz bomb had two shortcomings. First, it could not be set to hit a specific target, its aiming not precise at all. Secondly, although it traveled at 400 mph, it could be shot out of the sky by anti-aircraft artillery or fighters. Over England, it was not uncommon for a Spitfire pilot to actually tip over the flying bomb by disrupting the air flow over one of its wings.

Today was another typical routine of patrolling New York harbor and portions of New Jersey and Long Island. Calvin was halfway through his patrol route and cruising over Staten Island at approximately 300 mph at 20,000 feet when his headset crackled with a report from Air Defense Command.

"U-boat sighted off New York harbor near Swash Channel, 1.4 klicks south of Ambrose Channel and 4.6 klicks north of Sandy Hook, near Romer Shoal Light."

"Hot damn!" Calvin exclaimed to himself. He ejected his centerline gas tank and rolled *Glorious Gladys* over on her starboard side and within moments sighted the stubby lighthouse signal. He had barely acquired the surfaced German submarine in his gunsight when he saw a directed plume of white smoke or steam shoot from the forward deck of the submarine. The cruise missile accelerated to speed as it darted toward Manhattan Island at an oblique angle past him.

Calvin rolled the fighter plane onto its port side and pushed the throttle forward. He only had a few seconds to defeat the jet-pulse bomb. He approached to within 1,000 yards of the buzz bomb and fired a burst from all eight machine guns. Tracers showed the rounds falling just short or below the cruise missile. Calvin juiced the throttle until he was more or less dead-even with the speeding bomb. He could hear the throbbing of the jet engine (50 pulses per second). Or perhaps he was feeling the vibrations. The buzz bomb was bigger than he had imagined, painted a mottled green on top and light blue on the bottom. Of course, he had no idea that the warhead carried anything other than high explosives.

By this time his heartbeat was racing along with the high-speed chase. He could perceive the island moving under him. Ahead was another fighter moving swiftly toward him and the missile. The other aircraft, also a Thunderbolt, was firing at the buzz bomb and gaining rapidly. At this point, Calvin and his plane were expendable, and he accepted this without thinking. The other pilot, however, fared no better in hitting the missile.

For Calvin, it was gut-check time. He had perhaps one last chance to defeat the buzz bomb. He pulled up even to the port wing of the noisy monster and abruptly rolled to the left. He figured he had about a ten percent chance of disrupting the missile. He was amazed when the drone rolled over and lost elevation rapidly, in a powered spin.

Then he heard the other Thunderbolt roar past his position, still in a roll downward to port, and then a terrific explosion below him, perhaps 500 yards distant. He saw only pieces of the buzz bomb spread through the sky, the pulse engine the largest intact piece.

"Missile intercepted. Hit East River, north of Vinegar Hill, south of Corlears Hook."

"Roger that. Return to base."

"German U-boat?"

"Received confirmation—Sighted sub, sank same."

"Outstanding!" Calvin shouted.

He steered *Glorious Gladys* toward Long Island and glided through a long banking maneuver to his approach and laid the beast down with a near-perfect three-point landing. The squad leader was waiting for him near the entrance to the huge hangar.

One of the crew assisted Calvin in climbing out of the cockpit and onto the wing root. Sometimes sitting in that cockpit for some time affects your legs and balance, like gaining your landlubber legs after a long sea voyage.

"You are the man!" the officer shouted. He gave Calvin a vigorous handshake and slap to the shoulder. He then reached for his chest pocket and offered Calvin a big, fat cigar. "That was some mighty fine flying, Tuskegee man!"

"I can't hardly recall anything. I didn't have time to think about it much." His hands were shaking, making it difficult to light the cigar.

"Well, I'm sure there is a DFC in your future," he assured him, referring to the Distinguished Flying Cross award.

"There is one thing though," the officer noted as he wrapped an arm across Calvin's shoulders. "The DFC and the press coverage, yadda yadda, is for assisting in the sinking of a German U-boat off the shores of New York City. Heroic work. Credit goes also to the crew of the PBY that dropped those ash cans right on top of them. They had no time to submerge or get away. However, the buzz bomb will not be mentioned, ever. Top national security. The U-boat did not fire a missile. Got that?"

"Yessir," Calvin responded, a little confused.

"Nobody saw any missile. Right?"

"Right."

Not too many of the Tuskegee pilots in Europe could boast about sinking a German U-boat, he mused. Too bad he couldn't mention the German buzz bomb. Except to his proud father. Nobody would believe his story anyhow.

Many New Yorkers came forward to report seeing an explosion in the sky out in the harbor. The official response was that fireworks had been fired in remembrance of the President.

THE NATION MOURNS
Thurs., April 13, 1945, 1:00 pm Eastern Wartime

It was springtime finally and the dogwoods, azaleas, and yellow forsythias were in fragrant bloom throughout the city, but by mid-afternoon the heat and humidity made a promotional sign on the marquee most welcome in downtown Knoxville: "Air Conditioned with Refrigeration!"

The Tennessee Theater on Gay Street is a grand old palace for moving-picture shows and stage productions. Plush purple curtains flank the gleaming wooden stage adorned by ornate sculpted moldings and statuettes. Ushers escort attendees down the red-carpeted aisles to their padded seats. The lighting sets a contemplative mood. Although movies were the prime attraction, many celebrities and acts had graced its stage—Enrico Caruso, John Philip Sousa, Bob Hope and Doris Day, Harpo Marx, Mae West, Gene Autry, and W.C. Fields ("Who put pineapple juice in my pineapple juice?").

Today's matinee, "God Is My Co-Pilot," features Dennis Morgan and Raymond Massey. But first, the Movietone newsreel flashes onto the screen with dramatic martial music fading into somber tones of mourning. The baritone narrator assumes a tone of gravitas:

"Over the White House in Washington, the flag flies at half-staff as a grief-stricken nation mourns the death of Franklin Delano Roosevelt, President of the United States. Inside, in the historic Cabinet Room, Vice-President Harry S Truman takes the oath of office as 32nd President, administered by Chief Justice Harlan Fiske Stone. Mrs. Truman is at his side. President Truman asks the full Roosevelt Cabinet to remain in office, expressing his intention to carry on American policies as formulated by the Roosevelt administration."

Quiet sobbing fills the theater in echoes that bounce around the balcony and alcoves. Most Americans of middle age or younger could not remember anyone else serving as their President, through the Great Depression and World War Two.

"Franklin Delano Roosevelt, who became one of the greatest presidents of the United States, a friendly quick-smiling man who loved his neighbors and his family. This was a vigorous, dynamic man who lived the strenuous life to the hilt, despite the tragic crippling paralysis which almost ended his career at the age of 39. Much of his time was spent with his family. A nation and a world plunged into lasting sorrow by Franklin D. Roosevelt's death, offers deepest condolence, first to the Roosevelt family."

Meanwhile, halfway around the world, Adolf Hitler and his staff celebrated his 56th birthday underground in their Berlin bunker as the Soviets fought their way to the city center. The only news offered to the Fuhrer that day was bad news from his generals. Hitler denounced not only his generals but the German people themselves for failing him and allowing the Third Reich to fall. On April 30th, Hitler and his new bride, Eva Braun, killed themselves in the bunker rather than being taken alive by the Bolsheviks.

AFTERMATH

Knoxville News-Sentinel, Thurs., April 13, 1945

A four-car pile-up on Solway Pike just outside Clinton Engineer Works Wednesday resulted in several injuries, according to the Knox County Sheriff's Office. The accident occurred around 10:30 am just east of the Solway Bridge. One CEW vehicle was involved.

The Chicago Tribune, Fri., April 14, 1945

An explosion rocked a freight car of the *Southland Express* train while parked at Dearborn Station yesterday morning. Two unidentified men believed to be members of the southside Halliburton Gang were found shot to death at the scene. Armed men believed to be members of the northside Bennett Gang were seen by witnesses leaving the scene with several parcels believed to contain illegal whiskey. The investigation by Chicago P.D. continues.

The News and Record, Fri., April 14, 1945

A twin-engine airplane under distress was forced to land at night on the Hwy. 15 bridge over Buggs Island Lake at Clarksville early Thursday morning. The Boeing 247D was piloted by Earl "Bunny" Briscoe, well-known businessman of Lexington, Ky. There were no passengers aboard the aircraft. Briscoe, who has been investigated for organized crime activities, said he had taken the aircraft up for a cruise when he ran out of fuel. The aircraft sustained damage to the wings and propellers.

Knoxville News-Sentinel, Fri., April 14, 1945

Prominent Knoxville businessman Daniel Ross, 35, was found shot to death Thursday at his vacation home off the Foothills Parkway in Blount County. The assailant, who shot the victim for reasons unknown, apparently stole Ross's floatplane, which was found abandoned on Albemarle Sound in North Carolina, 420 miles away. There were no witnesses to the shooting; Ross reportedly was at his vacation home alone.

The Laurel County (Ky) Sentinel-Echo, Sat., April 15, 1945

Hunters in Laurel County Friday discovered the body of a Knoxville, Tenn. man in the woods near the main line of the Louisville & Nashville Railroad. The victim suffered many broken bones, including leg wounds, and most likely died of exposure in that remote part of the county. The victim has been identified as Dr. Martin Hamblen, 34, who was employed by the University of Tennessee and Clinton Engineer Works. The sheriff's office speculated that the victim had fallen off a train.

The Corbin (Ky) Chronicle, Thurs., April 20, 1945

The body of an unidentified US serviceman was recovered from Laurel Lake in Kentucky, two miles downstream from the Grand Gulf railroad trestle. The body was discovered by a local fisherman. The sheriff's office speculated that the male in his twenties may have jumped from the trestle just days before recovery.

The New York Times, Mon., May 21, 1945

The War Department has confirmed the sinking of a German U-boat approximately 30 miles off the New York Harbor on or about April 20th of this year. The submarine was sunk by a joint patrol involving a US Navy destroyer and US Army Air Forces flying boat. Officials noted that the German vessel was of sophisticated design, an electric boat which could travel from Europe underwater much of the time. The entire crew, except for two survivors, was lost. The War Department stated it has no plans to retrieve the sunken vessel.

The Oak Ridge Journal, Thurs., August 9, 1945

On Aug. 6, 1945 a bomb containing enriched uranium was dropped by a B-29 Superfortress over Hiroshima, Japan, resulting in the deaths of at least one hundred thousand residents. Although the bomb contained 144 lbs. of enriched uranium, it is estimated that the amount actually converted into explosive energy totaled less than one gram. The yield equaled 15 kilotons (30 million pounds) of TNT. Two days later, a plutonium bomb was exploded over Nagasaki, forcing Japan to surrender and ending the war. It is estimated that hundreds of thousands of young Americans, in addition to millions of Japanese, would have perished if the United States had been forced to invade the Japanese home islands.

Various reports by patrons of Pinky's Tavern:

- Large Donnie was apprehended by CEW MPs after the botched heist and gave up his associates readily. He served three months on a Federal prison farm before being shivved in the gut while working in a truck garden.

- Bum spent almost a year in a prison infirmary, recovering from injuries suffered from colliding with a car. He eventually became a prison trustee and was beaten to death by inmates in 1947.

- Pecker was picked up by CIC agents, interrogated, and sentenced to 20 years at hard labor. He escaped from the prison work camp in Macon, Georgia, and was never seen again.

- Hacksaw managed to avoid custody for several years before being killed in a drunk-driving accident with a school bus in Oshkosh, Wisconsin. Ironically, he was driving a stolen Duesenberg at the time.

- Tommy Tarantino guarded the contraband hootch on the train until one trip he fell asleep and choked to death on a toothpick, an incredibly horrible way to die.

The Miami Herald, Wed., Aug. 15, 2012

US Navy divers in the Gulf of Mexico have discovered the remains of what appears to be a large four-engine World War Two-era bomber 24 miles off the coast of Panama City Beach in 220 feet of water. The aircraft, found upturned on the seabed, bears no markings and apparently was painted black or a dark color. The cockpit instruments and interior markings are in the German language. US Navy officials have no theories as to how such an aircraft ended up in the Gulf of Mexico. No human remains were discovered. More exploratory dives are planned.

THE PAST IS PROLOGUE

The nurse gently woke me from my nap. The old man was fast asleep. I looked at my wristwatch and it was 8:30 pm. My digital device was still recording so I turned it off.

"I guess you better go now," she said. "Perhaps you could come back another day."

"Certainly," I replied, not really knowing if the old geezer had said all he had to say. But it was enough for now. "Please thank him for me."

I got up without disturbing the old man and made my way out the door and into my vehicle. I forgot to leave the bottle of whiskey. On the way home I figured what the hell and cracked open the small bottle of Evan Williams. The heat from the whiskey was soothing. The sleet had let up; it was nice and crystal clear now but cold.

I never did make it back to Norris. The old man passed away in his sleep a week or so after our extended conversation. I will write and publish his recollections as a journalistic article. I wonder if anybody will actually believe it.

ACKNOWLEDGEMENTS

I want to thank Ray Smith, Oak Ridge historian and author, for reading the original manuscript and offering many valuable corrections. Also, my friend Mike Reynolds, and my sisters Heidi Zimmerman and Karen Morrow, for reading the manuscript and making several useful suggestions. My writing buddy and pal Jay Thomas offered support and words of wisdom, as did writing colleagues Tess Sloan, Tina Curtis, Patty Ryan, and Bob Badeaux.

Atomic Express is historical fiction. What is historical and what is fiction?

Overall, most of the material dealing with the war, the combat, Hitler's birthday and death, the death of President Roosevelt, all of the weapons mentioned, the aircraft, is real. Most of the descriptions of CEW, the village, the security, the war production plants, and Norris Dam is real. The main concept of enriched uranium being transported by rail by MPs disguised as salesmen is real. Much of the descriptions of Knoxville, the train depot, the train itself, the university, the downtown theater, are real. The *Southland* was a train running between Knoxville and Chicago.

The Top of the World community exists, but it was developed in the 1960s, long after the Second World War. John Hendrix's premonition was real. The descriptions of the enrichment process are real. All of the facts in the White Paper are real. The General's secretary did know all about the Manhattan Project. The Communists in Georgia poisoned by rancid potato salad was a real event.

Operation Ultimate Vengeance is a fictional event, but Gruppe Seewolf was real. During the first half of 1945, the US military was concerned about a possible V-1 or V-2 weapon attack upon the East Coast. But no U-boats were outfitted to carry out such a threat. The Me264 four-engine bomber did exist but never flew across the Atlantic.

Most of the descriptions of U-boat pens in Norway and the situation in Berlin, including Hannah Reitsch, General Robert Ritter von Greim and test pilot Karl Baur, are real.

The descriptions of the German Bund in America during the 1930s is true, as is the FBI's dealings with Nazi spies and infiltrators. Claus von Kluge is fictional. The Soviet agent who revealed secrets at Oak Ridge is real although his name has been changed. Most of the details about the German section of Cincinnati are real.

Mitchel Air Force Base on the Hempstead Plains of Long Island, New York, did exist although it is highly unlikely that a Tuskegee Airman was stationed there. Oh, by the way, snapping turtle meat tastes delicious and it does not taste like chicken.

Most of the information about the "knuckleheads" and Big Dan the Hardware Man are fictional. Operation Brilliant was obviously fiction, as was Uhu, the superhuman Nazi infiltrator. Uhu is the German word for eagle-owl, which actually does exist in Europe. Many of the characters and action events, including the train and the airplane, are fictional. The book was written to include action events which are humanly possible although improbable.

The cornfield shipyard in Evansville, Indiana did exist, as did the WOOPS program with female guards.

Clarksville is the name of cities in Virginia and in Tennessee. The Wright Brothers Monument with beacon exists at Kill Devil Hills. There is a Dogwood Festival in Knoxville. General Neyland was a real person.

The details about the Electroboat submarine and the V-1 buzz bomb are real. In some actual cases, RAF pilots over England used their plane's wing to "topple" a buzz bomb.

Nothing in this historical fiction book should reflect negatively on the men and women who toiled during the war to build an atomic bomb at the several Manhattan Project locations. Dropping the bomb is still widely debated, but building an atomic bomb in the framework of three years was a stupendous feat of engineering and applied science nonetheless and CEW played a major role. There are historic sites in Oak Ridge today that can be visited. Oak Ridge National Laboratory is a major research facility today (www.ornl.gov). A video interview with Oak Ridge Historian Ray Smith can be viewed on YouTube under "Hidden History: Stories from the Secret City."

ABOUT THE AUTHOR

Mark Zimmerman is a retired newspaperman from Nashville, Tennessee, who now resides in Panama City Beach, Florida. He is the owner of Zimco Publications LLC, whose website is located at www. zimcopubs.com. *Atomic Express* is his ninth history book and first historical fiction. *Fortress Nashville* (2022) was named a Top Ten Civil War Book of that year. He is now working on a historical fiction novel about graverobbing, medical cadavers, and the attempted assassination of a high U.S. official.

www.ingramcontent.com/pod-product-compliance
Lightning Source LLC
Chambersburg PA
CBHW030647110726
47901CB00002B/607